Rafferty & Co.

Rafferty & Co.

a novel by

BETTY WAHL

NEW YORK

FARRAR, STRAUS & GIROUX

A section of this book appeared originally in
The Kenyon Review, in different form

Designed by Dorris J. Huth

Rafferty & Co.

1.

On the seventh day Alice saw Ireland, the green going down to the sea and the gulls above, come into view. The tender hurried alongside with a few end-of-season tourists bound for France and stood waiting to take off the passengers for Cobh. The other passengers lined the rails for a time and then drifted back to the tea dance.

As she made her way to the lounge in First Class where they had been told to assemble, she discovered several shawled women who must have come aboard from the tender. She slowed a little to glance at the bundles of linens and laces and odd, bumpy sweaters lying on the decks, but she would have plenty of time for such things later. Beyond the doors that had been closed to Tourist Class passengers during the voyage, she looked around with interest. The decor was plushier, but still of the thirties.

Rafferty had found a corner. The little girls, Stella and Vanessa, sat bundled in fawn coats and leggings, with brown velvet bonnets and brown gloves. "Everything all right?" he asked.

3

"Yes, except that someone forgot the clock."

"Oh, did I? Good thing you had a look."

The screws had stopped, and with them the noise that had given them all a measure of privacy in tight quarters. There weren't many passengers for Cobh, fifty or so, including the three strangers who must have been in First Class, a well-dressed older couple and a clergyman, a prelate, judging by his purple dickey.

"They're loading the tender," said a man who seemed to have been through it before.

"Oh?" said Rafferty. "With what?"

"Mailbags."

"If they don't get a move on, we won't get out of Cob tonight," said the First Class man.

His wife spoke to him in a low voice. "Well," he said, "why in hell do they spell it that way then?"

Alice could have told them that—the Cove of Cork, renamed Queenstown by the English, and now Cobh again, Gaelic spelling this time. She had it all from Rafferty, who, however, had a way of beginning with the Celtic migrations.

In the distance the dinner gong sounded, but not for them. After a time a coffee urn was trundled in, tended by a young officer with a single gold band on his sleeve.

"Do you know when we'll be going aboard the tender?" Alice asked.

"Ham sandwiches," he answered in careful, phonetic English.

"Thank you," she said and took one of the crustless triangles.

The man who knew what to expect appeared with a bottle of stout. "They're loading the tender."

"Oh?" said Rafferty. "Still?"

Suddenly they were hustled out into the corridors and hurried past the Tourist Class lounge to the strains of the Gypsy Trio and "Come Back to Erin." They went out into the floodlit night and down a heaving gangway to the boat below, with the mailbags. A last officer passed back through the hole in the liner's side, where

4

the waiting sailors seized the ends of the gangway and pushed it down onto the deck of the tender.

As the boats began to slide apart, Alice thought of the passengers sitting safely in the lounge with an after-dinner drink and the music. "Look at the lights," she said, turning the little girls toward the liner.

"I like this better," said Stella. "This is a *real* boat."

Alice felt it too. Even on the upper deck they were close to the black water rushing below and raising the faintly fishy smell of inshore seas, no longer the terrible nighttime ocean, but a place of lights, far and near, blinking in the water and above.

"Now, *emi*gration," an Irish voice was saying, "is the boys and girls leaving Ireland, and *imm*igration is the same ones landing in America. It's all the one thing."

"Yes," said Rafferty, "but someone moving into Ireland—"

"Ah, you'll find none of that."

It was too dark for Alice to see their faces properly, only the bowl of a pipe coming and going like the blinking lights.

"You weren't thinking of staying now, were you?"

"I was."

"Embassy?"

"No, I'm in tweeds."

"Buying or selling?"

"I want to make them here."

"Ah, modern American methods, nylon and all that."

"That's right," Rafferty said—to Alice's surprise, though there was no reason to explain everything to a passing stranger.

When it appeared that he would say no more, she took the little girls out of the wind, past the hatchway that led to the bright saloon below. The porters—black berets, heavy sweaters—were talking in the stern, a soft, singing speech with such a pronounced rhythm that she did not at first realize it was English.

Beside them the man who had made the landing before was searching the dim piles of luggage for his bags. Alice went to find

Rafferty, to ask him if he didn't think they had better start looking for theirs.

She found him at the front of the boat, drawn forward into the wind, straining to see or hear—what? She went away without asking.

ALREADY HE HAD CAUGHT THE SMELL OF TURF SMOKE, A SHARP, PUNgent odor, new and yet familiar. In a way he knew the whole island, its history built up like a pearl on its troubled people. Perhaps it was more precious to him, born where nothing had happened, where even the Indians had come from somewhere else. Here he could push back a long way before the road bogged down in Patricks, and gods and cattle raiders mingled and disappeared in the mists.

Somewhere too, across the narrowing stretch of water, were the rocky fields in which his own ancestors were buried. He wouldn't count on finding them, though, since all he had to go on was what his grandfather had said of *his* father's origins: ". . . if I said Cork, it was Cork, I was closer to it then." That had become even less of a clue when he had learned how many of the emigrant boats had sailed from Cork. The Raffertys, he now knew, had come from the West, Sligo and Donegal, one of those tribes that had never counted for much. There had been a Rafferty, Abbot of Durrow, in the eleventh century, and that was about it. The blind poet, Raftery, was usually confused with the Raffertys—not much of a claim, although he would like to visit the man's haunts in Mayo, if he had the time. But he couldn't even find out how much time he had.

"We'll have to call it something like *Research into the history of weaving down through the ages.* Doesn't sound too bad," Dr. Steichen, the president of Oakley, had said during one of their last interviews.

6

Rafferty, who hadn't come to talk of that, nodded.

"You'd better fill in Publicity with some dates and places. Too bad about the Guggenheim. That would have made a good release."

"Yes. Now, about the second year. I'd like to get that settled before we leave."

"I understand, but I don't think we ought to tie our hands that far in advance."

"No."

"Besides, you might find you didn't need another year, and then where would we all be?"

Dr. Steichen was sitting on his desk, swinging like a kid on a fence, tennis shoes and all, while Rafferty stood by the window with his seersucker suit sticking to his back. Summer school had come in with Dr. Steichen, a voluntary addition to the year's work that few of the faculty could afford to turn down.

"I was thinking," Rafferty said, "if I had the second year, I could get back in time to teach summer school."

"Good, I'll put you down."

"That's if I get the year. Otherwise I'd have to go back to Ireland in the summer."

"We'll see. Let you know at the beginning of the second semester."

Push him and get an outright *no*, Rafferty warned himself, and looked out over the dry campus. A block away in the parking lot, the students seemed to be playing tag in their cars, while a yellow haze rose above them. A single campus policeman would cost as much as an assistant professor, according to Dr. Steichen, who had suggested they all keep an eye on things and save the expense.

"You know," the man said, looking down at those damned rubber-capped toes, "you'd have more time there if you flew."

"That's right, but I don't like the idea of flying."

Dr. Steichen smiled. They all knew how he had flown to Wash-

7

ington when they were about to be done out of a new science building, how he hadn't even said good-by to Mrs. Steichen, had just bought a toothbrush at the airport and flew. "If your number's up, it's up."

"I know."

"That's what I'd do. Give you a week more. On the other end too. That's a good two weeks." Dr. Steichen nodded, convinced.

Two weeks. And for that he would have landed in the Old World still dressed in the clothes of his departure, the very air in his lungs unchanged. It was more than a day's journey from Oakley, where he was going.

He had wondered whether even the seven days of the voyage would be enough to let him change the pace of his life and thoughts—until he discovered the distillate of monotony in which the tedium of the old six-weeks passage had been marvelously condensed. Driven from his cabin by a faulty hot-air vent, he had found no escape from the ding-dong alternation of bingo and horse racing, cabaret and dancing, piano and band, while the boat moved without sails across the empty ocean, and the children hung on his neck like the albatross.

Then—it made no sense—that morning, at the first cries of the seagulls, his mid-Atlantic doubts had begun to drop away. And now, breathing the mixed smells of sea and land, he knew that there was no other way to approach the island, except perhaps in a long boat, rowed in on a rising tide, and himself leaping out at the shallows and splashing ashore through the surf.

He picked up his briefcase and, with an eye out for Alice and the girls, headed over to the side where the sailors stood ready with the gangplank.

8

THE NEXT DAY A BLUE ENGINE TOOK THEM THROUGH THE SOGGY center of the island, past castles and cows and bare-kneed boys waving, to Dublin.

A family hotel was what they wanted, "clean, comfortable, and economical," in the words of the guidebook, which listed more than a score. "I'll just check, before we get a cab," said Rafferty, slipping into a phone booth at the station.

Somewhere they had made a miscalculation, he said the second time he came from the booth to send her for more pennies. The tourist season had certainly ended, but the hotels remained unaccountably full.

They were almost alone on the platform now, and the man beneath the sign "Licenced to Deal in Tobacco" had settled back on a chair with his newspaper. "It's for the phone," she said when he stood up to get the change. "We're trying to find a hotel room."

"You've left it late enough."

"At this time of the year I thought—"

9

"You'd be all right, but for the All Ireland," he said and scooted down out of sight. He reappeared through a hatchway beneath the counter. "The football match tomorrow," he said, walking by her side. "You've come at a bad time."

The gateman agreed, shaking his head. "You wouldn't find a room in Dublin tonight."

"You should have come yesterday," said the man licenced to deal in tobacco.

"Or Monday."

"Well, then," Alice said, trying to keep a matter-of-fact voice for the sake of the little girls, "we'll just start phoning out into the country and take a train to the first vacancy."

"Ah, not at all, not at all," the tobacco man said.

"Not with the children," said the gateman, locking his gate and following them.

At the phone booth the two men took Rafferty's guidebook and began calling advice in to him. She would have felt better if they hadn't been consulting each other, guessing the rates of the various hotels, when the facts were right there, in the farthest column of the list.

The tobacco man ran his finger back up the page. "The lads won't be at the Imperial," he said, laughing.

"That they won't," said the other.

The Imperial was above the family hotels and, except that it offered no reduction for children, seemed to be about standard. "What do you mean about the Imperial?" she asked.

The tobacco man paused, as though now considering it for the first time. "You might stay there."

The gateman nodded, looked doubtful, and said, "You know, you might."

"But what's wrong with it?"

"Ah, there's nothing wrong with it. It's just—you might say— quiet, like." They both nodded. "You could do worse. Now, then," he called in to Rafferty, "you may as well try the Imperial."

10

The Imperial proved to be a trio of Georgian houses thrown together, the two extra stoops just ending in windows. Inside, the old elegance was still visible, and the glassed-in desk was standing there like a fish tank in the hallway. The lights were a little dim, and the bellboys were getting on, but Alice could see nothing that would explain why only this hotel had room.

Rafferty signed the book slowly, trying to pick up a little information about their fellow guests perhaps.

"You're welcome to stay as long as you like," said the Manageress, whose tucked navy blue dress had the frozen look of a uniform. "But, actually, we'd like to know when you're leaving. For the advance bookings, you know."

"We really don't know," Alice said. "We have to find a house."

The Manageress looked over at Stella and Vanessa.

"Oh, they're very careful children," Alice said. Rafferty saw to that.

"I'm sure they are. But landlords have to be cautious."

"Well, I've a list of agents to call, and I think we'll run an ad, too."

The Manageress nodded. "You'd want to hurry, the newspaper office closes at four, I believe."

"Thank you."

"You'll tell me when you know then, won't you?" she said and was gone.

They found themselves on the third floor, which was called the *second,* in room 17. The bellboy promised to look for a key. "Just shut the door when you leave," he said.

It was a nice room anyway, large enough to absorb a pair of double beds. Two great windows, hung with crisp swathes of lace, looked out onto the wide street and the Georgian row opposite. It was cold, though, and the gas fire that the bellboy had pointed out didn't seem to work.

"I don't think there's any gas coming through," Rafferty said.

"Did you put in a shilling?" asked a voice at the door. The Man-

11

ageress stood there with a mobcapped maid and an armful of linen. She turned to Alice and said, "It's warm in the lounge."

So they left Rafferty to get the gas fire going and went down to the lounge, a big glass-walled room across from the desk. Inside, the radiators hissed and a coal fire burned in a Hindo-Gothic fireplace with everyone there banked up around it. Alice kept going straight across to the bay window, which was stained glass—palm and pine where the saints should have been. She settled the girls on the long, fitted seat of tufted velvet, while the others watched. It wasn't like a hotel lobby at all; if she read aloud, she would be reading *Pinocchio* to the entire room.

The little girls, surprised at the sound of their voices rebounding from the glass, dropped down to a whisper and looked relieved when she brought out from her bag the familiar color books and crayons. Stella crouched over her book and worked painfully at keeping her colors within the lines. Vanessa didn't try. The green that had begun in a tree swirled through her pages like smoke, and she peopled the open spaces with green stork men, their legs erupting from their chins and stretching down to lilypad feet.

The woman nearest them smiled, a watchful smile. Alice wanted to reassure them all, to tell them she knew what they feared: the loud American who wants ice water, cold beer, hot rooms, and coffee, and leaves a wake of overtipped waiters and porters churning behind him. But Rafferty had sworn to respect traditions, to walk lightly and leave the land unmarked by their passage. Already they had surprised the waiter in Cork by asking for tea with dinner.

Maybe she had slipped a little in letting the girls wear slacks in this room, or maybe the trouble was just their age—or hers. She didn't know how old the other women were. Some were grey and some weren't, and there must have been a beauty shop nearby where the marcel was still going strong.

The men in the room were more clearly old. That could have

12

been what they were saying at the station: the hotel was a kind of old folks' home.

That was what made a country foreign. You didn't know what anything meant. Men who looked like bums were sober workmen, and the picturesque women in plaid blankets were the ones who wanted a handout. And these people talking by the fire? She hadn't expected Irish voices to sound like that. To listen to them, you would think they were English. Could *that* have been what the men in the station meant?

Whatever it was, she and Rafferty fitted in no better than the football fans, and it might be a good idea to move on when the match was over, to a family hotel—if she could find a way to mention it to Rafferty.

The phones were near the front door, in a room of their own, a square, one-window booth set down in each corner of the parquet floor. The ornate plaster ceiling was some fifteen feet above, and each booth had its own flat lid—and no light, as she discovered when she tried to read the list of estate agents.

By the time she had made the third call she had begun to get the picture. They could have a twenty-seven-room mansion, a three-room cottage, a few places that excluded dogs and children, and several that were much too expensive. No? She would want to run an ad, then, they told her. Her pile of the big, flat pennies went down slowly. She was thoroughly sick of reciting her "specifications": a small Georgian house ("Eight rooms," said this agent), close to Dublin ("That's right"), sea or mountain views ("Both"), and the question that always spoiled it, the rent. She asked him to repeat it. He did, and added, "There's no central heating, you understand." He would meet her first thing Monday, he said, the bus terminus at noon. "I'll take you up to Prisma then."

"Prisma?"

"That's what they call the house."

13

Twelve pennies to go. Nine, six, three. There were no other surprises.

She returned to their room, where Rafferty had the gas fire glowing cheerily, though it seemed little warmer. "There's exactly one house," she told him.

"Sounds about right." He showed her the paper, the long column of *Houses & Lands Wanted* and the short list under *To Let*.

She thought of the lawyer—*solicitor*, he called himself—who was handling things for Rafferty and had sent them the list of agents with a note: "Your wife will surely wish to choose a house for herself."

"We might as well put the ad in anyway. Otherwise, if there is something wrong with this house of yours, we'll have lost two days right there."

"Well, yes. I've been wondering, though, if it might not be better to put in just a box number instead of the name of the hotel."

"You know it's a lot easier to get people to phone than to write. We've agreed to admit we're Americans. What else is there to conceal?"

"No. You're right," she said. And he hurried out.

She opened the suitcases and began to unpack. Even if the house was as good as it sounded they couldn't be out of the hotel in less than four or five days. She had to buy a lot of household equipment—a chance to pick up some Irish linens, Rafferty had said when he vetoed taking trunks. "Luggage is what makes travel hell," he said and had nearly eliminated the problem, leaving her to cram everything into four suitcases. No wonder the clothes were wrinkled.

She unwound the cord from the new travel iron and looked around. The bedside lamp led her to what appeared to be the only socket in the room, a flat, brown knob with a pair of large round holes, into which the plug of the iron could not be forced. There was nothing she could do until she got another plug. In the

14

meantime the wrinkles might hang out, and the iron would go away, out of sight, before Rafferty saw it.

Shortly before they were to sail, Dr. Steichen had invited them to a party, not his party, but one given by a friend of his, "Pat" O'Reilley, a man they hardly knew.

O'Reilley had a shamrock on his mailbox, and the drinks he handed them were the greenest Tom Collinses she had ever seen. He had used a heavy hand with the gin too, and he soon had the whole group standing around the piano and singing St. Patrick's Day songs—in August.

After an almost static reprise of *Galway Bay*, O'Reilley cleared his throat and urged them all to lift the yoke of English tyranny from the six counties of Northern Ireland. And, having spoken of "pikes and staffs and our bare hands, if need be," he produced a box. "Something for you to use in our beloved Ireland," he said and thrust the compact weight of it into her hands. "Don't drop it, dear." Drop it? She wanted to throw it into a bucket of water and run.

"If you had any sense you wouldn't have taken that iron," Rafferty said later. "You could have said you had one."

"Just send it back, tell the man we don't have room for it," he said.

And, "You don't take things from strangers. There's no telling what that nut will expect from us now."

What *could* he expect? She would write a nice thank you letter, enclose some pictures, and put an assortment of Irish stamps on the envelope. What else could he possibly expect?

Rafferty had made it to the newspaper office well before closing time, only to discover that noon had been the deadline for ads, and theirs wouldn't be appearing until Tuesday morning. "So we're off to a great start," he said.

15

She nodded, but thought that they might go out with the agent, see his house, and have settled everything even before the ad appeared.

That night she asked the chambermaid, a red-cheeked girl from Wexford, how to go about getting a babysitter.

"You wouldn't want one of them," said the girl. She would keep looking in on Stella and Vanessa until her break, she said, and then they would go feed the ducks the scraps of the girls' breakfast toast.

And so, on Monday, with a spate of warnings—of the fire, of the streets, of strangers—they left the girls and found the Dublin end of the bus route.

When they arrived in the village, the agent was not at the bus terminus, which proved to be no more than a small "bus" sign at the curb. The bus took on a few passengers for the return to town, and when it had gone, they were alone, a brick wall behind them, and across the road, a few shops.

After a while Rafferty asked, "Sure you got the time right?"

"Positive."

"You know, I thought it sounded too good to be true," he said and took out the bus schedule.

A small black car charged into the road, darted back and forth, changing direction with grating gears, and stopped abruptly at their feet. "Bus early again?" the man inside called to them.

Bouncing in the back seat, Alice tried to estimate the distance they were covering. "You want to get up speed for the hill," the agent shouted, turning back to them—unwisely, Alice thought—as they tore along above the railway. The road made a sharp bend, the car lurched up the hill, pawed at the ground, and lost speed while the driver changed down from gear to gear until they inched up over the lip of the incline onto a short stretch of level ground with an even steeper rise ahead.

The man was parking the car. He had run two wheels up onto

16

the sidewalk and was going to leave it that way. "We'd better walk from here," he said.

Ahead of them the road rose up for a long way before it curved out of sight, hemmed in by old stone walls, except where a bulwark of concrete stood with a thin sheet of water flowing down it, as on the flank of a dam.

It was toward this, she saw with surprise, that the agent was heading, toward the rocks along the edge. She noticed then the Hellenic pillars that held an iron arch over the concrete and, in the thicket at the side, the sagging wings of the great gates.

"We should have been driving *down* the hill," he said, bounding from rock to rock. "Down the hill and just swing in through the gate."

Ruts in the surface above the concrete proved that wheeled traffic had passed there at some time.

The lane above was a high-walled passage, open to the sky. Somewhere the seagulls screamed, but she kept her eyes on the ground, a changing surface of mud, gravel, a few yards of cobblestone, and the granite of the mountain itself, slick with years, centuries perhaps, of use. Now and again a telephone pole appeared in the center of the road, which split into two narrow lanes to pass it. A weakness in her legs told her that they were still climbing.

At length they passed through another gate, this one with a small building the size of a garage at one side. The drive mounted the hill steeply, the hedge fell away, and they came out into the open at last. Alice stopped to catch her breath. Prisma stood above them, unmistakably Georgian, the rectangle repeated, contracted, enlarged, and finally abandoned for the one semicircle, which drew all the lines in through the funnels of its fan down to the door and back to the rectangles.

It was piebald, though, splotched with red and tawny yellow on the grey surface, which was a kind of plaster. As they neared it, Alice thought that the yellow seemed to be decay and the red, repair. "We'll look at the exterior later," the agent said, hurrying up to the door, and inside: "We'll start at the top." She took another breath and started up after him. The stairway paused at a windowed landing with a few doors off it (no view there, just the hill sloping up to a stone wall) and swept back on itself to head for the double doors above. The agent bounded up, flung them open and stood back, inviting them in.

Alice passed through the room without seeing it, drawn straight to a window and the vista below. Whatever was beyond the hedge (and a few trails of smoke suggested chimneys) was hidden by the sharp fall of the land. The lawn had become a terrace, propped out over the sea—the sea, islanded and notched with harbors, shone beneath them, its line of headlands receding to the south. Far below them the gulls wheeled, plucked at the water, and soared again, still below.

She looked up at Rafferty, and his gaze, fixed out over the water, made her think of the eagles who had once lived in these Irish cliffs. "Do you know," said the agent, coming up behind them, "you can see Wales on a clear day?"

The room itself was long with a pair of tall many-paned windows on the side and a wider one at the end. It had an enormous, classic fireplace of black marble, a pedimented doorway, and a plaster medallion in the center of the ceiling. Even without the view it would have been a magnificent room. Yet someone had stuck a double bed into one corner, with a dab of carpet beside it. Two straight chairs, a huge wardrobe, and an old wiry electric heater completed the furnishings. "You'd want a carpet in here and a fire in that grate," said the agent. "Mr. Hamilton had to be careful of the stairs so he and his wife spent their time down in the library, but you could easily bring the furniture back up here where it belongs."

Rafferty nodded. He seemed to be just as taken by the house as she was, despite the climb that had her still feeling a little shaky.

There was nothing in the rest of the house to come near the

18

drawing room. The rooms were plain and bright, the trim classic, the furniture sparse and dowdy. "And that's the lot," said the agent. They were standing in the "music room," one of a pair of connecting rooms—this with an old upright piano, the other, the "library," because of a glass-doored bookcase. From these lower windows they saw only a pleasant lawn rolling up to well-trimmed hedges. It was bigger than what they had been thinking of, she realized, and revised her estimate of how much house she could manage.

The agent had cornered Rafferty and was going into the technicalities. ". . . a year, say, with option for renewal, unless, of course, you're interested in buying."

"Excuse me a moment," she said, "but we haven't seen the kitchen."

"Ah, the kitchen," said the agent. "The ladies always want to see the kitchen." He tried to catch Rafferty's eye with a wink. "It's right in here."

He led them to the door at the end of the neoclassical hallway and—"Mind the step"—dropped them into darkness through a hole in time, down worn stone ledges with a smell of ancient excavations, onto the neolithic flags below. "The kitchens," he said, when they had come out of the dark into the grey. An iron stove rusted in a niche like a locomotive left on a weedy siding. Beyond it a fireplace was choked with rubble. The room was surrounded by doors, low filthy doors, and the agent danced from one to another, opening them. "There's the still room. There's the maid's room. There's the scullery. There's the larder. There's the pantry. There's the lock pantry—very handy with children. There's the fuel store." Alice looked through the doors without entering, like someone inspecting a fever hospital, afraid of what she might see. Her eyes had not yet adjusted to the gloom and she escaped with hazy images: the mottled sheen of a sink which seemed to be only knee high; a pale, battered enameled colander. Somewhere water was running, and though the agent scraped his feet a lot, Alice

19

was certain she heard scurrying sounds at the opening of some of the doors.

"It wants a dusting," said the agent, "and a little stove polish. You get a fire going in that"—he slapped the locomotive, showing its solidity—"and you'd be surprised how these flags soak up the heat. You'd come down to a warm kitchen in the morning."

But she was feeling her way up the stairs.

IT WOULDN'T DO TO APPEAR TOO EAGER, RAFFERTY THOUGHT, AS THE agent drove them back to the bus stop. Hold back a bit and they might get some paint in that kitchen. On the other hand he wouldn't want to lose the place. There shouldn't be too much danger, though, in letting it hang overnight and calling the man the first thing in the morning.

"We'll let you know," he said at the bus stop.

"No hurry," said the agent, with a disinterest that was anything but reassuring. If the car hadn't been moving away, Rafferty would have been in danger of committing himself then and there.

The car bounded down the road, honked at a blind corner, and hurtled from view.

"Well," he said, turning to Alice, "what do you think of it?"

He realized, as he said it, that she had been strangely silent the last few minutes. Now she spoke without looking at him. "What does that man think we are?" He hardly recognized her voice.

"What do you mean?" he asked, grabbing her arm and trying to see her face.

"That kitchen. He wasn't going to show it to us. If I hadn't asked he wouldn't have said a word."

"It was pretty bad. But if we play our cards right I think we can get him to paint it."

"Paint it? Paint!"

Now was the time for him to speak out, if he was ever going to speak. *I want that drawing room.* They could work out a kitchen

20

somewhere. They might adapt one of the bedrooms, or put a hot plate in the dining room, get a lot of chafing dishes. And what about the maid? It was agreed that they would be able to have a maid, and wouldn't she be the one in charge of the kitchen?

"What are you going to put the paint on?" Alice was saying. "Right on top of the fungus and the rot? Talk about whiting sepulchres."

"You haven't heard what I have to say."

"And how about the stove, and the stone floor, and the sink? Paint them in a contrasting shade? The only thing you could do with Prisma is dynamite it."

To say anything now would be the act of a brute. And the bus was coming.

"All right," he said. "But I think you'd better find the house by yourself. I can't put in any more time on it."

"Oh, Rafferty."

"It's not as though that's the only house. Ireland must be full of old houses. We'll see what the ad brings in."

3.

The first answer came the next morning before breakfast, a telephone call down in the phone room; there were no extensions. Rafferty, trousers pulled on over pajamas and his raincoat buttoned to the neck, hurried out with the bellboy.

"Well?" she asked when he returned.

"I don't know what to make of it." He handed her his notes.

"*Two reception rooms.* They must think we're the embassy."

"But only two bedrooms."

He had hardly unbuttoned the raincoat when there was another knock at the door.

She was dressed in time to take the third call, and in the lower corridor she came upon the Manageress, standing there like the captain on a burning bridge. She plucked the bellboy from Alice's elbow. "Mrs. Rafferty knows where the telephones are," she said and sent him running down the back hall toward the sound of exploding crockery.

22

When their own breakfasts arrived the boy looked breathless. "Sorry, we're behind with the trays this morning," he said, putting the second tray on the luggage rack and leaving at a trot.

Beneath their domed covers the plates were barely warm. Rafferty dented the pool of waxy bacon fat with his fork. "Look at that."

"I'm afraid our phone calls might be responsible," she said.

"Half a dozen phone calls? I'm not going to believe that."

"It's this time of day. The Manageress was upset anyway."

Rafferty skewered his bacon and toast on a fork and warmed them at the gas fire. She had to do the same for Stella and Vanessa. Nothing could be done about the soft-boiled eggs, never a favorite style, but, safe in their shells, the wisest thing to order from an uncertain kitchen. The girls could not be threatened—or bribed—into eating theirs. And so, rather than send them back, opened and studded with unmelting butter, Alice ate them herself.

They lay uneasily in her stomach when she went down to the lounge after breakfast to be nearer the phones and save the bellboys the long walk up to their room. They were tipping only sixpence, but better to be thought mean, Rafferty said, than risk upsetting the status quo. (And, in fact, one of the boys had told him, "You wouldn't have to give me something every time.")

She made her way to the windowseat while the others, already in their places by the fire, stirred beneath the morning's papers, shot out an eye, and returned to shelter. Most of them had the London papers—fortunately, considering the ad.

She still didn't know what to make of these people. They didn't act like transients. This morning they were bobbing up from their papers to read out a line or two, keeping an outraged eye on the government, the one in England. Because of it, she gathered, they would be here and not on the Mediterranean when the winter came upon them.

23

Winter seemed to obsess them. Somewhere, one of them read, a geologist had detected signs of a new ice age, and a letter to the editor brought them the disturbing news that the coats of the New Forest ponies were heavier than usual.

Out the beautiful old front windows, beyond the reflected lights of the room, the street glistened. A cart went slowly past, the driver's head beneath a dripping sack.

"If it were only a *dry* cold," said one of the women.

That wouldn't make much difference, if the other rooms were anything like theirs, Alice thought. The gas fire was a joke in a place that size, and they were never far ahead of its appetite for shillings. The Manageress suggested they try the bank for the coins and told them to feel free to enjoy the lounge.

She was everywhere they went: at the desk, beside the dining room, in the cold, green bathrooms. Once, when a vacuum cleaner on the stairs sent Alice cutting through the floor below theirs, she came upon the Manageress with a bellboy and a chambermaid, the three of them carrying a long length of lace down the hall. "Oh, Mrs. Rafferty, your room's above, on the next floor."

"Yes," she said, and hurried to the far stairs while the Manageress just stood there, waiting with her group and the lace, like a party of trainbearers who had lost the wedding.

And now she had the phone calls, a string of embarrassments, but also assurances that Prisma was not their only chance to escape. Tomorrow she would go out and see what they had brought in.

When she returned to the lounge after taking yet another call, one of the women asked, "Have you had many answers, dear?"

So it was no secret. "A few," she said. (And, in fact, not more than two or three met all their requirements.)

"It's very hard to find anything with central heating, you know."

"Oh, we don't expect that, really," Alice said, and the newspapers were lowered in several chairs.

24

"There's no letting in Dublin at all these days, as you know," said one of the others.

"Of course, if you don't mind saying *American*, you might find someone to reply." That was the old, white-mustached man who sat closest to the fire.

"Oh, we did." It was even money that they had read the ad aloud when she had been out of the room.

"You know they'll raise the rents for you then and central heating costs a lot to run anyway," said the old man, who twice earlier had said that he hadn't been warm since he had left Johore.

"One or two do seem quite high," she said, deciding not to protest her indifference to heat again. "But then we really don't know what we should expect to pay."

"No, you wouldn't," the old man said, not unkindly. There were nods around the room, and she waited for someone to enlighten her. She couldn't ask.

The door rattled then, and Rafferty came in with the two little girls. She had forgotten to tell him about the slacks. He crossed the room, holding out *Pinocchio*. "How's it going?" he asked.

"Fine," she said.

"Good. I've got to go out now, and you might as well all stay down here. It's freezing upstairs."

HE LIKED DUBLIN, ONCE HE HAD FOUND IT—NOT IN THOSE FINE OLD buildings, Leinster House or the old Parliament, where he had to keep reminding himself that he was looking at *originals*, but in the Georgian rows, mile after mile of them, the houses all the same and all different, like people. For a while in Dublin it must have been almost impossible to build a bad house. There was even one house that had a second slate roof sitting up atop the first, like a hat, and yet it looked right. He knew he would remember those streets forever, the two rows of facing houses with the rounded

25

mountains at the end, and the great Liffey gulls screaming in, as fierce as seraphim.

The ministry to which he had been writing was housed in a newer building of some non-vintage year, and was so poorly marked that he was carried past the door twice before he found it.

"You shouldn't be here until Wednesday week," said the secretary when she had read the letter he handed her. The other girl, the black-haired one, had stopped typing.

"I know," he said, "I was hoping you could put it forward. We'd planned to spend more time touring the country." Oakley to New York, New York to Cobh, Cobh to Dublin. He had had enough of the road for a while.

"You want a different time?"

The boy across the room put down his magnum of ink to give their conversation his entire attention.

"I'd like to see this man as soon as possible."

The girl looked at the calendar on her desk and at the letter again, and then back at the calendar—waiting for the date to change? "Kevin," she said, finally, "where's Mr. Duffy?"

The boy sauntered out the door and the other girl resumed her typing with the hollow slap of the keys on a yellow cardboard form. Duffy, Rafferty thought. Ó Dubhthaigh was Duffy.

Mr. Duffy came with ink on the side of his nose, and he looked stuffed, as though he had his clothes on over his pajamas. Rafferty tried to explain what had happened.

"We've given him time on Wednesday week," the secretary interrupted.

"Oh," said Mr. Duffy. "I'm late for my lunch as it is."

"Let me take you to lunch, won't you?" Rafferty asked.

"I don't mind. I won't be a minute," he said and darted out with his little bald spot shining pink behind him.

26

He returned shortly, cinching the belt of a double-breasted overcoat, not a tweed, but a pile fabric with a curious surface, like megalithic tomb carvings. The ink was nearly gone, his nose red, a dry wash.

"How much time do you have?" Rafferty asked Mr. Duffy. "I don't know any of the restaurants around here." They had reached the street door, and the walks, crowded earlier, now looked almost impenetrable.

"There's a grand place, just beyond," said Mr. Duffy, slipping himself into a gap in the walkers. Rafferty followed, dodging prams, umbrellas, and shuffling old men. Several times he lost his man and then recognized the coat ten or twelve feet ahead and moving fast. They crossed a couple of streets. Rafferty's tendency there was to outflank the crowd in the intersection and then find himself trotting along in the gutter, a prey to jangling bicycles and unable to break back into the stream on the walk. The second time it happened he thought he had lost him entirely, when a hand pulled him into an open doorway.

It was a good thing he had Mr. Duffy with him; left to himself, he would have passed up the place.

"There's no queue yet, thank God," said Mr. Duffy, pointing up the dark stairs.

The room above was obviously popular with the men. There was not a table empty, and more feet could be heard on the stairs behind.

"Ah, there," Mr. Duffy said, and dove into the back of the room with Rafferty in pursuit. There was a small open space on the narrow upholstered bench along the wall.

Two men were already on the other side of the table, which was none too wide. There was something beneath the table too, a dog. A good spot for a one-legged man, he thought, feeling around for somewhere to put his second foot. He tried to cross his legs and came up hard against the table. "Excuse me," he said to the two

27

men, who had ignored the bump that shook the dishes, but now looked startled by his apology. He rested his foot gently on top of the dog.

The waiter charged up, flicked his towel at the table, and put down jug-sized glasses of stout and slopping soup plates. Perhaps Mr. Duffy had a standing order.

"Your soup will be cold," warned Mr. Duffy, launching into his own without even unbuttoning his teddy-bear outfit first.

Cautiously Rafferty tried it. The soup was lukewarm and with neither texture nor flavor, surprisingly, since the sight of it had led him to expect something less palatable. Mr. Duffy, he was now thinking, must have brought him here for the atmosphere only. And, in a day when things were becoming increasingly standardized, he was glad to have come. There was no mistaking this for anything in Oakley. It might have been easier to carry on a conversation in a less picturesque spot, though. There was going to be no quiet cup of coffee at the end of this meal—to say nothing of the cigars and brandy that would have been a legitimate expense.

Over the chop, a neat shape of bone and fat, Rafferty tried to bring up his business. Across the table the man in an old bowler hat and spotted overcoat kept chewing, with his eyes fixed on the wall just to the side of Rafferty's head. Mr. Duffy nodded and slid out from under a few questions awkwardly enough to make Rafferty wonder whether he remembered anything at all, or perhaps, as his attention to his chop suggested, he was not to be disturbed while feeding.

The sight of two-handed eating still made Rafferty think of farmers at church suppers, men whose Old World manners he had in the past put down to untutored gluttony. Here, of course, he was the odd man out. Well, he might have to drive down the left side of the road, but he drew the line at holding the fork in his left hand.

While they waited for their "sweet," as Mr. Duffy called what had appeared across the table, shapes covered with the too-yellow custard that he had already learned to watch out for, Rafferty tried to bring up business again.

"Ah, yes. I'd like to run through the file again, and we'll see when we can reschedule you. You'd better give me the name of your hotel." He had forgotten all right—if Duffy was in fact Ó Dubhthaigh.

"Before I can do anything, I'll have to have your list of hand-weavers," he said.

"Ah, *yes*," said Mr. Duffy, with a different tone this time, coming in perhaps on the rising tide of recollection, "would there ever be anything, do you think, in a nylon tweed? Handwoven, of course?"

The dog beneath his foot stirred at Rafferty's annoyance. "I come from a long line of woolmen," he said. There was no point in saying more to this man: how his brother, Frank, was busy turning the mill into a parody of Progress—synthetic fibers, automation—a project so big that the money for the Irish weavers was, as Frank put it, a pimple on the elephant's ass. "I'd like to stick to wool."

"Yes, as you say. Ah, *there* you are," Mr. Duffy continued, though it wasn't clear whether he was addressing Rafferty or the pudding itself.

"They do a nice lunch," Mr. Duffy said later, as they left. (There was a queue, all right, all the way down the stairs.)

"Would you not go to the Gaeltacht, Mr. Rafferty?" Mr. Duffy was saying.

"That was my original plan"—whitewashed cottages, bare stony fields, *Man of Aran* and *The Playboy of the Western World* —"but I was told that if I didn't speak Gaelic, I'd have to have a native works manager, while I sat at a desk, preferably in Dublin."

"Ah, it's the young people, Mr. Rafferty. They'd see you with your clothes and a car and speaking the English. It's hard enough keeping them home as it is."

29

"And so it was agreed that the whole organization would stay here, in the East."

"Not that there aren't Irish speakers in the East, as well."

"That's right." He wasn't going down that road now. "It's the weavers I want, though. I was told there are a number near by."

"Ah, yes, we've got a list. I'll see you get it immediately, tomorrow, just as soon as we can find a few minutes for you," said Mr. Duffy, stepping out into a shoal of midday walkers who swept him on his way.

"WHERE HAVE YOU BEEN?" ALICE ASKED. "WE HAD TO EAT WITHOUT you."

"I took the man from the ministry out to lunch."

"You did? Where?" she said, thinking of their lunch down among the sauce bottles in the cold dining room.

"Some sort of men's grill."

"You mean a place where women can't go?"

"I don't know. There weren't any there," he said. "You sound as if you'd prefer we'd gone where there *were* women."

She laughed. "Dont be silly." It was annoying, though, that he had gone where she couldn't go. "Was it nice?"

"All right. A bit crowded, though."

"How much was it?" she asked, picking up her pen, to show him that it was as bookkeeper she asked.

"Thirteen and six."

Just under two dollars, she figured. "Each?"

"No, all together, including drinks."

"What about the tip?"

"Included."

"Well, it certainly couldn't have been very good." You never knew though, sometimes an inexpensive thing like cheese, bread, and beer made the best meal.

30

The afternoon had brought them a heavy mail, and more replies arrived the next morning, while the phone calls continued to trickle in and some unstamped envelopes came, marked, "By Hand."

After breakfast Alice hurried out to inspect a few of the nearer houses. It was only a short bus ride to the first one, Sandymount. She had found it on the map, near the sea, and hadn't expected the tight little row of red brick houses, with neither sea nor sand in sight. And yet, if you overlooked the fact that the house had no view and that the rooms were cramped and cluttered, it did have a kind of Peter Rabbit charm about it.

The owner, a fat woman with three fat dogs, had held Alice on the phone for ten minutes the day before, but hadn't mentioned everything. Yes, she said, as they sat in the drawing room beneath the round black eyes of two big china dogs on the mantel, the Raffertys could have the house immediately, just as soon as she moved out—and she would move out just as soon as she found a flat—and she would find a flat just as soon as she started to look for one—and she would start to look just as soon as the Raffertys agreed to take the house. And there she stopped, as though that were the end of the story, the pig had jumped over the stile, and they all got home that night.

One of the dogs at their feet in front of the fire snored, and Alice went out to the bus stop and tacked back across town on a trio of buses to the next house. There she discovered that "partially furnished" could mean a strip of "lino" in the hall and a pair of derelict wardrobes, too large to move.

By the time she was back in the center of town, it was after one o'clock, and Rafferty had an appointment coming up. So that was her day's work—nothing. She returned to the Imperial, and as she passed the lounge she saw Stella and Vanessa sitting primly inside. Rafferty was nowhere in sight, and the Manageress was materializing out of the shadows and was sure to see the unsupervised children.

31

She hurried around to the lounge door. "Daddy's at the telephone," Stella called down the length of the room. The residents looked up from their papers. One of the women was certainly out of her usual place, closer to the windowseat than before. What did that mean?

"Come on," she said. "We'll go up now."

"Did you find a house, dear?" asked the woman who had moved. Around the room the newspapers drooped.

"No," Alice said. "I was out looking this morning, but they weren't what we wanted."

"Here in Dublin?"

"Yes. One was Sandymount."

"Oh, you wouldn't like Sandymount," said another woman.

"No," said the first. "It's not suitable."

Alice nodded. "It wasn't," she said and shooed the girls out through the lounge door.

When they had gained the privacy of the back stairs she said to the girls, "Well, I certainly hope you weren't being a nuisance in the lounge."

"Oh, no," said Stella. "They started the talking."

"They did? About what?"

"Oh, you know. About being Stella Anne Rafferty and Vanessa Mary Rafferty, and how old we are. Only Nessa said she was five."

"*Almost* five," said the three-year-old.

"Did they ask about anything else?"

"Just what you and Daddy did. And I said Daddy was a typewriter, and you're a cook."

"Oh."

"That's right, isn't it?" Stella asked, bounding ahead to the landing so that she could see Alice's face.

"Well . . . yes."

32

4.

THE NEWSPAPER ACCOUNT A FEW DAYS LATER WAS NOT MUCH MORE accurate. *Mr. Rafferty is president of the Rafferty Woollen Mills in Oakley, U.S.A., and is Professor of History at Oakley University.*

"It's a good thing no one will be seeing that," she said. She wouldn't worry too much about Frank's finding his position at the mill taken over, but let Dr. Steichen read a story like that, and he would think that Rafferty had promoted himself from Assistant Professor and had been ashamed to admit that Oakley was only a college.

The picture was a poor likeness of himself, too, Rafferty said, although the pair of civil servants had come out well. "I thought we were getting somewhere when my man brought out the Brass, there," he said, pointing to the older man, "but he went to show the photographer out and never came back. I thought I was going to get the list until that happened. You know, I wouldn't be surprised if I didn't get it today either."

33

"Why do you say that?"

He just shook his head. "Well, we'll see."

When he had gone she took the girls downstairs for a while. The sun had come out during breakfast and was pouring in through the opened windows of the lounge. The fire was burning, too, and the radiators were hot. A few of the residents, outfitted in hairy tweeds, hovered near the windows, waiting for something—a car to take them to the country, she gathered. Before she had settled the girls into the windowseat a woman in lilac tweed was saying to her, "A charming picture of your husband this morning."

"Yes," Alice said, "I thought so."

"I should think you'd be going to the West, where the weavers are." The group at the window turned to her and nodded.

"Oh, we wanted to, but there's the language problem. We don't speak Gaelic."

There was a silence, an exchange of glances, Alice thought, and then a man in a magnificent orange tweed jacket said, "I think you must have been sent some outdated information. They speak English as well as you do."

"Well," she said, not sure how to take that, "we can't change now. The ministry said we'd need a native-speaking works manager, and we didn't want that."

"You're quite right," said another, a man in a splendid green tweed jacket and plus fours, very wide ones, in which Stella and Vanessa seemed unduly interested.

"The position is," said the orange tweed, "the government grants a subsidy in the Gaeltacht to every family that can convince the government inspector that they speak Irish in the home."

"Charming people," said the lilac tweed.

"You'd want to watch them, though," said the green tweed.

"They'll stretch the cloth, you know," said the orange tweed.

"No."

34

"Oh, yes. Tie one end to the cottage and the other to a donkey and just pull."

"If the cottage can take it," the other man added drolly.

They nodded, agreeing.

"Of course, you're better off in Dublin," said the green tweed, "but you have to have weavers."

"They've got a list at the ministry."

"Wicklow, I imagine," said the green tweed.

The orange tweed nodded gravely. "You'll have to watch for tinkers."

"Charming people," said the lilac.

Their car drove up then and they left. She saw them through the window, three of them folded into the back seat of a Ford Anglia, off to lunch in the Vale of Avoca. The others went back to their papers, and when the chambermaid finished her morning's work, she came in for the two girls so that Alice could spend the rest of the day inspecting houses. Rafferty would be back before the girl had to return to work. (She worked an eight-hour day, with a four-hour break in the middle of it, which made twelve hours, as Alice saw it, to the girl's amusement. She was not long up from the country, she said, and what would she do with her time if she had it all at once?)

They had had at least fifty replies to the ad, although a good half of the houses came to more than they could pay. Some of them might have been worth the money, but the man who wanted sizable payments made to a bank in Majorca didn't seem to have much of a place. Others quoted reasonable rents and then mentioned, in passing, the resident gardener or a ghillie (some kind of caretaker, she deduced) to be paid by the tenant, or that "rates," as they called taxes, were extra. When she had eliminated these houses and those which were too small and the ones shared with strangers in varying degrees of intimacy, she was left with less than a dozen prospects, spread throughout nearly every suburb of

35

Dublin. And, as the buses and trains started and ended in Dublin, it was a rare day that let her see more than two houses.

"They're not what I had in mind," she told Rafferty.

"No? Kitchens bad, I suppose."

"They're nothing like the one you have in mind," she said, although they were closer to Prisma's than she cared to admit. "It's just the idea of being in a beautiful country like this and living in a little grey house, squashed between two other grey houses."

"I see lots of red brick houses," Rafferty said.

"Well, they're grey inside. The wallpaper looks like lumpy oatmeal, and they smell of mildew."

Rafferty nodded and went on with his newspaper, the limp pages turning with an unnatural silence. The porcelain of the fire tinkled, cooling as the flame dropped, and she hurried to the black meter in the corner with another shilling before the fire could pop out.

"Two left," she said.

"I don't see why you don't go out and get a roll of shillings and stop talking about it."

"I've certainly tried. The bank would give me only five, and I don't think I could cash a check every morning. I got two at the P.O. today, but the American Express didn't have any, or that damned harpy downstairs."

"Alice."

"Well, it's her meter. She could provide us with change or tokens at least."

Rafferty shook his head. "I'll get the shillings."

"No, you've got enough to do." It was an hour's, two hours' work, just finding the shillings. You'd be better off chopping firewood.

"All right, then," he agreed.

"But you could ask every time you got change."

36

HE ASKED, WHEN HE REMEMBERED, BUT DIDN'T HAVE MUCH LUCK. People would be more willing to oblige a woman, he thought. Besides, Alice could have them all out of that hotel any time she wanted to.

He wondered how the idea had got going that women were the civilizing force. Businessmen's wives, prodding their husbands on to the symphony, was that it? What about the quiet job of day in, day out, wing clipping that most of them did? Some of his friends didn't even feel the shears any more. "Don't you think we ought to be going home now?" or "Yes, it's nice, but where will you put it when you get it home?" All they could do was hole up in their offices at school and say they were correcting papers. Even Alice noticed it. He couldn't help thinking that she would have seen this situation in a much clearer light if it had been happening to one of their friends.

He hadn't dared hope that they would find a house like Prisma, not one they could afford. There might not be another drawing room like that in Ireland. How many houses had more than one real room anyway? One couple in Oakley took people upstairs to a back bedroom to point out a narrow view of the river. And another had built their living room around an exposed chimney breast of old firebrick, *c.* 1895; and that was *it*.

Forget it. He had enough to think about without that. It wasn't only Mr. Duffy and his receding appointments. Out of half-a-dozen important contacts on his list—spinners, dyers, finishers— the only one he had been able to reach first try had been the garage man, who had given him a complete, orderly, and logical explanation of why the car he had ordered and paid for before leaving America was not ready for him. It had been annoying at the time, but the garage man was rising in his estimation, now that he had seen a few other firms in operation.

"Just stop in at the premises when you get to Dublin and we'll work out the details," a Mr. Callahan had written, and a Mr. Lynch on the other side of the Liffey had used almost the same words. When he dropped in, Mr. Lynch's secretary said, "Ah, yes, we've been expecting you. The moment he comes in I'll tell him you were here, Mr. Mahaffy."

He hadn't caught Mr. Lynch yet, but he had seen Mr. Callahan once, had been taken to lunch by him, the sort of thing he had had in mind when he had asked Mr. Duffy out. Mr. Callahan had a longer dinner hour, a much longer dinner hour, so long that Rafferty began to be troubled by it.

"Ah, there's nothing that Miss Madigan can't handle."

"Listen," Rafferty said. "I'll walk you back there, I could use a little air."

"Capital. Just as soon as I finish this. You'd better have another," he said with a flick of his finger that brought the waiter over with two more brandies.

Rafferty thought of a stream of clients dropping in at the premises to see Mr. Callahan. Didn't the man know he had the Rafferty business in the bag? But Mr. Callahan was already well into a story, too good to break in on, and when they parted at last, he said to Rafferty, "Just stop in at the premises tomorrow or the next day and we'll work out the details."

Outside the light was going, and back at the Imperial he found that he needed a nap. He waked to find the shutters closed and Alice sitting icily in front of the fire.

"Listen, I don't feel much like dinner. You go on and I'll put the girls to bed when you get back."

"What time do you think it is?"

Rising on his elbow he could see that the girls were asleep. The tiny travel alarm beside the bed seemed to say 10:15.

"Men's grill again, I suppose."

"No, a very nice place, I'll take you there sometime."

So that was one more thing he had to do.

There wasn't a thing he could think of that he had actually accomplished, except the trip to St. Patrick's to see Swift's grave and to Christ Church for Strongbow's. His solicitor hadn't been expecting him until the following week and had gone fishing in Galway, taking with him the lease and key to the building that was to be the Dublin workroom, or so the secretary seemed to be saying.

The building was a carriage house in the mews behind one of the Georgian rows. Number Eleven. He had picked it from the short list that the solicitor had sent him in the summer and had been taken back a bit by the discovery in the following letter that, although he was buying the building, there was to be a clause forbidding its use as a dwelling house. Perhaps it was just as well, he thought, as he made his way down the mews. Some of the buildings looked abandoned, and those in use were mostly for commercial purposes, though he did have a near miss with a pan of dishwater flung out into the gutter from one of the doorways. On second thought, however, he could see how the possibility of having to live there might have had considerable educational value for Alice.

In Number Eight the tenant was an agreeable young man in business with an acetylene torch and a few other pieces of related machinery. He let Rafferty have a look through the building to get some idea of what to expect in Number Eleven. If they were as alike inside as out, then the "enclosed delivery space" which had appealed to him was a cobbled stable yard, closed to the public view by a pair of high, massive doors (on his own building the hinges sagged suspiciously) but open to the sky, in that climate more of a recommendation to a bootlegger than to a wool factor.

"Mind the step," the young man called in a hollow voice from behind his welder's mask.

There was a great deal of room upstairs, fine for office and inventory, with plenty of room below for filling the beams.

"It just depends on what condition mine's in," he told Alice.

"You really can't tell from the outside." At least he hoped not.

"I know," said Alice, feelingly. "You could use this time to see if there's anything better before you actually buy it. Better to lose the deposit and have done with it."

"I went around to a couple of the estate agents after I left it and looked into some other places. At that price they're all pretty much the same, once you get around the way they describe them." Out and out lying was what he would call it, and he hadn't looked any further.

SHE MIGHT HAVE SAVED QUITE A BIT OF TIME IF SHE HAD HAD THE vocabulary down in the beginning. A "reception room" was no more than a catch-all term for those rooms, rectangular boxes with one door and a fireplace, rooms that happened to be a living room, a dining room, a library, for as long as they were furnished that way. And any bit of ground, no matter how small, was a "garden" if it wasn't actually paved or graveled, and if it was, it was a "yard." So she shouldn't have said, as she had several times early in her search, that she wanted a "yard for the children."

The good houses must have been passing from hand to hand without appearing on the rental market. What they were offered, no one else had wanted.

The problem was not that she had been accustomed to luxury. Their place in Oakley had been an ordinary upstairs, adapted by a handyman who had left the closets in the living room and the kitchen, and installed a sink that wouldn't drain when the plug was in the bathtub.

Fortunately Frank was footing most of the hotel bill. Until they found a house, was the agreement, but he hadn't meant indefinitely, and even if he had, she still had to deal with the gas meter. Sometimes it seemed that the only business of her day was to bag seven or eight of those coins: silvery, the size of a quarter, the Irish ones with a bull, the English with a king or queen. They all

40

worked in the meter, but where were they? Locked into the gas meters of Dublin?

The big stores were hopeless, giving her no more than a "sorry" when she asked for a shilling in the change. She did best in the smallest shops—newspapers and a pyramid of oranges, a single light bulb and no heat—where old men or women, sometimes with the thumb and forefinger sliced from a glove so that they could handle the coins, would search through the cardboard cash box for her shilling.

Back at the hotel, with her parcels (biscuits, cheese, and fruit for a lunch by the gas fire, a respite from the Brussels sprouts in the dining room), she found herself wondering if there were not another door, one that wouldn't take her through the narrow straits between the lounge and the office. Beyond their glass wall the residents stirred on the tree-of-life carpet. The mood of the sunny morning had not returned. She wondered if she had profited that day from the newspaper story that had made Rafferty seem a man of substance, or if they could have felt a passing kinship with her, all of them strangers among the Gaels.

It was a few steps farther on, where the hall widened again, that the Manageress lay in ambush. "Ah, Mrs. Rafferty. Any luck today?"

"I'm afraid not." Back in the lounge the residents seemed to be watching her over the tops of their newspapers.

"You *will* let me know," said the Manageress. "You're welcome to stay, of course, but we would like a date, just for the books."

"I'll tell you the moment I know," she said. "The house I saw today wasn't suitable," she added, to show that she was trying, but the Manageress had faded away. Alice started down the corridor.

"You should take the lift," said the Manageress, coming back.

"I thought I'd see if there was any mail."

"Your husband took it when he went up."

"Oh, thank you." Alice turned and headed for the lift, which was hardly a convenience, being at the wrong end of the hotel and leaving her to climb up and down a staircase which stood like a twelve-foot stile in the upper corridor, at the juncture of the houses that formed the hotel.

"You'll be going to Leopardstown tomorrow?" asked the boy in the lift, which rose slowly.

"The races? I have to stay with the little girls."

"Take them along, they'd enjoy it."

"Maybe," she said, knowing she would do no such thing.

"You'd want to watch Birmingham Boy," he said, stopping at her floor. "The brother knows the lad."

"Oh, I will, thank you," she said, and stepped out, wondering what she could have been warned of—and then remembered that a *lad* was a stable boy.

In their room Rafferty put down the paper. "Any luck?"

"You share a kitchen," she said, dismissing the house she had been out to see. "But I got a tip on a horse."

"Great." He picked up his coat. "I'll be back in time for dinner."

"Anything happen here?"

He shook his head. "Not unless you count the changing of the curtains, a three-man act, a little long for my taste," he said, looking over at the windows, where the curving folds hung almost as if they had been carved.

"You should have seen it, Mama," Stella said. "The bars come down like swings."

"Oh, well, the way things are going, Mama will get to see it the next time," Rafferty said and slipped out into the hall before she could ask him what he meant by that.

5.

SOMETIMES THEY PASSED LIKE RELAY RUNNERS, HANDING OVER THE girls, pulling on a raincoat, and hurrying out the door.

"Any luck?" Rafferty asked on his way out.

"No." He could have the details in the evening.

"There's another letter for you on the mantel. Something's going to pop up one of these days."

"I suppose so," she said, shutting the door behind him. The ad might continue to pull in a reply or two a day, but they weren't really in the game.

She checked on the little girls, who were napping, and turned down the fire to save the gas. The envelope on the mantel was of pale blue paper, the address written with blue ink in square handwriting. She dropped it unopened into the wastebasket. She didn't want to look at another house—not that anything had happened in the morning that hadn't happened before. A pleasant woman had shown her through a little grey house, semi-detached.

She had once thought that the word carried overtones of remoteness. "Completely attached" would be a better way to put it, the two houses a pair of Siamese twins, joined at the hall doors; street after street, town after town, in concrete, pebble-dash, and sometimes red brick, they waited for her.

Inside, the two "reception rooms" lay one behind another, their wallpaper the color and pattern of oatmeal, their windows looking out onto hedges ten feet away, so that the light slanted down, as into a well. If the upper windows, above the hedges and walls, sometimes opened out onto scenes of amazing beauty, these upper rooms, small and single-windowed (and often with hand basin, h. & c.) could not be imagined as anything but bedrooms. And over all there was a smell of damp and mold, and the question of why, in a housing shortage, this house was available.

What if she had not seen Prisma? Was she expecting those hedged-in reception rooms to stand up beside that drawing room above the sea? Sometimes she felt that Rafferty was still seriously considering Prisma—and blaming her for finding the kitchen impossible. Yet, even now, some twenty kitchens later, it kept its reading of absolute zero, which made it possible to see the merits of the others, those square rooms with red tile floors and a black stove in a niche and, just standing there like the furnishings in a doll's house, a square electric cooker, a rectangular deal table, and two bentwood chairs. The sink was off in the damp closet that they called the scullery. The dishes were in the pantry. The food went into the larder, the coal in the fuel store, the maid—if you could get her—in the maid's room.

She went back and fished the blue envelope from the wastebasket. *Two reception rooms,* she read, *garden in rere, usual out offices, semi-detached.*

What about the West? Depopulated, the papers said. Rafferty would have to go it alone there, without the help of the ministry, which might not be a bad idea.

She wadded the empty blue envelope and missed the wastebas-

44

ket, just as there was a knock on the door. It was one of the bell-boys, carrying a black book and a small box of tools or something else that clanked. He eyed the bed where the girls were sleeping and said in a low voice, "Gas meter." She nodded. Could it be that the meter actually was faulty, and they were now to get a reasonable return for their shillings? At the meter, after a few clicks, there was a rush of coins into the box. The bellboy knelt on one knee to count them, and Alice watched, ashamed of her own interest.

"How many?" she asked.

"Forty-seven!" He noted it in the book.

"Here. Let me buy a pound back," she said, going for her purse. He smiled, shook his head, and tipped the coins into a canvas bag which she hadn't noticed earlier. "What difference does it make, as long as you have the right amount of money?"

"She has to have it this way." He tightened the neck of the bag.

"The Manageress?" she asked, following him to the door. He nodded. "When do you take it there?"

"After these." He pointed down the stub end of the corridor. "They're four, five bob, mostly."

"I think I'll go down and ask her to sell me some back."

"You could do that," he said, but she could see that he was surprised by the idea.

The dead weight of the coins dragged at her suit pockets, and her cheeks tingled in the cold air of the corridor as she sailed by the glass-walled lounge, down the hall to the back stairs.

"It's impossible," the Manageress had said with a finality that would have sent a beggar on his way, but had had no answer to *Why*, just vague talk of "routine" and "uses." It had all been no credit to the Manageress, who had been concealing whatever was her real reason. After what she had gone through to get those shillings Alice did have a moral right to expect their return. She wished she had not used those words, however, wished that she had not gone down at all.

In the room the little girls were still asleep. It was hard to realize that she had been gone for no more than five minutes. She put three of the shillings on the mantel, the other forty-four she slipped into a back pocket of a suitcase. There was no way to tell Rafferty what she had done. The shillings would last them a week, but she could not think of remaining there that long. They could move to another, more congenial hotel tomorrow. And then?

HE RETURNED JUST IN TIME TO TELL HER: "I DON'T THINK I'LL GO down to dinner. I had some stout and a sandwich and I'm not hungry."

She nodded.

"I'll put the girls to bed," he said. He had something else to make up for her trip down to the dining room. "Look," he said, "four shillings for the kitty."

"Oh, good," she said in an offhand way, as though she had never mentioned the subject before. "I've been thinking," she said then. "I phoned the agent this afternoon and told him we'd take Prisma."

"Good girl," he said, hugging her. "I knew you'd come around."

He was hungry after all, he realized as soon as the others had left the room. For a moment he considered following them down —and considered the explanations it would entail. He uncorked a Guinness instead, took a bag of biscuits from the wardrobe, and ate, watching the crumbs. Alice would think he had planned it this way, anything to escape the dining room.

Tension, that was what had been spoiling his appetite, the thought that the one house he had ever cared about was slipping from his grasp, and at a time like this. The list was lost. "It's not

46

lost," Mr. Duffy had said that afternoon, "it's just a question of putting my hands on it." The solicitor was expected back from his fishing trip in the morning—just as he had been expected every morning for a week. And the car—the garage man had kept reassuring him until he had given that screw a few turns too many. And now he was trying to imagine what the fiddle might be. Whatever it was, they probably wouldn't have the car for the move out to the house.

He wondered what could have made her change her mind, probably nothing more than a slow piling up of straws, until she knew that she couldn't do better.

H.W.R. Forbes, said the sign downstairs, gold on black, *Conveyancing, Wills & Testaments, Comm^er for Oaths.*

He didn't look as though he wanted to be asked how they had been biting. It was hard to imagine the man with fishing gear at all, let alone spending an extra week at it when he could have been conveyancing.

"You'd better take a look at the mews building before we carry on with the documents," said Forbes.

"I will." He wondered if that was the sort of advice they were paying the man for.

"And if you intend to use the stairway, it might not be a bad idea to have it braced." Rafferty nodded. "There's a man near you there who might give you an estimate. He's done work for me."

The key was something to see. It felt like a wrench in his pocket, and he was surprised to find that it fit the keyhole nicely. It would not turn the lock, though. Damn Forbes, he thought, rattling the key, and was just giving the door a kick for good measure when the smell of pipe smoke told him that he was not alone. He turned his head and saw an old man with a raisin face, right at his elbow. "Yes?" Rafferty said.

"You'd want a eyelet," said the old man.

"Eyelet?"

He nodded and went on his way, shuffling quickly down the alley.

Gimlet, he supposed that was what the old snoop meant. But he wouldn't know how to go about picking a lock, and didn't like the idea anyway. He looked at the key again. It was labeled properly, and it did fit the keyhole. He assaulted the door once more, turning the key clockwise, counterclockwise, forced it a little, worried about damaging the lock. The key was indestructible. At last he stepped back to see whether there might not be some other means of entry. The old man was returning, he saw to his dismay, and was still talking about the eyelet. It was, however, an oil can that he held.

"Oh, *oil* it," Rafferty said.

The raisin face smiled and nodded, "Eyelet."

He was right. The lock, oiled and eased back and forth, yielded at last.

"That was a great help," Rafferty said and, thinking a tip might be in order, reached into his pocket.

"Ah, no, Mr. Rafferty," said the old man and went off with the oil can.

What was he to make of that: expected, recognized, and aided? He must have had curiosity and gossip to thank. The thought occurred to him, and not for the first time, that it might have been wiser to have written fewer and vaguer letters to the ministry.

The building hadn't been as bad as he had feared, but then he had had a lot of time in which to imagine the worst. It was basically sound, and the roof was watertight. A week's work or so, he figured, would put the interior into usable condition. Forbes's man, *Wm Ryan, Carpenter & Joiner,* as his gold and black sign put it, had agreed to take the job. Ten days, *he* figured. His tools were already on the premises, and Willie didn't look as if he would have enough others to continue working elsewhere while staking

48

out the job in this fashion—an unworthy thought, Rafferty admitted, but one born of his recent experience.

All in all it had not been a bad day, though Mr. Duffy had sent no message, and the spinner's man was still in Donegal, or Sligo, his own office wasn't sure.

As soon as he opened the door to their room he could see that Alice hadn't done as well. "What's the matter?"

"I thought you said we could get linen sheets," she said, hammering each word into the air. "Do you know what they cost? Seven pounds and *up*. Irish linen comes from the North. Belfast."

"I'm sorry. I guess we'll have to buy cotton," he said.

"And do you know what *that* costs? Just plain, coarse cotton costs as much as I'd pay for the best percale at home."

"That's too bad," he said. Did she mean that he, in his business, ought to have known that? "Do you want to go up to Belfast tomorrow? It's only two hours or so."

She shook her head. "Customs."

"All right. I'm sorry I didn't let you take the trunk."

At that she began to cry.

"Oh, for Pete's sake," Rafferty said, the things you could find yourself thinking about. "Listen, we knew there were going to be unexpected expenses. Now we know what one of them is: sheets."

"Oh, it isn't just the sheets," she said. "I mean I'm worried about the move. I wish we had the maid now."

He nodded. "I can understand that."

"I don't think we ought to run an ad?" she asked.

"No."

She looked ready to sink into despair again. Damn. "The thing to do," he said, "is go down and ask the Manageress about an agency. She'd know."

"No. No, I don't want to do that."

"Come on, right now, before we go down to dinner."

"I'll do it tomorrow."

"No. Now." He took her by the arm. He had never felt so much

49

the necessity to get things done. Ongoing, that was what they had
to be if they were to survive in this country.

THE MANAGERESS HAD BEEN SURPRISINGLY PLEASANT ABOUT IT.
"You're in luck," she said. "There's a woman there in the village
where you'll be, the news agent, Mrs. Redmond. Sometimes she
sends us girls."

They would wait until they had moved then. It wasn't just the
maid or the sheets that had her down, it was Prisma. A house
mattered more to a woman, a thing she could never say to
Rafferty. He would just answer, "nesting instinct," or something
else that would make her want to kick him.

They couldn't have found a better house, considering that they
had come for something old, something you couldn't find in Oakley. She had to stop thinking about it, stop wondering if a grey
semi-detached place might not be better after all.

"Get the sheets?" Rafferty asked that evening.

She nodded.

"Good," he said, and put his own parcel down with the others
stacked on the couch. "I found some more soap."

She laughed, and a sheepish grin crossed his face, but neither of
them said anything. He had been making his contribution to supplies by indulging in a weakness for soap. Tablet by tablet he had
been bringing it in: Pears, Yardley, Cuticura, Imperial Leather,
Windsor Brown, castile from Castile, the kind you cut into bars
yourself. Even if they got the year's extension they would never
use it all before they left.

The stores had delivered the bigger bundles to the hotel, where
the bellboys carried them past the lounge and up in the elevator.
On the last day she brought in a few final packages, some turkish
towels in a curious pulpy cotton that she had put off buying in the
hope of finding something more familiar.

50

"Oh, Mrs. Rafferty."

Ambushed.

"Buying a few linens, I see," said the Manageress.

"Yes, we thought we'd get them here, rather than bring them in."

"Wise of you," said the Manageress. Alice just smiled.

"I hope you've found the staff properly attentive."

"Oh, yes." She wondered if now, on their last day, there was to be an era of good will. "I'm a little embarrassed to be requiring so much service."

"I wonder"—the Manageress furrowed her brow—"if you aren't being perhaps a little too generous?"

"Generous?" She couldn't mean that.

"To the staff," she said. "Tipping."

"Oh, no! I'm sure we're not." Not by their own standards, but by the Manageress's standards? By those of the residents who were, for once, not watching the glass partition? The sixpences for announcing the phone calls, the half-crowns for carrying the breakfast trays up to the third floor and down, the extra florins to the chambermaid for watching the girls—for the whole staff not much more than ten dollars since they had arrived. But in that place it must have been noticeable, and the Manageress might fear that they would leave in a tidal wave of generosity from which the staff would never recover. Otherwise why mention it now, on the last day?

The Manageress had faded away before she could answer. Alice dutifully headed for the elevator.

By the time she had made her way up and over the stile on the third floor she was considering the matter more coolly. The Manageress hadn't said *you are*, she had said, *I wonder*. They were American, therefore they must have been overtipping. No one had told her that it was only a spate of sixpenny bits.

It was naptime, and she let herself into the room quietly. Even before she shut the door she saw the curtain, the jagged piece of

51

lace hanging from the center of one of the crisp arcs, and the hole above it.

The girls were asleep.

"I'll be back for dinner," Rafferty said in a low voice and picked up his coat. He stopped as he passed her at the door. "Is anything wrong?"

"No," she said and shut the door behind him. She hurried to the window to see how great the damage was. She had scarcely touched the curtain when whole rows of loops began spilling from the ends of broken filaments and stretching out into brittle kinky thread. And farther from the tear, with the flexing of the curtain, the starch flaked off, spiked threads rose from the pattern, and hitherto invisible rents appeared.

It was not the work of children, but of sun, washing powders, and age. For a long time it had not been lace. Below stairs there must have been a giant ironing board, on which the curtains, gelatinous with starch, were laid out, the straggling threads carefully arranged where they had once belonged and the whole thing set with an iron while the Manageress stood by.

How could she tell the Manageress about the tear? The curtains were hardly more than starch, but the illusion was accepted. And the Raffertys, who ran preposterous ads and asked for keys and wanted their shillings back and automatically overtipped, could be expected to destroy the curtain. She got out her sewing kit, a toy sold for travel.

The little girls woke, denied ever going near the curtain. Rafferty returned, took the girls to dinner, came back and put them to bed, and still she worked. At first she had only widened the rip until she learned to guess which loops might be expected to bear the weight of another, which must be tacked to a bolstering thread, and, most difficult of all, which were to be left alone. The alternative was four twelve-foot lengths, forty-eight feet of six-foot cotton net—and the admission of guilt.

"There," she said, at last, stepping back.

Rafferty put down his magazine. "It looks a little wrinkled."

Alice sighed. "I've been working for six hours."

"God knows you've been working. I couldn't have done it. But it does look a little wrinkled. That's all I said."

"I suppose it does." It did.

"Where's that iron you got from O'Reilley? What did we bring it along for?"

"I don't want to handle the lace again."

"Just take a book, make a little ironing board. Hold it right up to the curtain."

She got out the iron. "I don't think this plug will work here," she said.

"Just take the one from the lamp." In the dim light of the overhead bulb he changed the plug while she padded a book with a hand towel. The cord just reached the window. The iron began to hum, to buzz, perhaps its normal sound, or perhaps if she shook it—there was a blue flash, the piercing smell of electricity gone bad, and the room was lit only by the gas fire.

After a while Rafferty said, "Maybe if we opened the shutters . . ."

The street lamp outside the window gave them nearly as much light as the overhead bulb had.

"Oh, the iron's *hot*," Alice said, licking the hand that had bumped it.

"Well, hurry and do your job then."

She did, by the light of the street lamp, while he changed the cord ends by flashlight.

"What will we do about the lights?" she asked.

"We'll have to tell them in the morning."

She slept badly, troubled by noisy dreams, and awoke, remembering the iron and the accounting for the fuse that would have to take place. The curtain did look indistinguishable from its mate, almost, she was thinking, when she noticed that the overhead light was on, glowing faintly in the daylight.

Breakfast came late. "Sorry we're late this morning," said the bellboy as he set down one tray and went out for the other.

"Somebody fused the lights," he said, returning. "Blacked out us and half the Killarney." He pointed toward the hotel next door. "They couldn't use the electric cookers until the ESB gave us the power again."

As soon as he had finished breakfast, Rafferty left them to do the final packing while he went to sign the lease. "Considering that it's fixed," he said as he was leaving, "there's no need to mention the curtain—or anything."

She was afraid, though, that it might be mentioned to her, and she was relieved when she had paid the bill with no mention made—of anything. She and the girls sat in the bay window of the lounge for the last time, waiting for Rafferty, who was taking a long time. Their small pile of luggage and large pile of parcels stood beside the door. The Manageress was nowhere in sight, probably gone to count the towels, inspect the curtains.

"I imagine," said one of the women, "you'll be buying linens and laces while you're here?"

"I thought I would at first," said Alice, "but they seem awfully expensive."

The woman gave her a tolerant smile. "Dear? Yes, if you just consider the original sum, but they last forever, you know."

"I know," said Alice, wishing the Manageress would reappear, satisfied by her inspection.

Rafferty appeared first. She saw him through the glass, and when she started to leave with the girls he waved them back to the windowseat and came in to them.

"What's the matter?"

"Everything's all right," he said. "We're not going to sign the lease unless you want to."

"You haven't signed it yet?"

"You remember the lawns and the hedges at Prisma, how good they looked?"

54

"Yes, but what does that have to do with the lease?"

"Well, there's a full-time gardener. He lives in the little lodge by the gate. Comes to about two hundred pounds a year."

"Oh." She added the two figures together. "I wasn't even *looking* at houses in that price range."

"Do you want to look? We could stay here, or go to another hotel, if you'd rather."

She had never seen him look so sad. "What do you think, Rafferty?"

"I think Prisma is worth it." He was facing straight ahead, toward the colored glass, his blue eyes focused far beyond the palm and pine.

"All right, Rafferty."

She stood up and started for the door, watching for someone to say good-by to, but no one looked up from the newspaper, and so they just left.

6.

"You'd want to be a goat," the cab driver said, standing beside his opened door and taking a good look at the ramp that led to the outer gate. Until then he seemed to have been a very agreeable man.

"Oh, you can't make it from here," Rafferty said. "That's what I was telling you. You've got to approach the gate from the top. It's banked that way, see?"

"I see," he said, and opened the back door. "Now, you get on up to the house, and I'll see to your kit."

"That'll be at least five trips," she said. Why couldn't he just take the car and have done with it? "It's a long way up."

"That's me intention," he said, "and that's what I'll do."

So they started out, Rafferty and the driver loaded like coolies, and Alice with a little girl dragging at each arm. Gusts of wind came down the boreen like bobsleds, kicking up the leaves into their faces. It was going to rain too. "Look, we're almost there," she said, hitching the girls forward a few feet. The wall of the lane had become the side of the lodge; she would have assumed it was a garage, just glancing at it. Inside the gate a ladder stood against the hedge, and the clippers lay on the ground in a litter of freshly cut twigs, but the gardener was nowhere in sight. Time enough for him later. She let go of the girls—they could take as long as they pleased now—and hurried around the last curve.

She had forgotten how it looked. The driver came up beside her, set down the two suitcases, and began to flex his fingers, restoring the circulation, she feared. She looked away, up at the roof, where the remains of a patent chimney cowl whirled in the wind. They had brought the man to that absurd driveway, given him those leaden bags to carry, and now he could see what was at the end of the road: Prisma, the stained plaster, the leprous grey, grey against the grey sky, hollow, uninhabited, a deserted house.

"Begod!" she heard him say, and turned, embarrassed, to take the blame. "That's a *grand* house."

He meant it.

Load after load he brought up the boreen. "Just leave them in the hall," she said.

"No, no. Where would you have them then?" he insisted.

"That's a grand, big room," he said, putting a bundle of blankets in one of the huge, empty bedrooms.

"Ah, you'll be snug in there," he said, carrying the typewriter into the cramped library.

Well, wait till he saw the kitchen, she thought, sending him down there with a package of linen. He came up, smiling. "That's a fine stove you've down there. Imperial Iron."

All too soon he had brought up the last load and left—with half the tip Rafferty wanted to give him. The rain came, driven in gusts, and slapped the windows like a cat-o'-nine-tails. Looking out from an upstairs window where she was shaking the mop, Alice saw the hedge clippers still on the ground, gleaming wet, beside the deserted stepladder. She found it hard not to believe that from the height of the ladder the gardener had seen them

57

coming and had disappeared before he could be pressed into service as a porter.

She pulled the mop in out of the rain. Its clotted head could use a good washing, but not today, not with the kitchen still to face. There wasn't much dust upstairs anyway, too cold for dust, or too damp, she thought, polishing a frost of mildew from the leather seat of a chair.

Her fingers felt so blue and brittle that she could no longer think of washing the drawers, and she contented herself with rapping them out on the hearth, dislodging some grain and a dead, dried mouse.

The germicidal properties of newsprint were well known, she reminded herself as she folded it to fit the drawers. And Rafferty's soap, unwrapped and used as sachets, made the drawers smell clean anyway.

The drawing room, a big furniture-moving job, was too much to tackle at the moment, so Rafferty was seeing what could be done in the library. He would give the girls a picnic lunch there, and she would have the rest of the day to do something about the kitchen. She unfolded one of her new aprons, a flowery pink model in a stiff, canvassy material. She had been fitting herself with a decent white one in the shop, when the sales clerk came up saying, "For your maid, Madam?" She shook her head and he hustled her a few feet down the counter and gave her a choice of pink or green, in this model. It sat on her like a cutout for a paper doll.

"Will you *look* at Mama," Rafferty said, when she stopped in at the library on her way down.

The little girls were sitting on the hearth rug. It was an island in the sea, they told her. Rafferty, three feet away, was conveniently inaccessible. He had a bag of what he said were called *flex, adapters,* and *lampholders,* with which he was trying to do something about the lighting.

"You'll get your feet wet, Mama."

"Yes," she said, "I'm going down now, Rafferty."

"I've got the fire going down there," he said. "The gardener was looking for you."

"For me?"

He nodded. "He'll be back."

A burst of activity in the chimney sent three or four bubbles of smoke out toward them. So that was why the room smelled like a roundhouse.

"We'll have to get some turf for the fire. You could get sick from this," Rafferty said.

"Well, I'm going down now."

"Yes, you said that."

So she went out of the room, down the hall, and flipped the switch beside the basement door. And when she spotted the empty socket overhead, she started down in the dark. The first step was only half a step down, a real boneshaker that cost her most of her momentum.

There was a chance that she had been carrying around a false picture of the kitchen. After the first shock of it, she hadn't taken in much detail. She hadn't even noticed the electric stove, the "cooker," that the agent assured her was there. What else had she missed?

She pushed open the kitchen door and looked into the noontime twilight. A crack at the stove glowed red, and the window was lighter than the walls, and—no, she couldn't have overlooked a tree, pushing up through the middle of the floor.

"*There* you are," it said, and started moving toward her, its feathery crown shaking. She dodged the fronds as they thrust forward, and came upon the small man behind.

"Oh, you scared me. I thought you were a tree."

"Ah, no, the garden's beyond," said the man who must have been the gardener, and with another, "*There* you are," he pushed

59

the leaves right into her arms. They sprawled damply, soaking her sweater sleeves while she struggled to bunch them again. Was it a symbolic plant, like laurel or holly, a bardic welcome?

"Greens, for your tea," he said.

"To eat," she said firmly, giving him a chance to say that he hadn't meant that.

"Danny's me name," he said. His black beret, pulled down like a bathing cap, kept her from guessing his age, fifty, sixty, seventy.

She crammed the last of the leaves into the crook of her left elbow and held out her hand, "I'm Mrs. Rafferty." She smiled to show that she didn't blame him for his sudden and expensive entry into their lives.

"You'd want to close the draft then," he said, nodding at the stove. Perhaps he hadn't seen her hand.

A slide, down near the glowing crack, looked likely, and when she pushed it, the sound of the fire was muffled. The stove was much more complicated than the old log burners she remembered. "Do you understand this kind of stove?" she asked.

"No," he said, "that would be Cook's job."

"I haven't got a cook. Not yet," she added. She feared that she wasn't coming up to his expectations. "Did the Hamiltons take their cook to England with them, would you know?" she asked.

"Ah, no, they didn't."

"Is she working anywhere, now?"

"No. I'd say she wasn't."

Her first two fingers pulled themselves together, crossing for luck. "Is there any way I could get in touch with her, do you think?"

"Well, now, I wouldn't know that, though I've heard of it, mind you. Cook's dead, as you know."

She looked at him.

"She was making a pudding and she dropped dead. Right there, where you're standing."

60

She hopped to the side—again; he would think she was all nerves. "When was that?"

"Four years ago last Whit."

A slight interregnum there, she thought, but let it pass.

"Saturday's me half day," he said, moving toward the entryway. "And I have me Sundays too." He raised the latch.

"I'll see you tomorrow then, Mr. —" She waited.

"Danny's me name."

"Yes," she said, nodding. "Good-by." She didn't see how she could call him that, at his age.

"Bad day, Mis'ss," he said, and stepped out into the rain.

All night Prisma creaked like a ship in a storm. Their windows rattled until Rafferty wedged them with paper, and then they hissed. The hot-water pipes cooled, snapping like footsteps, as the heat retreated to the boiler at the kitchen stove. The chimney boomed, low, hollow, an alphorn. There were skittering sounds beyond the ceiling, beneath the floor, in the wall behind their heads. Somewhere a door slammed. And again. They got up and searched the house, leapfrogging the light bulbs ahead from socket to socket, seeing nothing, hearing nothing now. Back in bed, warming the sheets a second time, they heard it begin again, and let it go.

By morning the wind had settled down to a steady blast from the east. The sea below rolled on toward the invisible shore in dark, heavy waves, too slow for the wind, which tore the foam from their tops. Seagulls wheeled and fed in a frenzy. Stella and Vanessa squealed in the eastern rooms and walked on air, slapping web-footed pajamas onto the billowing carpets. The skylight dripped into the upper hall.

"I'm not mad," Rafferty said to her in the kitchen, "but I've got to get going." He was slicing the outside from a loaf of bread, dropping the gnawed crusts through an open hole into the Impe-

61

rial Iron. Alice, feeling incognito in her paper-doll apron, cut the tiny toothmarks from a pound of rashers. "Now we know what the meat safe's for," he said.

"It wouldn't have made much difference with those holes in it," she said.

"I'll bring home some screen." He finished peeling the bread and cut two naked, crustless slices with which he made himself a jam sandwich. Fortunately Alice, foggy with fatigue after dinner, had put the butter into the covered soup tureen, and the strawberry jam had a tin lid. The floor rolled with rice, like church steps after a wedding. The sugar was a dead loss, but the oatmeal, broached late in the night's revelries perhaps, had only a small hole in the corner of the bag. The tea was untouched. Alice looked into the teakettle on the electric stove and saw that the bubbles were gathering on the bottom.

"Stop worrying about the tea," Rafferty said. "I'll get something to eat in town."

"It didn't seem this slow yesterday," she said, hoping she was right. Could the wind have cut the voltage somehow?

"I'll get you a bread box, and a dozen mousetraps and some light bulbs."

"And a broom. And hangers."

"Okay. Write it down and anything else you think of. I'll phone you around noon."

"All right." She looked into the teakettle again.

"Forget it. I've got to go. There's a train in fifteen minutes." He hurried out the kitchen door and up the stairs. She heard him lurching down the hall above, thrown off his stride by that trick step on top.

"IT'S A DREADFUL THING, MR. RAFFERTY," SAID THE BLACK-HAIRED secretary. "It's hard on you, Mr. Rafferty," agreed the redhead. He doubted that either of them could have repeated a word of what he had said. The only one who showed much interest was the office boy. Mr. Duffy was unavailable, and not for the first time.

"Now look," he said. "That list was promised to me before I left America. We certainly wouldn't have come to weave in Ireland if we hadn't believed that there were weavers available here."

"Would you not?" she said blandly.

"This is the tenth time I've come to this office," he said, feeling that, like an anniversary, it ought not pass unmentioned. "Ten times, ten delays."

"That's a terrible thing, Mr. Rafferty," said the black-haired girl, and the redhead nodded, both of them extruding the steady drip of their quieting sympathy, so that only they, who didn't listen, would have to hear him.

The frosted glass and plywood partition at the end of the room would not be soundproof, he thought, and raised his voice. Had it ever occurred to anyone that he might write to the newspapers, he asked. *It's being retyped, Mr. Rafferty. It's in the post, Mr. Rafferty. It's on the minister's desk, Mr. Rafferty.* How did they think that would read? Either he was being told barefaced lies, or this office was in a state of absolute disorganization. Even now they were thinking of nothing but their eleven o'clock tea break.

"There's nothing wrong with tea," said the redhead, her face clicking into life. "It's been proved, by surveys and things, that two tea breaks a day contribute greatly to efficiency."

"Efficiency! *My God!*"

The door to the inner office opened then.

A young man in a black suit and a maroon sweater stepped out, and the door was closed behind him by other, invisible hands. "Oh, Mr. Rafferty," he said, his face reddening as he crossed the room. "Would you ever mind waiting outside for a bit?" He opened the door to the hall and went out with Rafferty. "It upsets the girls, like."

63

Rafferty looked at the man, who had the hair and pleading eyes of a spaniel, and said, "I can appreciate that point."

"Oh, I knew you would," the young man said gratefully. "Interferes with their work," he went on, blushing more fiercely. "Maybe you could . . ." His hand indicated the bench across the hall.

Rafferty nodded. The young man looked down at the knob of the door, hesitated, and went in briskly.

It would have been a mistake to have pressed his point. The others in the inner office would have liked that—if he had just blown himself out and gone home.

What were they doing with the list? Perhaps he would work it out in time, like the delays on the car which made sense when he saw how the garage man might have been able to take care of one of his regular customers a few weeks early by diverting the car on which their dollars had secured immediate delivery. The tone of the man's denial was all the proof he needed. There would be action there soon, he felt.

But what profit could there be in withholding a list of unattached handweavers? Half a dozen letter writers had offered him that list, in letters that sometimes agreed on nothing else. It hardly seemed that they could have got together on the carrot to be held before him.

No, the list was lost, and it was easier to put him off than to find it—*had been* easier to put him off. The clerks and office boys passing with teapots might have been told to see how he was taking it. He was just fine, thank you, sitting there, smoking his pipe, not noticing the cold at all. In time Mr. Duffy himself would have to come out.

The wall was a swampy institutional green, a color that took on patriotic overtones here. PLEASE ENTER said the door from which he had been ejected. What was he doing here—a man with a wife and two children? He should have spent the year in a library

64

somewhere, writing a damned good book on the decline of the crafts.

Footsteps approached from beyond the turn in the corridor again, and he centered his open notebook on his knee, a man who knew what he was doing. The footsteps neared and slowed. A pair of very good brown shoes stopped beside him, not Mr. Duffy's.

"Mr. Rafferty?"

He looked up. It was the senior civil servant, the one who had gone to show out the photographer two weeks before.

"Yes," said the man, when he had taken Rafferty into his own office. "It looks as though we've been taking you over the hedges and into the gorse."

"It does," Rafferty said.

"I shouldn't wonder if you doubt that there actually is a list?"

That was the way it was, he told Alice that night when they were sitting in the library. You were at the end of your rope and along came a human being. The man had promised to run the list to earth himself. He had an appointment for eleven the next morning.

"Yes," Alice said, "but it does sound a little familiar."

He shook his head. "This is a different kind of man."

"But what if there is no list?"

"There is a list."

"But just *suppose* there were no list. What would you do then?"

"What would you do?"

"I don't know. You could probably get a second-semester job somewhere, if it were known that you were available. And we'd just pay off the lease and the gardener and go."

"And what about Frank? It's his money."

"What with taxes and all, even a dead loss doesn't cost him more than thirty cents on the dollar. We could pay that back someday."

65

"My God!" He jumped out of his chair. "You've got it all figured out, haven't you?" And he had thought all he had to do was get them into a house.

"No. It's just that when things are going the way they are, you ought to have an alternate plan."

He was set to pace the floor, but what with their chairs, the lamp table, the light cord, and the turf basket, he found himself rotating on the hearth rug. "What do you mean, *going the way they are?*"

"Well, the mews building, and you haven't got the car, and the list, and Prisma, and no maid and the gardener."

"What's wrong with the gardener?"

"Nothing. Just three pounds ten a week."

In the water-spotted print above the fireplace, Grace Darling, the lighthouse keeper's daughter, rowed through the storm. "All right, then. The mews building is being repaired. The car *is* coming, I've seen the shipping notice. And I can't do anything with the list until I get the car anyway." Alice nodded, and he moved over to the arm of her chair, started to sit on it, felt it wobble, and stood there instead. "I know that this is a difficult house for you, but we will be getting a maid. Think of what it'll be like, living up in that room. And even now, with the turf fire, a comfortable chair, a glass of Guinness, and a lamp to read by— Is that the lease you've got there?" he said, breaking in on himself.

She nodded. "I wanted to see what it says."

"There's no way out of paying the gardener."

"I know. I was just going to ask you where the greenhouse is."

"What greenhouse?"

"It says here, '. . . to keep in good and tenantable repair order and condition the glass in the windows of the house lodge and greenhouse.' No commas."

"The lodge would be the gardener's house, but I haven't seen any greenhouse. Must be out near that toolshed in back."

Alice nodded.

66

"You know, that could be another one of those things, 'good and tenantable repair order and condition' and we don't even know what it looks like."

Alice just smiled, her little now-you-see smile. Damn.

7.

SOMEWHERE ON THE HIDDEN PATHS OF THE KITCHEN GARDEN THE gravel crackled, and the gardener skittered from the gap between the toolshed and the hedge. "You've come for more greens," he called, hurrying to meet her.

Alice shook her head. A kind of cabbage, the grocer's boy had said. "Bile it with the bacon." It was easily the most unpopular dish she had ever fixed. "You know," she said as the gardener reached her, "that was such a big bunch that we haven't finished it yet."

"Have a fresh lot," he said. "There's a great deal more in the garden."

There was, a frothy green sea of it. "No, thank you. It's the greenhouse that I've come out to see."

It was in sight now and she could hardly believe it, a little beauty of glass and copper gone green with age, an octagon with a cupola on top. From the distance it seemed to be in good condition, though some kind of rigging was strung inside. She stepped past the gardener and went on toward the greenhouse, only to come upon him a moment later, trotting around the bay tree to open the door for her.

Inside, the flats were dry and dusty, and earthenware pots, once piled, lay fallen in serpentine columns. And here there really was a tree, growing out of an octagonal tub beneath the cupola, a palm tree so old and fat that its trunk had had to be bound together with iron hoops like a cask. The lines that she had seen from the outside were attached to the hoops, and seemed to have no other purpose than to hold a striped collarless shirt and three grey woolen socks. Overhead, in the draft from the open door, the palm fronds clashed together with the sound of dry paper.

"Before my time," said the gardener when she asked what kind of palm it was.

"Then it doesn't ever have dates or coconuts or anything?"

He augered away at an ear with his little finger and said nothing.

"What I mean is—palm trees do grow outside here?" He nodded. "So there must be some reason why this one is indoors, using up all that space. It must be a lot of trouble just watering a thing like that."

"Hoo, hoo, hoo," he laughed, a mirthful owl. "Them things grow in the desert. They don't need water, like a camel." The roots went down then, through the tub and the terracotta floor.

Here, from the inside, she could see that the building was not quite a perfect octagon. Cut off by the hill, it ended abruptly in a stone retaining wall. Between the buttresses were shelves, filled with apples and pears. "Those'd be for Mr. Hamilton," the gardener said, making it clear that the fruit, having been picked before their occupancy began, was not theirs. Surely he didn't intend to ship it to England.

"It seems a shame to let all this space go to waste," she said. "You could put in lettuce or something."

"Ah, it wouldn't be worth your trouble."

69

"Or tomatoes." Before he could dismiss that too, she went on, "I think I'll have a try at them, myself." She raked a loop of fallen palm leaf through the soil of one of the abandoned flats. "I raised them from seed once, yellow plum and oxhearts and Sioux Fires. . . ." She went on, it didn't matter what she said. The greenhouse was like one of those private roads where the ownership had to be reasserted for twenty-four hours every year, before custom became a right. "They might do well here," she said and left, ducking beneath the striped shirt on her way out.

WHEN RAFFERTY RETURNED NEXT TO THE MINISTRY THE SECRETARIES seemed to look on him with a bit more respect. Perhaps it was all in his mind, for the senior civil servant was not mentioned, and he was shown into the office that Mr. Duffy shared with three others.

"There, we've found it!" he said, handing over the list. One look at the list and Rafferty forgot to point out that he had been given to understand that it never had been lost. It was not a list of unattached handweavers. It was—and Mr. Duffy did what he could to muddy the waters around this fact—a list of small farmers who had answered "yes" to the question: Would you be willing to take up some cottage craft, such as handweaving, to supplement your income?

"In other words, they don't know how to weave, and they certainly wouldn't be likely to have looms," Rafferty said, and he thought, My God, I'm taking it calmly.

"I wouldn't say that," said Mr. Duffy. "There was no special category for that percentage who were actually weaving at the time of the survey. Actually our main concern at the time was bacon production. And in any case you'll find any number of disused looms out in the country."

In ordinary circumstances, in any logical, reasonable conversation, he would have gone for every one of those statements,

70

Rafferty thought, and let them pass. "And what about the date?" he asked, pointing to the top of the list.

"What about it?"

"That's four years ago."

"Ah . . . yes . . ." Mr. Duffy was counting, or drumming, with his fingers. "Four years past. Actually it's better that way. They've had time to think it over. Those that take you up would be the steady ones."

Rafferty just nodded. There was nothing he could say. In fact, as he left the building, he was surprised to realize that his only feeling was a numb relief at coming to the end of a game long since lost. He was free to do something, anything, besides haunt the corridors of the ministry.

He went on to the mews building. There was a sign on his door these days, hanging by a wire from a nail: *Wm. Ryan, Carpenter & Joiner*. The builders' suppliers had to know where to make deliveries, Willie said, in answer to objections. And when Rafferty had singled out the nail, as being likely to leave a hole, Willie had just laughed himself into a coughing fit. It was no wonder these buildings got into the state they were in.

He opened the door, quietly he thought, but he was greeted by the sound of falling masonry and a long whistle from the upper part of the building. "Would youse look at that, Your Honour!"

"Be there in a minute, Willie," he called. He took his time, hung his coat on the back of the door and put on a shopman's tan smock before he picked his way through the rubble and up the swaying stairs. "What would be the pint in working on them, Your Honour, if you'd burn the building down the first time you was to light a fire?" Willie had said, and disclosed the fact that he was also a mason and plasterer.

Now he was standing on a low bench, working at the top of the wall and knocking out a last bit of brick as Rafferty approached. "Look at *that*. You'd a been roasted alive in your beds."

71

Rafferty nodded. He had had a hard time the first few days, until he had realized that Willie's comments were all-purpose remarks, not necessarily applicable to the situation at hand. He was used to these "unveilings" too, in which, after a ceremonial tap or two in his presence, some appalling situation would be revealed in its full horror, a sort of cornerstone laying in reverse. This was a bird's nest, or so Willie said, hardly one of the wonders of nature, if true. When he looked up at it, the wind blew back down the remaining stub of the chimney, through the clustered sticks, and sent the dust of the bird's bad housekeeping into his eye. The whole place was a shambles. The entire course of the chimney, a bent aorta, cracked and clogged, had been excised from the brick wall. Only the building next door kept the wall from collapse.

"I got the list of weavers today," he told Willie. "We'll have to start bringing in the yarn next week."

Willie nodded, pulled a stick from the chimney, and threw it down into the rubble. "The plaster won't be dry, I'd say, but if you keep the fire down you'll be all right. It's an easy go from here on in."

"Fine," he said. He figured three weeks, four weeks, and another one to cart off the rubble.

He had been in Ireland nearly a month now, and he was farther away from producing anything than he had been when he landed. He could hardly bear to think of how he had badgered the yarn people, getting them to promise early delivery, lest he find himself with a dozen weavers on his hands and nothing for them to do. Now, if they came through—and *they* would—he was going to have to pay storage on the yarn somewhere. He should have fixed the stairs himself. A couple dozen spikes might have done the job, and he could have stuck a stovepipe out a window.

Watching Willie poking around up there, dismantling the so-called bird's nest, stick by stick, straw by straw, as though he were looking for the needle, Rafferty wondered if he would ever have the use of his own building. The numbness was wearing off, and the whole situation was getting to him. He had come over five thousand miles in search of weavers, and there were no weavers, just a couple hundred pig farmers who had once told the bacon survey that they would like to make a little extra money. And supposing a dozen of them agreed to weave for him, what then? His practical knowledge of weaving was not what Frank assumed it was. He had done a lot of reading, but the only handweaver he had ever seen in action had been in an Indian exhibition in a Santa Fe Railroad waiting room.

He left Willie in what he had once thought of as the "office" and went across to one of the "storerooms." It wouldn't have taken Willie long to have fixed the door; a quarter inch off one end, and they could have shut it. They could have put the yarn in there. Instead he had nailed the door open, driven a spike right into the floor for a doorstop, and put two torn bags of plaster in the middle of the room.

There, standing and using the gritty window sill for a desk, he started to work on a want ad. He would try it in one of the provincial papers, where the weavers would be more likely to see it. But after a minute or two, Willie got his hammer going again, and Rafferty put away his pen. He hoped the building next door was as deserted as it looked.

As he opened the outside door to leave, the knob shook in his hand with another crash upstairs—chimney pots falling in? Or perhaps the whole gable end? He hesitated, half in and half out, wondered if he should scream for help first, before he ran upstairs. Then he heard the long whistle and "Would youse loo—?" He shut the door noiselessly and hurried down the alleyway, staying close to the buildings, until, hearing a door open somewhere behind him, he broke into a run for the last twenty yards or so, up the slippery cobbles, beneath the arch, and out into the busy street beyond. Only then did he notice that he was still wearing the smock.

An hour later his want ad, composed in a restaurant over a quiet pot of tea (he referred to himself cautiously as an "export firm"), was in the post to the *Wicklow People* and the *Longford Leader*. At the garage he had seen the car, a small estate van, or station wagon, as he thought of it. Tomorrow he could get it. In the meantime the shopman's smock was locked into the glove compartment, staking his claim. Now, a quick word with the solicitor, and then he would be off to get some maps.

"Ah, Mr. Rafferty. I was just about to send round to you. Sit down, won't you?"

Forbes held out a thin hand to his chairs, two Georgian, with horsehair seats, and one a Vienna bentwood. Rafferty sat on the bentwood, hiding it from view.

"I've found the boy for you, Mr. Rafferty."

"Boy for me?" Unreasonably he thought first of a weaver, though it could only be another tradesman, a plumber, perhaps, to keep Willie company.

"A school leaver, a boy to go for the messages."

"Oh." Surely the man ought to have a better picture of Rafferty's Woolens than that. "I'm going to have only two men working in Dublin, and my wife is keeping the books at home. I don't think I need an office boy."

"Oh, you do. You do. Now this boy will come for two pounds and four shillings a week."

"I don't—"

"I know. You can get a boy for much less, but there's no telling what you'd get. Now this boy's from a good family, first job, unspoiled. I'll send him over to your premises this evening at four. You'll be there?"

"No," he said and won Forbes's attention at last. "I'm not going back there today. I can't even find a place to stand where that maniac isn't about to pull a couple of tons of brick down on my head." He hadn't intended to complain of Willie, but perhaps it was just as well that Forbes knew what his man was up to.

74

"You wouldn't let Willie Ryan at the chimneys, would you?" he asked sharply.

"He said—" Rafferty began.

"That's a job for a mason."

"He said—"

"No. Did you get a price?"

"I did." He waited. It was Forbes's man, Forbes's move.

Forbes was nodding, thinking. "I'll have a word with the man," he said.

"I wish you would," Rafferty said. He could see that whatever it was that he should know about Willie, he was not going to find it out.

"Yes, I'll speak to him this evening, and we'll put the boy in to keep an eye on him. Yes."

MRS. REDMOND, THE WOMAN THE MANAGERESS HAD RECOMMENDED, had a newspaper route on their hill. The morning papers were delivered by the wavering beam of a flashlight to the sound of short-legged running which continued out the gate and down toward the house at the end of the lane. The fee for delivery was sixpence a week, and, considering what you had to pay boys these days, Mrs. Redmond had told Rafferty, it was more of a favor to her clients than anything else.

Put off by the woman's link with the Imperial, Alice had lost some time in trying to find another employment agency. "Empliment agency," said the butcher, unwilling to let go of the word. "Empliment agency. They have them in London and Manchester. Mrs. Redmond beyond is the one to find you a girl."

The news agency was a tiny shop, the width of its door. The papers to be picked up were fanned out on the counter, names penciled on top in the order of an unvarying precedence in which Raftery, as Mrs. Redmond seemed to think it was, lay on the bottom. Bottled sweets filled the shelf behind her and, clipped to the

75

lines overhead, were a few magazines well out of reach of browsers. On the side walls there were tacked a scattering of notices: hunts, point-to-points, meetings of organizations whose clustered initials must have made sense to someone, and a plain sign of black, white, and red urgency, "Save Irish Horses from Export."

There was nothing to indicate that Mrs. Redmond was an employment agency, and Alice approached the problem from a distance, giving her every chance to be the first to mention it.

Mrs. Redmond nodded enthusiastically. "Ah, yes. It's the central heating you miss," she said. "It's unhealthy." She threw it away with a wave that pulled her blue smock back from the wrists of a workman's heavy sweater.

"No, I like the open fire, really," Alice said. "I can never get out of the kitchen to enjoy the fire, though. If I just had—"

"—a mouser, a female. A kitten'd be no use to you."

"Yes," she said, "but I was thinking more of the whole problem, not just the mice. A maid."

"Indoor or outdoor?" Mrs. Redmond asked, shifting to a business voice with a prerecorded sound.

"We've got the gardener, so she'd be indoor, of course."

"*Indoor,*" said Mrs. Redmond, "means she sleeps in. *Outdoor* means she leaves at night."

"Oh," Alice said. She wouldn't put anyone in the basement maid's room, but there was a nice room on the landing, beside the bath. "Let's say *indoor*. That way I'd have a babysitter in the evening."

Mrs. Redmond nodded. "Actually, up on that hill, I'd say you wouldn't get a girl to sleep in. She'd go to the pictures or a dance and then she'd have a long way up in the dark."

"We'll make it outdoor, then," Alice said, wondering why Mrs. Redmond had bothered to ask.

"That would be dearer, you know. The girl will have to pay for her own lodgings and breakfast."

"All right. Whatever you think is best. Just so I can get help."

76

Mrs. Redmond nodded. "Give me three or four days," she said.

Alice had pictured it all before they had moved into Prisma: how, as soon as she had finished the breakfast dishes, she would leave the kitchen and go up to the drawing room.

She would sit there in the window and sew or do Rafferty's accounts while she watched the children on the lawn below and looked out over the sea beyond. For lunch they would toast bread and cheese at the fire, because if there was one thing she had learned at the Imperial, it was that you didn't have to sit down at a table three times a day. That would leave the dinner and its dishes, two or three hours a day—and only until she found the maid.

She had made just one mistake: you couldn't leave the kitchen. "Abandon all hope . . ." There should have been a sign up beside the bulb that couldn't light the steps from where it was, on the outside of the door frame. The end of one meal merged with the beginning of the next, if she wasn't already a full meal, or two, behind in the cleanup. The big black and nickel locomotive, the Imperial Iron, had the water tank at the boil before you could fry an egg on the top plates, so she had to use the slow-witted electric cooker and lost her day in twenty-minute dribbles, waiting for pans to heat—or to simmer down a little.

Even when she left the room, the kitchen kept right on making work, the stove needing coal, the ashes sifting out onto the flags, the moisture condensing on the walls and rolling down to feed the mildew that crept up from the floor. She had shut off all the little rooms, except for the scullery, a dank, mossy cavern, some thirty feet from the stove, where she found the sink, at about knee level, just right for the trolls. She had given up hope even of taking over the main kitchen and tried no more than to hold her own in the center, to keep a kind of Pale of cleanliness and order while the mice waited at the borders for their chance, when they advanced, ravaged, and retreated, leaving their dead in her traps.

77

Whatever she resolved in the morning, the dinner dishes stayed unwashed all night, and she began the day in the hole, deep in the hole, for she had to do the shopping first. Prisma was a good three-fourths of a mile from the shops, and at that angle, even the trip down was difficult. You had only to think of the view from the drawing-room window and realize that the village was at sea level to appreciate the climb.

"Every damned morning," Rafferty said. "You used to go shopping once a week."

"I know. But there's no refrigerator, and the mice, and I can carry only so much." The car was going to make a terrific difference.

"Get them to deliver. Just phone. They're delighted to deliver, they told me."

"I know." It solved the grocer's and butcher's problem of what to do with the things that no one would take if they could see them first. "I'd rather go myself."

"All right. It's your time, but I can't stay here with the girls while you go out. I've got to get moving."

She took them down the hill with her once, and came home humping the day's bundles up the hill in hundred-yard stages and doubling back to carry Vanessa, who had simply stopped climbing and wouldn't start again.

After that she left the girls with the gardener. "I'm no baby-minder," he said, not annoyed, just stating a fact.

"Well, they don't need minding. They'll play outside until I get back."

When it rained she put them out in the greenhouse and gave them spoons to dig in the flats. "They're in the greenhouse, Mr. Molloy," she would call to the gardener as he plodded around in the mud. Sometimes he nodded, and sometimes he didn't even do that, though she couldn't be sure, for the rain got on her glasses. You couldn't carry string bag and basket *and* umbrella.

She had learned his surname when he had brought her his book for the unemployment stamps, another weekly payment that she hadn't expected. Part of it should properly be deducted from his wages. She would certainly be a fool if she got softhearted and paid it all herself, thinking only of his meager three pounds ten, and forgetting that he had his house, with electricity and water, and fruit and vegetables.

It was always at least ten before he appeared in the garden. Things were late here, of course; some of the shops didn't open until ten. They, however, didn't close at twelve. He had to make his own meals, he said, and that kept him occupied until two, when he returned to work. He finished around four. "The light's going," he said once, and as the hill faced mainly east, it was going, though it would be quite a while before it was gone. And Saturday was his half day. That made twenty-two hours a week, she figured, and even at that there were more hours than there was work. She would hear him scritch-scratching by the hour, probing the pebbles of the driveway for incipient weeds or raking out the marks of a delivery boy's bicycle or of the little girls' feet, and finishing with a final half hour's passage, swinging a wide-toothed rake in overlapping arcs until the entire drive had a pattern like fish scales.

So she didn't feel too guilty when she left the little girls in his charge, only a little surprised at herself for doing it. Of course, it was a temporary arrangement, just until they got the maid.

8.

THE BOY WAS SMALL FOR HIS AGE (IF HE WAS FOURTEEN), LOST IN a man's suitcoat, the sleeves shortened until the cuffs came only an inch or two below the patched elbows, while the skirts swung unaltered around his bare knees.

"Well, Brian," Rafferty said, thinking of the figure that the boy would be cutting around the shop, "we're going to have to get you one of these smocks. It's a dusty job."

"And a brush." He said *broosh*. "There's no brush."

A hair brush? Surely he couldn't expect the company to provide that, however much it was needed, or even a clothes brush. "What kind of brush?"

"A floor brush," Brian said, looking over in the direction of Willie, who had had the new tiles and bricks delivered on top of the old rubble, a living illustration of how the towns of antiquity had risen from the plains onto hills of their own refuse.

The new smock fit the boy like a hand-me-down. "If I took it

80

back and got one that fit you here," Rafferty said, pulling the shoulders up where they should have been, "then the sleeves would be too short."

Brian was amused. "It's a grand fit, Mr. Rafferty."

"And here," he said, sliding a comb into the breast pocket, "a new comb with every purchase today."

"You mean you want me to comb me hair," he said, and before Rafferty had to answer he had hurried off into the washroom, from which he emerged looking like an otter, sleek and soaked, and pleased with himself.

The floor brush, a heavy-duty janitor's broom, was wielded with such enthusiasm that the next morning, when Rafferty eased the new car into the cobbled yard, Brian was outside neatening up the pile of rubble.

"You'd want to get a bucket, Mr. Rafferty, and a floor-cloth, and something for the windows."

"Wait till I get out of the car, will you?" he called. He was anxious to get started on the weavers, and he already had a long list of things to do first. Well, Brian was supposed to be the messenger, wasn't he?

They went in, and he added Brian's three things to his list and then explained it all to him. "And try to get the best value, and make sure you note the price of everything," he said and handed the boy the list and the money. "I'll be out in the country when you get back. You can give me the accounting this afternoon."

Brian slipped off his smock and trotted out the door. Rafferty followed him through the gates. "Slow down," he called. "You'll wear yourself out." Brian turned back and shook his head, laughing, and trotted out beneath the arch. He was wearing an outsize pair of rubber boots in which his bare legs moved up and down like piston rods. They would have to get him some decent clothes.

In just a day he had made a difference around the place. Even Willie had been affected—or perhaps Forbes had spoken to him —and the rebuilt chimney was nearly up to the ceiling of the

81

lower room. With any kind of luck he might not have to pay storage on the yarn after all. And, with the tide running his way, even the weavers might follow in their turn.

And then he saw the list, on the window sill, where Brian must have put it when he took off the smock. Damn. The boy had worked like the devil for a day, and he had thought he was on to a more vigorous subspecies of the race. No telling what might happen now if Brian decided to trust his memory. Rafferty sat down in front of the window to wait his return.

Then he noticed that Brian, who must have seen that he had been trying to work at the window sill, had lined up the ink, glue, and paper clips along the back. The boy did have something. It didn't make a bad desk, a good sixteen, eighteen inches deep and well lighted; no place for his feet though.

He took out the list of prospective weavers and the one-inch map from his briefcase; there was a lot of work for him there. He hadn't realized at first that the farmers were arranged by the size of their acreage, from two acres, one rood, three perches, on up to twenty acres, which must have been the stopping point of the survey, or of the typist who had made his copy.

Their addresses sounded like poetry, and proved to be places too small for the road map. He had to look for them on the unindexed Ordnance Survey maps, searching road by road for whatever place names he could find, some threaded out along the flank of a mountain and others crammed together in type so small that even the magnifying glass was barely adequate. (What a printing job!) The general idea wasn't going to be enough, he could see, having discovered a Ballymoney, a Ballymooney, and a Ballymooneen, as well.

After half an hour or so, when it appeared that Brian would not return until he had exhausted his memory, he went out to the car and brought in the owner's manual. It was the first new car he had ever had, and the little girls had been quite impressed when he had arrived at the front door with it the night before. He didn't intend to do that again, it was possible that he had already invalidated the warranty by taking the car up that road. It all depended on what was meant by *ordinary usage.*

The owner's manual was written on the premise that he was dying to get under the bonnet and tackle his sparking plugs with his spanner. His enjoyment of the unfamiliar words gave way to an uneasiness he had felt before, after an hour with *The Home Medical Encyclopedia:* any comfort in knowing a remedy for familiar trouble was more than outweighed by the discovery of dozens of hitherto unimagined difficulties. He was happy to put it down when he saw Brian pass the window.

"Well, Brian," he said, meeting him at the door.

"Oh, I thought you was gone, Mr. Rafferty."

"I intended to go, but you didn't take the list."

"Oh, no, Mr. Rafferty. It's there, be the window," he said, sounding unperturbed, and went over to the sill.

Rafferty pulled it out of his pocket and held it up.

"You had it in your pocket, sure you did," said Brian, exploding at the joke.

It dawned on Rafferty that the boy must have thought he was being accused of having *taken* the list. "Listen, Brian, you were supposed to take the list with you. That's the point of it."

That, it seemed, was just as funny. "I'd look a right eejit, Mr. Rafferty, walking around with a scrip of paper like that."

"What did you think I wrote it for?"

"I thought it was for yourself, Mr. Rafferty."

"In other words, *I* looked a right eejit."

"Ah, no, Mr. Rafferty."

"Well, let's see where pride has led us."

"Mr. Rafferty?"

"Let's see how much you forgot."

Brian, however, seemed to have remembered everything, and

how much it cost, down to the postage on the individual letters. "I saved you nearly three bob there," he said.

"Oh, no." Not the mail.

"Oh, I did. Your man wanted two and three for the little blue one. 'Get along,' says I. And he says that only for the air post you'd save three bob on the lot. So I says to him, cute like, you see, 'Them's important letters, there. You won't be putting them on the cattle boat.' And he says to me, 'None of that. It's your first-class ocean liner.' Well, Con Murphy's brother went to America, and Con said it took five days, and they had meat three times a day. Oh, they did," he said, misinterpreting the growing disbelief that Rafferty must have been showing, "three times a day and only five days, and wouldn't one of them be a Friday."

"But the envelopes were marked *Air Mail*," Rafferty said.

"That was the worst of it, Mr. Rafferty. Your man had me ink it out, and the striped edges too." He held out a hand, much the worse for post office blue-black.

In some circumstances you might say that time was money, Rafferty heard himself saying, going on like some button-shoed admirer of *Poor Richard's Almanac*. He didn't believe in commanding uncomprehending obedience, he said. He was surprised to learn that Brian thought that the trans-Atlantic liners made daily departures, like the Holyhead Mailboat, and hadn't known that most of them took more than five days to make the crossing. Brian listened, nodding, and he talked on, gathering impetus from Brian's interest, as he did when he found a class really involved in the subject at hand. It was almost half an hour before he realized that he should have been rewriting the letters.

Too bad he hadn't kept a carbon of his letter to Frank, he had spent quite a while getting it just right. If the situation were to appear with complete clarity, there was a chance that Frank would decide to cut their losses and get out. He had stopped the looms on a run of blankets at 3:45 one afternoon, just twelve min-

84

utes after the accountant had brought in the figures he had asked for. It would be wise, however, to let it be understood that there was a shortage of uncommitted weavers, and they might have to train part of the work force.

In its way the letter to Dr. Steichen was more of a problem. It had been just a note, tossed off on impulse, as it were, saying they had landed safely and mentioning, by the by, a few of the setbacks to his timetable (always remembering that in a town like Oakley what he said to Dr. Steichen might reach Frank, and vice versa) and not actually bringing up the second year's leave of absence, but making it harder for it to slip from the man's mind. Now this little arrow might take a month to fall to earth, giving Dr. Steichen every excuse to think that time had solved whatever problems there may have been when the letter was written. He couldn't send a duplicate, and the man was sure to think they had decided he wasn't worth an airmail stamp.

It was afternoon before he finished redoing the letter to Frank. By the time he drove up into the hills it would be almost time to turn back again. He might do better to see about finding a garage in the village, and in the morning, first thing, he would go directly to the country.

So the car didn't make any difference, and she still had to walk up and down the hill once a day. Rafferty said the exercise was doing him good. Perhaps it was. Perhaps it was doing her good too, but she was going to bed at ten, nine-thirty, or even nine, and lying there, sometimes too tired to sleep, just listening to the noises in the walls and the wind, the sash rattle and chimney boom.

In the dark mornings, waked by the clink of milk bottles, she would go down to the kitchen, stomping on the stairs and rattling the knob to give the mice warning, before she crossed the dark

85

room to the light chain. The Imperial Iron would be cold and unable to fight the damp chill that the flags seemed to draw out of the hill itself.

The electric cooker waited on its delicate Queen Anne legs to begin its unhurried day. Its oven was so hopeless that she had put adhesive tape on the vents to keep out the mice and stored the crackers and biscuits in it. And in the grill alternate coils were burnt out so that it would have taken a chess player to work out the moves for grilling anything. It was a rare morning that didn't find her scraping a slice of toast over the coal bucket and hoping it would pass.

Mrs. Redmond, who had seemed to think at first that they needed an experienced girl to handle the job, was now saying that a school leaver, a girl of fourteen, was what Mrs. Rafferty required. "That way," she said, "the girl won't have to forget everything she's learned and start in on the American ways."

"If that's what you think. It seems awfully young to me."

"Ah, you needn't worry. It's best to have them completely unspoiled."

"That's what we'll do then, if you're sure you can find one."

"There's no problem. Just give me three or four days."

WHETHER IT WAS FORBES'S LITTLE TALK OR BRIAN'S JOB AS MONI-tor, Rafferty didn't know, but before the week was out the chimney had been rebuilt and the incision covered with an undulating surface of bright red plaster. This would become white as it dried, Willie said, a suggestion so preposterous that it had to be true.

In the meantime Rafferty started on the list. He was hardly out of Dublin before he was lost in a landscape of bare, worn hills with no people, and for a long way, no signposts. He drove for miles without seeing another car, along narrow stretches, mountain on one side and gully on the other, where he wondered if two cars could pass. Then the road widened and he began to feel the

86

awkwardness of having the steering wheel on the right, only to realize that he had borne to the right at the widening of the road and was tooling along around blind curves on the wrong side of the road.

The first farmer remembered the bacon survey well. He took Rafferty out for a look at the pigs. So did the second, third, and fifth. Pleasant little animals he found them, though he was troubled at first by the small eyes. They were white pigs with the clean pink of their skins shining through, unexpectedly lithe and alert. (If these were the much-mentioned pigs of the Irish kitchens, it was certainly no worse than having a dog in the house.)

When they left the pigs, though, and Rafferty tried to move on to the weaving, he found himself in a rolling, misty landscape, unsignposted by *yes* or *no*. The man from the ministry might have asked the farmer whether he had any interest in someday doing a thing like weaving, and the farmer might have told him that he had nothing in particular against the idea—since that was what the man from the ministry had wanted to hear. To speak concretely of a loom, of lessons, of yards per week, was another thing entirely.

From farm to farm he went—when he could find them—and seemed to accomplish little more than prove his tolerance for ritual cups of tea, an honor to them, the senior civil servant had assured him, tea with an American. He hadn't realized that that would be his role. In Oakley, with his tweeds and pipes and heavy shoes, he had heard that visitors to the college sometimes took him for English, or Irish—his name, of course. Here he was just The American, or, as he had once overheard it, The Yank. Even when he distributed a handful of sweets, still in their Irish wrappings, the woman would say to her bashful children, "Look what the man's brought you from America."

And so they wanted to talk about skyscrapers and Red Indians, and were disappointed that the only Indians he knew of lived in tarpaper shacks and came peaceably to town in jalopies. Or they

87

wanted to talk about their own relatives in America, and couldn't understand how he had never been to Philadelphia or Cleveland. He was relieved one day to be asked about Chicago and be able to say from his own experience that Marshall Field's did indeed exist. Better to have denied Chicago entirely, though, he saw a few moments later when he had to admit that he had never heard of Nuala Byrne nor even of Mrs. John Anderson, Jr., her great friend.

Why should that make them sad? It was a very big city, he told them. His few friends were connected with the universities, and he was not often there.

Too bad that most of the talk had to run along those lines, so fruitless for them and him. He kept trying to get in his own topics. Did one family know, for instance, that he had seen a hinge like the one in their boreen in an illustration of bronze-age artifacts? No, he said, when he had explained the bronze age, he didn't mean it was that old, and in any case it was iron, just that the survival of the style was interesting. To him alone, it seemed.

And when he came upon a thatched roof he liked to tell the people there how nice it looked, how wise of them to keep it, and asked them if there was much thatch being done nowadays, and what was done about repair. Finally, from a farmer who stood less in awe of The American than most, he got an answer: when the thatch, which was already wet and weedy, began to fall into the last of the inhabitable rooms, they would replace it with a roof of corrugated iron, and regret only the expense.

It was a good thing that he had got only smiles the first few times he had brought up the subject, or he might have pulled out some of his half-baked ideas about the Simple Life.

More and more he was finding that there was a lot he didn't tell Alice at the end of the day, to protect her, and because it seemed indecent to speak of the details of poverty that he had spied or overheard. Still, a day with him might have done her a lot of good. She had a way of getting going on things about the house,

88

like her electric stove—not that she didn't have a point there. He had tried to make a pot of tea one night after she had gone to bed, and he would agree that the stove was a real stinker.

"But you know," he said to her, "some of these women don't have anything but an open turf fire with kettles on cranes to cook all the food for their families and for the pigs too."

She laughed at that.

"I mean it," he said. "They have a big black pot there, full of potatoes, turnips, grain, and God-knows-what, from the smell of it. They have to cook it for the pigs every day."

"Well," she said, her admission that her case was less than perfect.

"I'm not saying there isn't something wrong with your stove, just that there are worse things." Things such as women no older than Alice handing him a cup of tea with the horny hands of an old blacksmith. *That* wasn't right, and the worst of it was that he was trying to help, offering their husbands a job that would pay them a decent wage for the wet days and hours and half-hours unused by the farm. He should have picked up his dozen men before he had made twenty stops, instead of this massive sweep, sowing the idea broadcast and wondering if there would ever be a harvest. Even his ad in the provincial papers had produced nothing.

He had been at it nearly a week before he got his first *yes*, a bachelor, perhaps significantly, for the loom would take up a lot of space in the one room that most of them had for living, dining, and cooking.

No one, however, had said *no*, which had led him at first to think that there was a great deal of interest in his project.

After a while he had begun to cross off the ones that he suspected weren't really interested, or whose wives weren't, but he still wasn't covering the ground the way he ought to have been. He wasn't good at closing those leisurely interviews, and sometimes he couldn't even find the farms.

89

It was hard to fit the country in with his idea of Western Europe as being overpopulated. High demesne walls sealed him into narrow deserted roads, or the country opened out into a vista of ruined castles, ruined manor houses, ruined cottages, sheep, rabbits, or just upland bog and an empty road. Directions could seem crystal clear, a simple "left, right, right," and founder on the definition of a road. A pair of sharp eyes was not much of an asset, though he might have spied the foot-high stump that was still the Big Tree to two men in rubber boots. But how see that McBride's Pub was run under the sign of Guinan's or that the gates of Balmoral Lodge had been repainted Rinn-na-Mara by its present occupants?

Once, when he was halted at a desolate crossroads studying the map, a pleasant old man had appeared beside the car and directed him down a boreen which ended at the grass-grown ruins of a cottage.

"That'd be Old Corrigan," said a man at the next farmhouse. "It isn't often that strangers see him."

"No?" said Rafferty.

"You see, that family," he pointed to Rafferty's list, "would have been there when Old Corrigan was alive."

"He's not alive now?"

"No."

"A ghost?"

"He's harmless."

"I should think you would have noticed something," Alice said when he told her.

"I didn't. He was a nice old man."

"I don't suppose you noticed if he had a shadow."

He shook his head. No sun anyway. "And there was another man today. He had a little cartful of turf and was walking beside the horse, a pony really. 'How far?' I asked him, and he said, 'I'd make it three, maybe four mile, but for a grand motorcar like that, there wouldn't be a mile in it.'"

Alice laughed.

"In a way he's right, you know. All my life I've suffered from the other kind, the people who think you can put a number on anything. But when I'm out on those roads, and the dark's coming on, I'd like a fact, just once, a fact."

She seemed to feel that a lot of his problems could be solved by noting the direction of watercourses or even the position of the sun. "The sun? How many hours of sunshine a day do you think we have anyway?"

"I just mean you should keep the brighter sky vaguely to one side or the other," she said, her hands busy with the silverware. He was supposed to think of her knife as a bank of brighter clouds. Good Lord, he wasn't leading the Lewis and Clark expedition.

"Eat up," he said, throwing a bone into the turf fire. They were still eating in the library, since the dining room would have meant another fire, maybe other things too, for the dining table was missing two of its eight legs, and the doorknob came off in his hand.

He inspected the bottom of his second chop. He had been pretty forbearing about the meals lately, he thought. "You know," he said, "these'd be a lot better if you'd burn the fat and leave the meat raw, instead of the other way around."

"It's that *damned* stove," she exploded, banging the table.

"Watch it." He steadied the table with one hand and his knee while he straightened the weak leg. They had brought the table over from between the windows, where it had been borrowing stability from the wall behind. He shouldn't have mentioned the chops.

"Why don't you get someone in to have a look at your stove?" he said.

9.

THE MAN FROM THE ELECTRICITY SUPPLY BOARD SWITCHED ON THE
stove and tested both burners with the horny heel of his hand,
feeling here and there, like a doctor looking for a weak pulse.
Then he poured a few drops of water onto the cast-iron plates and
stood back for a time, until a breath of steam rose from the water.
"*There*," he said, as if everything were all right now.

"But it takes forty-five minutes to boil a kettle of water."

"It would that, if you take it from a cold start. But it's hot
enough then, so it is?"

"It certainly is. It takes another half hour to cool enough so that
you can leave a pan alone on the stove."

"You wouldn't want to leave it in the middle of the plate. You'd
put it to the side, like that."

"What about the grill?"

"You wouldn't want to touch that. You'd pay a couple of quid
for a new one, and no telling when you'd get it."

Hoping to get something out of the service call, she brought in

O'Reilley's iron. After the man had removed a single screw, even she could see that something was wrong. There were blue-black burns on the metal inside and bright splashes of melted solder.

He looked puzzled though. With his thumbnail he dislodged the brittle insulation and crumbled it to a sandy powder between his fingers. He turned the iron over and over. She began to wish she had not brought it out. "Oh, *there's* your trouble." He ticked the name plate at the back of the iron with his screwdriver. "120 volts. That's 220," he said, pointing to the wall socket.

"Everywhere in the house?"

"The whole country. It's a good job it didn't fuse the lights."

"Can it be fixed?" she asked before he could carry on along that line.

"I'll fix it so you can use it." He yanked the cord free. "Now, you put your iron on the cooker there, only mind it doesn't get too hot. See, your plate's hot now." The drops of water were trembling. "You'll get used to it." The stove? The iron? Both? He began packing his things. He had a bag like a doctor's, but his coat was an old canvas one, torn off above the knee.

"The trouble is, I'm used to gas," she said.

He looked around the room and went over to examine a stub of copper pipe high up in the wall. "There's your man," he said. "You'd be stuck without him, being on top the granite, like. You ring the Rathdown Gas Company. They're in the book."

"Thank you. Now, what do I owe you?"

"Nothing. There's nothing I could do for you. Just ring the gas company and they'll have you back on their mains in an hour or two."

Rafferty had problems enough of his own without being asked to buy a new stove, she thought, but she had left the stew unattended for twenty minutes, and, in the ensuing explanations, the question of the gas stove arose.

"Sure," he said, "anything, if it'll make a difference."

93

The next morning, when she returned from her shopping trip, the gardener was inspecting the hedge at the inner gate, and he fell in step with her going up the drive. "Trouble in the house yesterday?" he asked.

"No." As if there hadn't been trouble ever since they had entered the door. "What do you mean?"

"I thought I saw the ESB."

"Oh, that. I had him in to look at the electric stove, to see why it's so slow."

"Slow? Cook never said anything."

"No. Well, I'm thinking of getting gas."

"Oh, that's lovely stuff, the gas. I'd have it meself, barring the explosions."

When she phoned, the man at the gas company wasn't greatly interested in her description of the copper pipe. "Actually you might be in a better position without the old line. I'll send a man out in the morning."

It was afternoon before the doorbell rang, and Alice was taken aback by the sight of the man at the door. It was time she got used to the way the workmen dressed: the black berets, trousers tucked into long grey socks by way of bicycle clips, and the overcoats, the tattered canvas on the electrician and now this one, an ancient double-breasted model in an eye-catching state of disrepair. And yet—if Rafferty could only see it—there were places where the worn tweed still glowed in its soft, bright colors, and the pattern stood out like a patch of pavement at Pompeii.

"Mr. O'Reilley sent me," he was saying, for the second time. He seemed to expect more than the nod she had given him.

"We'd like the stove downstairs. I suppose you'd like to see the pipe," she said. Something was wrong, she saw. "Cooker," she said. "You don't call it a stove. You call it a cooker."

No, that wasn't the answer. He was feeling inside the coat and drew out a letter, with an American stamp. "He says in here," the

94

man said, tapping the envelope, "just tell them Pat O'Reilley sent you."

"Oh yes," Alice said, remembering O'Reilley's party, afraid that she knew now what the man must be. "I thought you were the gas man."

"Ah, no." He laughed at the idea, and she thought of Pompeii again, seeing his teeth. "Is there any way I can help you? Mr. O'Reilley said he heard you was having a hard time."

O'Reilley had heard? Was this going to be Dr. Steichen's answer, did he hope they would be *sent* home? "No, thank you. We're all right. Mr. O'Reilley shouldn't have sent you out here."

"You know how to find things? You have the bus book?" He was embarrassed, as though he didn't see how *he* could help *them*. "If you find you need me, just send a message. Here's the place." He slipped out the letter and handed her the empty envelope.

"Thank you."

He began going down the steps sideways. "You could tell him the next time you write."

"Yes."

"Tell Mr. O'Reilley I was here," he said, anxiously, she thought.

"Oh, yes. I will. And thank you."

He picked up a black bike from beside the driveway and pushed it down to the gate.

She was just going back into the house when the gardener rounded the corner, rake in hand. "I didn't see that one before," he said, nodding in the direction of the gate.

"He knows someone we know in America." She looked down at the envelope. "He's from town, from Dublin."

The gardener nodded. "Pity he didn't go to Himself at the premises in town instead."

"Yes, it is." Rafferty would have known what to do.

"Bad job that hill, for a man his age."

"Yes." He looked about as old as the gardener.

95

Back in the library she pulled the fire slowly forward, trying to keep it intact, and built a three-block pyramid of turf behind it. Was she on to an old technique? In this room there was no chance of heating the air, which came through uncounted holes and scarcely paused on its way to the chimney. Only the radiant heat was real, the red glow of the fire on her shins and face.

She would have to write O'Reilley and tell him that the man had come up to Prisma, a long and pointless trip on a bicycle, for a man his age. She was annoyed with herself for not thinking of that until the gardener had pointed it out. She ought to have asked the old man in for a cup of tea. He might have been counting on it. Still she didn't like the idea of him and that overcoat in her house.

They had really made a mistake when they had gone to O'Reilley's party, first the travel iron that wouldn't travel, and now this. It was embarrassing, just the thought of how O'Reilley had gone on about England and the six counties of Northern Ireland. "What if England had kept the New England states after the Revolutionary War? The exact same thing." It wasn't. It was more like their keeping Canada, she had thought, and said nothing. A little man, O'Reilley, he kept shouting and pounding the top of his baby grand piano, damning England, damning the king (and not wanting to be corrected to *queen*), damning the Dublin government for going along with it, and praising only the IRA, his last hope. "I give them all the help I can," he said and then turned to Alice. "I'll give you their address before you go. You ought to have at least one friend when you're in a strange country. Just tell them Pat O'Reilley sent you." He must have forgotten, and she had never given it another thought, until the man had pulled out O'Reilley's envelope and said, "Just tell them Pat O'Reilley sent you."

She picked up the envelope. Johnnie O'Connor, it said. It was hard to imagine him as a runner for the IRA, but, of course, that would be the last thing he would want to look like.

96

"You know," she told Rafferty at dinner that night, "if I'd re-membered to ask O'Reilley for the IRA address he wouldn't have sent the old man out."

"I wouldn't be too sure of that," Rafferty said. "But you'll have to write O'Reilley now, get him to call off his dogs. Tell him we have all we can handle now, without risking trouble with the gov-ernment."

"How could we get into trouble?"

"I don't know, and I don't want to ask Forbes. And don't for-get that everything you say will go on to Steichen and probably to Frank as well."

"The old man certainly looked harmless."

"Have it your way. And, by the by, what did the gas man say?"

When she phoned the next day, he said, "Tomorrow."

For several days it remained "tomorrow," with apologies and plausible excuses. Then one morning it was "some time next week. . . . Ah, we won't disappoint you, Mrs. Rafferty."

HE CAME TO KNOW THE HILLS THE WAY THE CAPTAIN OF A TRAMP steamer knows his handful of islands. Ballybritton, Ballybyrne, Ballyconnell, Ballycumber, Ballyhorsey, Ballyknocker, Bella Byrne's Bridge, and Black Tom's Cellars.

The odd patch of blooming heather which had been there when he had begun his journeying was gone now, and the coarse moun-tain fern, the bracken, had died and turned red. Close up it might have been only a sparse tangle of bedsprings rusting in a dump. But on those high little roads he could look ahead and see the hills crowding behind each other, the rounded nubbins of ancient mountains, all in the color of the orange tweed worn by a certain kind of old men and women, a scene to start amateurs on water-colors, and stop professionals with its vulgar perfection.

He had picked up quite a bit of the lore of the place—from books, he had to admit—and when you thought of those hills, pastures for a few dozen sheep now, having once supported hundreds of families in each valley, it was no wonder that the history was often bloody or, at best, depressing. Sitting by their turf fires, he would question the cottagers. Why did a certain road look different from the others, he would ask, and be told about different dates of surfacing and where they had got the gravel for the tarmac.

"I don't mean the surface. I mean the way it goes up over the hills, the way the stone walls look at the side." There was something Roman about the road, not that straight, but still an engineer's road, and *old*, he thought. "I mean something in its history, something different."

"Ah, no. You think so? Ah, no, it's all the one road."

Or, standing in a doorway, he would say, "See, over there, on that hill, near the top, how the ground looks almost striped?"

"The rocks."

"No, above them. Those regular lines, in the bracken?"

"It's only the bracken."

"Yes, bracken. But the bracken itself seems to be in stripes, like that roof there," he said, seeing almost the same effect in the rusty corrugated iron roof of an outbuilding.

"Ah, there'd be no houses there."

Rafferty would have left it at that, but the farmer, to close the subject, went on, "Just shadows in the bracken."

"Yes, that's what I mean. What makes the shadows?"

"The sun," said the farmer, flinging an arm toward where it ought to have been. "The clouds."

Perhaps he had stumbled onto something unmentionable, fairies, or whatever they called them. This thing, this appearance, was always high, in the wasteland, above the highest tilled fields, even above the grazing land. "And even when you know it's in a certain place, you don't always see it there," he found himself

98

trying to explain to a man he had met in a Dublin pub. "I'd almost say they were corrugations of some kind."

"That's right. The potato trenches, lazy beds," said the man, whose name was Fogarty. "Before the famine they used to till that land. God knows how they did it."

"And why didn't the farmers tell me that?"

Fogarty shrugged. "They probably don't know."

"They don't and you do?"

"You historians can talk about your 'oral traditions,' but if you have a language change it comes to the same thing as a population change. I'm writing a paper on it someday."

"Oh, I won't poach." And he asked about the road.

"The military road," Fogarty told him, "built in the eighteenth century to subdue the Byrnes and the O'Tooles. Oh, the military had their troubles up there. You're moving through some of the most-mapped country on earth. When the Cotswolds were still a few puckered lines, the elevation of every Wicklow molehill had been charted—for the use and enjoyment of the tax collector and the military."

So it was an engineer's road.

"And mis'ss?" Alice paused on the steps to hear him out. "They was potato parings on the compost."

"Yes." And why not?

"I keep a clean garden."

"Oh, you do, Mr. Molloy. Very clean." But no one could keep a clean compost, if that was what he was getting at.

"If you was to do it right, there'd be nothing, only the grass clippings in it."

"You mean you don't want potato peelings in the compost?"

He nodded. "Just greens. Cabbage leaves, that class of thing."

"I see. And what do I do with the rest?"

"You burn it, in the kitchen. That's what Cook did."

99

"Yes," she said, drawing out the word into a knife's edge, despite herself. You don't fight with a gardener, Rafferty said—but it wasn't his problem.

The man was moving off with his rake toward the beech tree. He would be at it all afternoon, raking a few bushels of leaves and dragging them in the wheelbarrow up to the cleft in the rocks where he had his bonfires. She ought to be happy, she told herself, that at least one person still enjoyed the sort of leisure that the house had been built for.

RAFFERTY HAD A LOT OF QUESTIONS ABOUT BRIAN, BUT FOR WHAT HE was paying the boy he figured he didn't have a right to ask them. (Forbes had warned him not to raise the wages. "He's well above the average now, and you do have to deal with other firms. . . . The Irish invented the boycott.") Bit by bit he was putting together a picture.

He had come to Dublin one day during the lunch hour, driven from the hills by bad weather, and had found Brian sheltering beneath the arch at the entrance to the mews. Willie always locked the building when he left for lunch, he said. Then why wasn't he somewhere eating his own lunch? He had eaten it. Already? What had he had? A bar of chocolate, a large one. "I don't get hungry, Mr. Rafferty. Sure I don't." And even supposing a chocolate bar—and a cigarette—could be considered an adequate lunch for a growing boy, why hadn't he stayed inside the building rather than risk adding pneumonia to malnutrition? "I didn't like to bother Willie about it." What did he eat for breakfast? Tea, and toast and jam, if there was time. And what would he have at night? "She makes a lovely tea, Mr. Rafferty. Bacon and cabbage and potatoes, as many potatoes as you can eat, and sometimes a sweet. And we have supper too." What? "Bread and butter and tea."

So he had unlocked the door and put Brian by the fire with the

100

two sandwiches, one cheese and one tomato, that Alice had made for his own lunch that morning. And then he had gone out and found a small restaurant which he paid by the week to put a proper lunch into Brian.

And, not long after that, when Brian had been working a month, and it was apparent that none of his wages was going into clothes, Rafferty took him into a clothing store and had him fitted with a tweed jacket.

"They'll only pawn it, you know," said the clerk, who would almost have preferred to lose the sale, Rafferty felt.

"She will, you know," Brian agreed, "unless I'd keep it at the premises."

"You might have some sort of uniform made," the clerk suggested.

"What good would that do?" Rafferty asked.

"Oh, they don't like to take the uniforms. There could be trouble."

In the end they had compromised, and beneath the inner coat pocket and inside the corduroy pants were sewn large cloth labels: *This garment is the property of Rafferty's Woollens.* The shoes would be safe, Brian said, as long as he had only the one pair.

The transformation was startling, but, as they walked back to the mews together, he told Brian that there would be no real transformation until he managed to go back to school somehow.

"Awrr," Brian said.

"I mean it. I was a poor boy myself."

"Ah, you wasn't, Mr. Rafferty. Sure you wasn't?"

"I was. I couldn't afford a store-bought cigarette until I was twenty-one."

Brian slid his nicotine-stained fingers into his new coat, Napoleon fashion.

At least he had thought they were poor when he had to give up the room that his scholarship entitled him to because he would

101

have had to provide his own bedding, and they hadn't had a sheet in the house—just flannelette mill ends with seams down the middle. But they had gone into the winter with more than five hundred jars of fruit and vegetables down the cellar, and the house safe in his mother's name. And if it had been a question of no college at all, rather than just a two-mile walk home at ten every night, they would have found the sheets somehow.

Brian broke into a laugh beside him and dug his elbow into his arm. "You smoke a pipe, Mr. Rafferty. You never smoked cigarettes at all."

He shook his head. "We're not playing word games, Brian. This is a serious matter. I had a nickel package of Bull Durham, and I rolled my own cigarettes and they looked like hell. And I never had one of those until I was seventeen. The point is that without education you'll never be anything more than a navvy. Every time you open your mouth and say 'You was' you're advertising the fact that you quit school."

Brian looked sad. "I'd never do the scholarship paper, Mr. Rafferty. You'd want to be keen for that, all right."

"THE SEAWEED'S HERE," SAID THE GARDENER, POINTING DOWN TO-ward the gate where a small cart stood, overflowing with reddish-brown gelatinous lashes. The driver of the cart was standing beside the horse's head, giving his attention to him.

"Yes, Mr. Molloy," she said and waited. She had never seen him that early in the day, and something that looked a lot like a pajama sleeve protruded from his raincoat.

"That's ten bob," he said.

"I'll have to go up and get it," she said and went back into the house. She just hadn't wanted to ask him why. The last storm had left the beach a mess, she knew. Could it be that they, as householders, had an obligation to share in the cleanup?

"Seaweed?" said Rafferty, who was just getting out of bed.

"You're going to give him ten shillings for a cartful of seaweed?"

"Well, yes. I mean he's so definite about it."

"All right, but I suggest that you find out what it's for."

"Ah, it's a grand manure," said the gardener, taking the ten-shilling note.

They piled it next to the compost heap, where she saw it when she went out with the cabbage leaves.

"THE BOY'S GOT A SENSE OF ORDER," RAFFERTY SAID TO FOGARTY.

"You're lucky there."

"He should never have left school. He'd make a good engineer or something like that."

"I know. Waste." Fogarty nodded sadly and strummed a fingernail on the paper clip that held his left shirt cuff together. He was a barrister, the barman had told Rafferty, told him to go over to the Four Courts if he wanted to see Fogarty in wig and black gown.

"What's it cost to keep a boy in school?"

"Oh, I don't know. You just might find a place for under twenty pounds a year, maybe fifteen. Plus books. Could easily run fifty quid per annum."

"I could manage that."

"You could. I could. But we're talking about your Brian's father, assuming he'd want to do without Brian's wages."

"I mean I could send Brian to school next year."

"Best not."

"Why not?"

Fogarty shook his head. "You wouldn't understand, maybe when you've been here a year or two more . . ."

Rafferty didn't push it. It would take more than just time for him to start justifying middle-class privilege.

"I'd try to get him into the Tech, if I were you. He can go at night, keep right on working."

103

"Oh, now, I've taught night school—get broke enough you'll do anything, even the Federalist Papers. You start out bringing in folding chairs for the overflow, and by the last month you're down to half a dozen ladies. Real students of history, I thought, just wondered why, in that case, they seemed so slow on the uptake. Turns out they've got their husbands washing the dishes and putting the kids to bed so that they can get out and improve their minds."

Fogarty laughed. "It's nothing like that here. And the teachers have got to be good, they're dealing with boys who've never learned to study properly."

And who isn't?

"You coming now? I've got a brief for tomorrow," Fogarty said, picking up his bag.

"Might as well." He drained his glass.

At the corner Fogarty headed north to catch the train to Howth, and Rafferty headed back to the mews for the car. There had been talk of getting together in the evening with their wives. But when he considered the trip in, all through Dublin and out the far side, a big crescent, it didn't seem a good idea. "Easy enough if you had a boat," said Fogarty.

He wasn't particularly anxious to meet Mrs. Fogarty. He had assumed, though, that there was no way of avoiding it; he had nearly forgotten what it was to begin a friendship without looking forward to its fruition in the "evening," them and us, and a heavy bit of pastry at eleven-thirty. And then Alice would feel obliged to respond with her black bottom pie, even though he had been made well aware of what no more than boiling an egg meant in that kitchen.

"There, what about that?" he said, and handed it to her. "Doesn't even have a mate."

She looked at the rubber boot, dried and cracked like an old

104

mud puddle. "No reason for keeping it," she agreed. The problem wasn't quite as simple as he was making out, however.

"And what's this?" he asked, shaking a rusty can and tilting it so that the light fell inside. "Rusty carpet tacks. Bent. They've been used. Here."

She took the tin in her other hand. She wondered if he had considered how you threw out carpet tacks—just dump them in the ashpit and hope that whoever emptied it would be careful with them?

"And what about this?" he asked, holding out a soup plate with a large notch in the rim where the two cracks had crossed.

She shifted the tin beside the boot, taking care to touch them as little as possible, and took the soup plate from him. "It can go out."

"And what about this? Looks like part of a broken playpen."

"That"—she had an answer this time—"is what the inventory refers to as a *clothes rack.*"

"Oh. It's more complicated than I'd thought, then. Well, we'll just put that in here," he said, opening the door of the still room, and shoved inside it the collection of loose rods. "The principle is still the same, just pick 'em up and throw 'em out. I'd do it, but I can see you've got all these reservations, and we'd end up having a fight."

He left her standing there, holding everything, and she heard him out in the hallway with the turf barrel. So she carried the boot and the soup plate out to the ashpit and placed the tin of tacks back on the kitchen floor, more or less out of sight in the heart of the debris. Later, she could put it inside one of the paint cans, after she had opened them all to discover what could be thrown out.

It was easy enough to come in from the outside and cream off the top, pick up half a dozen things that obviously had to go out and simply pronounce them disposed of, without going into the mechanics of that. What would you do about that perfectly good cover to a soup tureen? And would you throw out that electric fire that seemed to need only a new cord and plug? You might fix it, but then you would be dealing with 220 volts, and even if you just blew the fuse, it might not end with a private, candlelit search for the fuse box. It could mean the ESB, and the gardener with his questions.

She spent a good eight hours a day in that kitchen, and she had learned that everything there had a long fuse on it—like the scullery door. She had put on rubber gloves and used boiling water with soap and ammonia. The water turned black and softened the dark padding around the frame, which was not felt at all, just dirt, grease. And then, from the clean, cream-colored casing, the latch plate had fallen and revealed that the wood beneath would never hold another screw. Glue proved to be not nearly as adhesive as mutton fat and dirt, and the door was now held shut by a little hook, like a screen door.

And even assuming you were omniscient and knew just what to throw out, and you had screwed your courage down to a resolute disregard of spiders and mice and fungus, then what? Why had someone chosen to start a rubbish tip there instead of carrying it a few feet farther to the ashpit? What was it covering up? She wasn't going to mention that, but it was the sort of thing that had to be considered. And time. Here she was at eight-thirty with half an hour's work ahead of her, burning the garbage, clearing the work table, mouseproofing the food. And that didn't count the dishes which, she knew now, would have to wait in the scullery all night. You simply had to stop sometime.

10.

MRS. REDMOND MUST HAVE BEEN HOPING THAT SHE WOULD TAPER off a little, Alice thought. She dreaded the daily stop there herself, more so since the time she had wondered aloud whether she ought to run an ad. Mrs. Redmond had had a great deal to say about that. Obviously, as Rafferty pointed out, it was to her interest that they did not run the ad, and her stories of what had happened to people who took a chance on a strange girl were a little too pat, with the unconfused outline of fables. All the same, Alice had dropped the idea.

"Where are all the girls?" she asked one morning.

"They'd be in England," Mrs. Redmond said.

"They prefer it there?"

Mrs. Redmond shrugged. "You know what happens to the Irish girls in England." Her tone suggested it all. "It's the money," she said, "much more than they can get here."

"How much would they be making then?"

"Oh, it might be five pounds."

"Supposing I offered that much?" She didn't see how she could, though.

"Oh, you wouldn't do that, sure you wouldn't?" Mrs. Redmond stood up and leaned across her counter with a sudden affability. "There's no need for that, dear. Everything's dearer in England. A girl'd have to pay her fare there, and the extra for the National Health, not that they think of that, mind you. Oh, you wouldn't have to pay anything like that much." It wasn't easy to avoid Mrs. Redmond's eye in that tiny shop, and, seeing she would be given no chance to reply, Alice fixed her gaze on "Save Irish Horses. . . ."

"You'd want to be patient," Mrs. Redmond said, when she had said everything else. "I'll find you someone at a proper wage. There were two girls in to me yesterday. It happened that the older one wouldn't take a place with children. I told her you had just the two, girls, like. But she'd had enough, five boys and the mother never home. And the younger . . ."

Well, that was it, she thought, climbing the hill, there would never be a maid for her, not as long as the old status quo had a thread left to starch. The arrogance that had built her kitchen was still there, but without the reservoir of barefoot, twelve-year-old girls to be forever grateful for a bed in one of those back basement rooms with two square feet of barred window just below the ceiling.

The girls who remained would go on working where they had always worked, and, even if it meant that each year there would be less and less of them, Mrs. Redmond would do her best to keep them from hearing that there were places where they might have at least a decent wage. What was she to make of Mrs. Redmond? *She* would know too much to believe in the lace curtains, and she knew, or thought she did, what she was condemning the girls to in England. What reward could she be expecting in this world or the next?

It wouldn't have mattered so much to Alice, if they had not

made it impossible for her to do her own housework: the stoves that wouldn't let her leave the kitchen, the sink—was she supposed to kneel at the sink? That Ma Perkins apron was no accident, either. It put her in a class with women who went around the house in carpet slippers and curlers.

What she ought to do was to run an ad: *own room, interior sprung mattress, central heating,* the works, and £5 *a week.* Put it in, right below *Can Lady recommend competent cook-general for Colonel's family?* and *Viscountess requires nursemaid.* No need to pick up the answers, and every time she went down to that damned galley, she could think of how the boat was rocking up above.

She recognized the coat through the narrow beveled glass at the side of the door. The letter to O'Reilley had never been written— no hurry, she had thought. Why couldn't the man have come a few minutes earlier, while she had been out? She could pretend that he had, just not answer the door—and have him come out again, yet another useless trip on his bicycle.

"Mr. O'Reilley sent me. He wondered how you was getting on."

"Yes." She forced herself to say, "Won't you come in for a cup of tea, Mr. O'Connor?"

"Thank you very much," he said, and stepped in, pulling off the beret and loosing the white hair like the stuffing of a burst cushion.

"The kitchen's this way." She started down the hall. "You know," she said, not knowing what to say, "I keep thinking you ought to be wearing a trenchcoat."

There was a silence, a prolonged silence as the hall seemed to unroll before them, lengthening as they went. Perhaps he hadn't known that she had been told what he was, or perhaps it was simply not to be mentioned. When they reached the door at the end she turned back and saw the old man looking down at the ruin he was wearing.

"It's a fine coat," he said, "but it's seen better days."

Was it possible that he didn't know about the stereotyped revolutionary's trenchcoat, had never seen an IRA movie, and thought she was commenting on his rags? "Oh, it's a beautiful coat," she assured him. "I told Mr. Rafferty about the tweed the last time you were here."

No response.

"He's here to make tweeds, you know, Irish industry for the Irish," she added, hoping to break through to his sympathies.

He ran a finger along the soft, glowing colors that Rafferty would have given his eyeteeth for, and nodded. "You wouldn't find a coat like that now."

"It's too bad," she agreed. "Mind the step." They started down in the dark. "I'm afraid the kitchen's a mess. I had to get out and do the shopping first."

It was hardly an adequate excuse for the roomful of bundled garbage, heaped laundry, and dirty dishes, more than any one meal could produce.

She switched on the electric cooker and crossed to the scullery. "I'm afraid it'll take forty minutes to boil the water," she called out while the kettle filled, a slow process with the water pressure what it was on the hill. She wondered if he would take it amiss if she started cleaning the room while she waited for the cooker.

"Oh, not that long," he was saying in the kitchen.

"By the clock," she called.

"Twenty-five minutes, half an hour at the most," he insisted.

"I had the man from the—" she began, coming in with the kettle. O'Connor was standing in front of the Imperial Iron. "Oh, that thing won't boil water, ever."

He laughed. "Look."

In fifteen minutes the kettle was singing. A few taps of the hammer had loosened rust-cemented joints, and most of the ornamentation proved to be functional doors, slides, and knobs. "Can you remember? That one's for the back boiler. That's for the oven.

You'd want to get used to it. Ah, you can wet the tea now." A plume of steam was bursting from the spout. "How long was that?" he asked, looking up at the stopped clock.

"Less than twenty minutes!"

"That's a grand stove," he said, patting it, "and if you didn't have it, the fireplace'd be better still."

She looked over at it, the mound of broken bricks in the grate and two iron teakettles, dusty and rusting, and just smiled. "I'll get the bread and butter," she said. She wished he would take off his coat, but she wasn't going to speak of it again, however obliquely.

When she came back from washing a few knives in the scullery, he was standing there looking at the pan in which she had grilled (toughened, Rafferty said) last night's steak. "That's a grand lot of dripping there," he said.

She wondered if he could be hinting for the waxy yellow fat. "Would you like to have it?"

"That's very kind of you," he said, transferring the tin to the hot stove, and went over to the table where he gripped the loaf with nails bordered in black and cut a few pieces of bread. She had meant only to give him the fat in a jam pot, but there he was, he and his coat, suddenly in charge of her kitchen.

The pan of bread sizzled with what she had to admit was an appetizing smell, and, after a minute or two, he piled the bread on his plate and stood, waiting for her to sit, she guessed.

She sat down. She had spent half an hour with Mrs. Redmond, lost fifteen minutes on the gas company, most of it just waiting while the phone crackled, and now this, and on a day when the little girls were outside, happily employed. She would have to work right through their naps to make it up.

"You should have a maid," he said, talking with his mouth full.

She didn't know what to say to that, where to begin.

"You know, a girl to help you with the housework. She'd do the washing up for you, and the laundry, and she'd mind the children

111

too," he said, looking over at the table of clay and color books.

So she told him. Mrs. Redmond. The gas company. The cooker. The sink. The compost heap. The shopping. And Mrs. Redmond.

"That one's no intention of getting you a girl."

"But what if she thinks it's the only way to stop me offering five pounds?"

He just shook his head. "You won't have to pay five quid. Run an ad. Say you're American."

"You don't know what you'd get that way."

"You'd be all right, you could always sack the girl."

"I was thinking more of the criminal types. Someone who'd just wait until you went out shopping and then have her boy friend come and clean out the house."

He nodded and drummed the table with his dirty fingernails. "You know, I think I could get you a girl. She wouldn't be no fancy parlormaid, but you wouldn't have to lock up the plate."

Could he? "The thing is—" she stopped, looking for the right words. Difficult as things were, they could be worse if the house were turned into a stop on the underground railroad, or whatever it was they had. "I wouldn't want a girl who was involved in politics."

"Oh, you wouldn't that," he agreed. "There's no good in them once they go that way."

"And I'll pay you what I was going to pay Mrs. Redmond."

"No, no, not at all. But you could tell Mr. O'Reilley."

"I certainly will."

"Just tell him I was able to offer you a little assistance."

She nodded.

"Now," he said, "indoor or outdoor?"

Later, when she had said good-by to O'Connor in the driveway, she saw the gardener coming toward her. Sometimes she thought it possible that his chief function wasn't gardening at all.

"Oh, Mr. Molloy," she called out, "I've been wanting to ask you about the Brussels sprouts."

"Not ready yet," he called, shifting his trajectory so that he shot into the orchard and out of sight.

That night Rafferty agreed that Mrs. Redmond had no intention of supplying a maid. "But that doesn't mean that your friend in the IRA's the answer. Suppose he sends you a secret agent to carry on business from our kitchen?"

"I thought of that, and he promised that he wouldn't."

"All right, if you want to trust that kind of man."

"He's nothing like that. If you could see him you'd know. I don't think he's anything more than some kind of office boy."

"Except that he's in an illegal organization, given to blowing up innocent people."

"If you want to put it that way." The question was, who else was taking an interest in her problem?

"I'm not blaming this poor old guy, no telling what he's been through, but your friend O'Reilley ought to have his head examined."

Her friend?

"And for God's sake, will you write that letter to him, before he can send more help?"

HE HAD TEN MEN NOW, TEN MEN AND TEN DISMANTLED LOOMS. IT seemed a good place to quit. There were no new names on the list, just men who hadn't said *no*. To hear them go on, you would think the whole county was talking of nothing but whether to weave for Rafferty's Woollens. From most of them he never would have had an answer, he thought. They didn't want to weave, but they didn't like to disappoint him, and besides (as Fogarty said), who knew but what a *no* might in some way make them ineligible for an as yet unborn government dole?

In the mews Willie had all but finished; even the vein of dry rot that the plumbers had struck was playing out. They had the looms, the yarn, wrapping paper, twine and brass shipping scales, and a black, errand boy's bicycle, the kind with a small front wheel under an enormous wicker basket and, in the triangle of the frame, the firm's name in white paint: Rafferty's Woollens, 11 Ormond Lane.

Brian was growing a little restless. "I think me and you could put up one of them yokes downstairs, and then you could get started."

So he explained it again, how he had been running the ads throughout the eastern part of Ireland, and if all else failed, he was going to have to go, cap in hand, to some of the other firms and beg for the loan of a man to teach the weavers.

"Do you not know how to weave yourself, then, Mr. Rafferty?"

He shook his head. He couldn't have imagined that it would come to this.

"There must be thousands of weavers," Brian said, kneeling beside the office fireplace where he was piling the last sods from the turf basket on top of the full one he had just brought up. "Would you ever have the priest ask the people at Mass?"

"I was thinking of the woolman. He knows where all the weavers are."

"That's a grand idea, Mr. Rafferty. Look at how he found the looms."

"That's what I was thinking. I wish he'd show up. It's been three weeks now. If we'd been weaving we might have been running short."

"Oh, there's a great deal of wool there, Mr. Rafferty, so there is."

"Yes." He couldn't expect Brian to understand a hypothesis. "You shouldn't be smoking, Brian," he said.

Brian looked down at the cigarette in surprise. "Oh, I didn't know I was, Mr. Rafferty. I've tried to give it up. Honest, I have." Before more could be said on that subject he was out the door with the empty turf basket.

The office was a pleasant room now, about the size of Prisma's

114

library, but, having been built for servants, had a low ceiling which kept the heat down where it was of some use. He had found an old leather-topped Regency table for less than the going price of a new desk and had bought, here and there, four unmatched, but similar, Regency chairs. That was all he had in the room, except the long counter for inspecting and packing the tweed. It was opposite the fire, behind his back. In front of him were the calendars, one on each side of the fireplace. He had bought the first one, a dusty wreck of a mahogany box with printed linen rollers inside, and spent half a day gluing and polishing it, and adjusting the knobs for the months, the days of the week, and the date. By the time *Monday* confronted him for the second time he realized that it was a calendar for which time did not exist, as circular as a clock. The yesterdays turned from the windows and slipped into the future. It was a calendar for a place where the inkwells were filled on Monday, where the bills went out on the first and were paid on the tenth, and not much else was happening.

He never knew where he was, looking at it, and so he asked Frank, who sent him a big broadside of a railroad calendar with the year at a glance. The days moved from the first of January (red) to the thirty-first of December (black). He knew where he was now all right. The past grew larger and the future smaller until he could hardly bear it. He would never finish in a year.

And he wasn't as certain of the woolman as he had led Brian to think. The question of the weavers was not exactly a virgin topic, but every time it had come up something had happened before he could ask the woolman's help. He couldn't remember enough to be sure that it had always been an act of God, like Willie's dropping the sink, or whether the woolman himself might sometimes have been responsible.

He went downstairs. "Be back in an hour or so," he said to Brian. He would swing over to the quays, look through the places that would be having auctions within the next day or two, come

115

back over the metal bridge and look at the secondhand books at Webbs, and then it would be nearly time for lunch.

WHEN SHE CAME HOME FROM SHOPPING, ALICE SAW THE GARDENER at the front gate, adjusting the ladder against a stretch of hedge that already looked perfectly clipped.

"Where are the girls?" she asked him.

"They're beyond, in the kitchen."

"But they're not supposed—"

"It's all right. That one's with them."

The girl was sitting in the center of the kitchen with her sheepskin boots planted flat on the floor and her green coat buttoned to the chin.

"That's Mary Flaherty," said Vanessa, pointing her crayon at the girl. "She's twenty years old."

Stella drove her elbow into Vanessa's ribs, and Mary Flaherty blushed. "Mr. O'Connor sent me," she said. "He said it would be better than Liverpool, and I could see Mammy and me brothers every night."

"And you have references?"

"What's that?"

"A character," she said, not liking that, Mrs. Redmond's word for it, "a letter from your last employer, the people you worked for last?"

She laughed. "She couldn't pay enough to keep me in boots, and I said I couldn't stay. The way it was, she said she wouldn't stamp me book until I paid for the dishes the dog broke, but I know me rights."

"Yes," said Alice who had lost the thread of thought. "I suppose Mr. O'Connor knows you?"

"Oh, he does."

"Then we'll let that do for a reference," she said, and the girl

116

grinned and nodded, as though together they had outwitted some officious regulation.

"Do you want me tomorrow, or should I wait until Monday?" Mary Flaherty asked, when they had settled everything else.

"What's wrong with today, right now?" Unfortunately the girl had had time to take in the state of the kitchen. "You can use one of my aprons," Alice said, and when she made no answer to that: "We'll call it a whole day, of course." And when Mary still seemed to be just thinking, Alice added, "I know the room's a terrible mess, but I won't be able to have it any cleaner tomorrow. I just can't get the work done."

"You're stuck?"

Alice nodded, and the girl began to unbutton her coat.

Half an hour later Alice all but skipped up the stairs, right on up to the drawing room, where she stood looking out at the grey sea for several minutes. The gardener below was on his ladder, leaning right over the hedge and talking to someone, probably a delivery boy headed for the house at the end of the lane. The boys came up, pushing their bicycles, and flew down, empty bottles clattering in their baskets, their bells warning pedestrians into the grass as they swerved past potholes and boulders in free flight.

It was not to be a clean break with the kitchen, not yet. She would have to do the cooking for a while, and a certain amount of supervision. *Steep the delph*, she had never said that, but something she had said had led Mary to think she wanted all the dishes piled in the washtub and left to stand in hot, but not soapy, water. And a quick job she made of that, just the time it had taken Alice to put a couple of sods on the library fire.

She was working for less than Alice had counted on paying too, and even then she felt that the girl had been surprised to get what she had asked for. Let a girl like that into Mrs. Redmond's clutches and she would be lost, done in by her own decency. The woman would harp on her lack of references until the girl felt no

117

better than a stateless person. And yet, in these times, when a maid worth a reference should be worth holding on to, you might wonder just what a reference meant. ("I'll forget about the candlesticks, and you'll forget about the two months owing, and I'll give you a good character.")

She went down to phone Rafferty then. "That woman was stringing me along for months," she told him, "and the old man found someone right away."

"Good, now will you write to your friend O'Reilley this afternoon?"

"I will, right now," she said and asked him to tell Mrs. Redmond when he stopped by for the evening paper.

"Afraid to face the old girl yourself?"

"It's her own fault. I certainly gave her enough time."

"All right. I'll do it. You'll have to go in sometime, though."

She wrote to O'Reilley that afternoon and thanked him for everything, the party, the iron, and the assistance his man had given her in finding a maid. The girl had been prepared to go to England to find work, she told him, letting him enjoy his part in one of the few positive acts of the IRA. In the circumstances it seemed callous to tell him to call off his dogs. He would see that they were in contact with his man, and there would be no need to send him out again.

He had been out, poking around a table of used books, and when he returned to the shop, the woolman's dusty blue van was parked in the cobbled court, a little too close to his own car. Inside the building, the woolman was having tea with Brian and Willie, too late now to get the man upstairs for a drink and a private talk.

"How's it going with yourself?" asked the woolman, putting another—the third?—spoonful of sugar into his tea.

"It couldn't be much worse," he said, deciding to jump right in.

118

"I've got ten men willing to weave and no one to teach them. I haven't even got a lead."

"Ah, you'll find someone, so you will," said the woolman. "It takes time for the word to get around."

"Yes, but if someone like yourself were to help pass the word around, it might move a little faster."

"Faster? You haven't been here more than—" he paused as though counting, and Rafferty waited for him to discover that it was nearing three months—"say, four months, have you?"

"No," he said.

"You might compare it with fishing," the woolman went on.

"With a bare hook. In a bathtub."

"*Fishers of men,* that's what it says. You try one pool and you try another. A certain amount of waiting."

"You can say that again."

"So we'll postpone the reorder until the next time." The woolman was rising a good hour earlier than was his custom. "You'll be all right for two, three weeks anyway."

"Oh, yes," Rafferty said. "Though if we get a good crop of moths this summer, we may get right through that inventory."

"Ah, you're doing a grand job, all the same," the woolman said and left.

"Well," Rafferty said to Brian, "we didn't get much help there."

"When your boyo says *fishing,*" said Willie, putting down his teacup, "what he means is *poaching.*"

"Poaching?"

"That's your God's truth," said Willie and disappeared back where he ought to have been.

Rafferty stood looking at the closed door.

"He don't know," said Brian, "he just picks up things."

Rafferty shook his head. He could see why the woolman wouldn't want to take a man from one of his own customers, but if he were to do the dirty work himself . . . it was too bad that Willie had chosen to put that word on it.

119

He hadn't come to Ireland to tear into the other weaving firms' labor. He had come to insure that weaving could continue, by starting a few men on the sort of tweed for which he saw a big market. All he wanted was a little help, a man for six weeks, two months.

The woolman had as much as told him that he wouldn't find one here in the Dublin area, where his want ads had been kicking around for months with never a word from a weaver. Try another pool, he said. Farther West, where the weavers were.

Otherwise the ten farmers would never learn how to weave and Rafferty's Woollens' entire contribution to Ireland would be the great employment scheme for Willie Ryan and a job for Brian, who should never have left school.

11.

"If i'd known that you were going to look for a girl on your
own—" Mrs. Redmond launched into the topic as she receipted
their month's newspaper bill. Time enough had passed for anyone
else to have forgotten the matter.

"It was nothing like that," Alice said. "I just happened to mention it to a friend that we were looking for a girl, and he happened
to know of this one."

"I hope you're not paying her too much."

"No, it's less than I'd expected, as a matter of fact." Wild horses
would not drag the figure from her.

"Good. Now, mind you check her references."

"Oh, yes, I have." She was ready to go now, but Mrs. Redmond
had the receipt just out of reach. "I wouldn't want you to feel I
was prying," she said, "but things are different here, you know.
You may have noticed that with your gardener."

"Yes," Alice said.

"You get along all right, don't you?" Mrs. Redmond said sharply.

"Oh, yes. Fine."

"Good." She went on then to discuss the position of the household help in what she said was America, a Gulliver land where the assiduous practice of equality had led to a situation in which grossly overpaid and overfed maids took orders from no one. It would have been so easy to have avoided all that, Mrs. Redmond said, granted, of course, that the basic wage was not excessive.

Alice nodded and said nothing.

Now, if the family had steak, she should be sure to provide a bit of mince or sausage for the girl. "They prefer it, actually," she assured Alice. All breakages should be deducted from wages in the very week they occur. Never advance any salary, however ingenious the plea. And in the event of continuing illness, paleness, or fainting spells—Mrs. Redmond leaned forward in a confidential manner, the receipt falling from her hand, unregarded on the counter.

"Oh, she has terribly good health," Alice cut in, and picked up the receipt.

"Yes, yes," Mrs. Redmond said and settled back in her chair. "Of course, you never know for sure what you've got."

"I know, but she seems to be quite perfect."

That was not the way she usually thought of Mary Flaherty. Cheerful, hard-working, yes, but not perfect. She had done everything, she said: cook, clean, mind children, the lot. And Alice had made the single mistake of accepting experience for competence. She couldn't very well say now, after all this time, that there was hardly a thing the girl did that didn't leave her amazed that anyone could go about it in that way.

They had had a few unsatisfactory talks about things that could be no longer evaded. "Now," she said, trying to be impersonal, "if

122

someone washed the frying pan first and then washed the glasses in the same water, they'd naturally look a little dirty."

Mary held up one of the greasy glasses, examining it as though she were an expert about to pronounce it rare old Cork glass. "It's the bad light in here," she said.

So Alice rewashed one of the glasses in clean dishwater and held it up beside one of the others.

"There's not much difference in it," said Mary. "Sure there's not?"

Then Alice put both glasses behind her back and brought them out again. "Now, see if you can guess which one was just washed."

Three times she picked out the correct one, instantly, triumphantly. And Alice, with what she thought of as a fine restraint, smiled and said no more. *Quod est demonstrandum.*

Or was it? Three days later, catching Mary in the act, she said, "I thought we'd decided we weren't going to wash the frying pan ahead of the glasses."

"Ohhhh."

"It makes the glasses dirty."

Mary nodded, and Alice started to leave. "They's just one thing, Mrs. Rafferty."

"Yes?"

"You can't get the frying pan clean when the water's all mucky and cold."

She was relieved to find a logical explanation. "Just take clean water when it gets too dirty."

"There's soap in the water."

"Of course."

"You mean take soap twice for one washing up?"

"Yes." She thought impenitently of Mary's eventual return to ordinary employment, profligate of soap powder—if she could remember.

Head down, eyes shut, and full speed forward, she cut through

123

the work. Alice, who hadn't been to Dublin since they had left the Imperial, had headed for town as soon as she felt right about leaving the girls with her.

"What do you want me to do today?" Mary asked, as she was leaving.

"Do?" They had been going through the regular schedule for two or three days, and she had to hurry if she was to ride in with Rafferty. "Just do what has to be done."

She returned in the afternoon to find Stella and Vanessa and Mary, all with broad conspirator's grins, stalking her down to the kitchen.

The debris was gone, all of it, swept bare to the corners. (And there was a solid floor beneath it.) The ashpit overflowed and the orange turf ashes permeated everything, putting second thoughts out of the question. And just as well.

The gardener, shaking his head, got the seaweed man to haul it away. "Seven and six," he said to her. "He wouldn't have asked but five bob, only for the turf ashes. It's dirty stuff, the turf, and the man's a bit chesty."

"I know, Mr. Molloy." This wasn't the first time he had spoken against the turf. "I like the smell of it, though."

"Oh, it's a fine smell all right, but you can't warm yourself on the smell of it."

"I suppose not." She found that the man annoyed her a lot less now that she had some free time of her own, and she didn't have to keep stoking the garbage into the Imperial Iron. That job didn't seem as hard for Mary; she had a suspicion that sometimes more than just the greens found its way into the compost heap.

It was as babysitter that Mary was most successful. She had an apparently endless tolerance for nonsense. If the girls decided to have a "washday" and left all their dolls' clean clothes wadded in a bowl of soapsuds, Mary was quite content to dry them over the stove, iron them afresh, and dress the dolls herself. And she actually liked getting the girls dressed for a walk: fawn leggings, fawn coats, velvet bonnets, and gloves.

"They should have raincoats," she said, and Stella and Vanessa kept begging until Alice bought them shiny black double-breasted slickers with fishermen's hats and high rubber Wellington boots. Mary took the girls out every day after that. Alice, remembering only too well the time she had been up and down the hill with the girls, didn't see where the pleasure came in.

"Where'd you go today?" she would pump them at night, while they got ready for bed. Sometimes it was the park, where they found conkers and pine cones for their "collections"; or up the hill, a few sodden blackberries there, consumed on the spot; or down to the pier where they collected stones that looked a lot prettier when wet, and once received a live crab in a paper sack, gift of a fisherman. ("Put it back in the sea or eat it," said Rafferty when he was shown that. At the time it had seemed easier to put it on to boil than to send Mary back down the hill with it. A mistake. It wasn't just the work, cracking and extracting, but the indecision. *Everything is edible but the lungs and the stomach*, said the cookbook, without offering a diagram.)

Mary found a friend, Lily, who usually shared their walks. "She's fifteen," said Stella. "*Fifty*," said Vanessa. "She still wears her school tunic," Stella said. "Maybe she's a teacher."

In any case Lily pushed a pram. The baby was not popular with them. It was a spitter. "Cormish is his name." "Cormac?" Alice asked. "*Cormish.*" They agreed on that.

There was another fact. "You tell her," said Stella, moving out of sight behind the open door of the clothes press.

"*You* should," said Vanessa.

"Tell me what?" Alice asked.

"What Lily did," said the voice from behind the wardrobe door.

"All right. What?"

"Well," Vanessa said, "Mary Flaherty bought some sweets—"

125

"That's like candy," said the wardrobe door, "but we said we didn't eat it."

"And Lily was going to eat one," Vanessa said, slowly, paused, and finished in a rush, "and first she took out her teeth."

"My goodness," Alice said, and Stella, seeing that it was not an obscene topic after all, came out to discuss it.

RAFFERTY HAD BEEN SUMMONED TO THE MINISTRY, TAKEN IN PAST the secretaries and Mr. Duffy and his crowd, right in to the senior civil servant, who shook his hand. "Sit down, Mr. Rafferty," he said.

He handed him a newspaper, folded to the want ads, a black crayoned ring marking one of them.

"Well," said the civil servant, when he had given Rafferty time to read it, "Rafferty's Woollens?"

"Yes."

"Six weeks' to three months' work in the Dublin area?"

"Yes."

"In the *Donegal* paper?"

"There's another in the Galway paper," Rafferty said, making sure that all charges would be disposed of at once.

"Good man," said the civil servant and took the Galway paper, with its crayoned ring, from a drawer. "Galway and Donegal, the heart of the Gaeltacht."

"So, I've heard."

"And you'd take these men out of the Gaeltacht and bring them to Dublin."

"For three months, at the most, and then they'd go back."

The civil servant shook his head. "They never do."

It was more than bureaucratic concern, Rafferty felt, and said nothing.

"Have you ever considered contract weaving?"

He didn't like the sound of it. "What do you mean?"

126

"You design your own patterns and one of our handweaving firms produces them for you."

"That doesn't get it." Did *this* man think he would go for that?

"No, I imagine it doesn't."

"You know we were sent some pretty fulsome accounts of the labor situation here, right down to a list of available handweavers —which is hardly what I was given," Rafferty said. He didn't like the way he was being cast as "difficult."

"Yes, an unfortunate misunderstanding."

"But not made in my office."

The senior civil servant committed himself only to the extent of a nod.

"You can't expect me to sit back and take it quietly."

"I'll find you a man, someone to teach the others—you're not still talking about twelve experienced weavers, are you?"

And why shouldn't he be? "No," he said, "just find me one good teacher."

"And when you get your replies you'll ignore them, or write that the position's been filled."

He nodded. He could always keep the names and addresses for future reference, just in case.

Rafferty went away thinking of Galway, the little he had seen of it, stone-walled fields, the whitewashed, thatched cottages familiar from so many pictures, which had, however, never conveyed to him the enchanting scale of the place: the roof beams no more than a pair of men could lift, the eaves within a man's reach, the doors head high, the towns only a good walk apart. The cow was the measure of the pasture, the spade the measure of the field, the scythe the measure of the meadow. Even the mountains, by happy accident, were neither farther nor higher than they looked.

Why then leave? And they did leave land that could have supported them in something better than the grinding poverty too many of them found in Dublin. Was it simply the universality of bad taste, Dublin the neon bauble? Or was everything too clear in Galway, a man's acreage, his crops, his bullocks, his very place (older than this one, younger than that one) in the procession from cradle to grave? In Dublin he could be anyone, and the man beside him, shoulder to shoulder in O'Connell Street, might at this moment have come from doing, might be about to do—who knew what? If enough people were gathered together something must be happening, something more than the long patient queues standing in the rain to see a three-year-old American movie would seem to indicate.

No, Rafferty said to himself, he would burn the answers unopened.

THE PROBLEM WAS MOSTLY ONE OF VOCABULARY, ALICE THOUGHT. To steep meant to soak. A serviette was a napkin. A napkin would be a diaper. A jug was a pitcher, and a jar was a hot water bottle. Find the word and you'd found the idea.

She looked a long time for the words that would mean *rinse* to Mary. She described the process: to rinse the dishes . . . to rinse the clothes. The item, already washed in soapy water, already clean, was immersed in clear, hot water, *steeped* in hot water.

"There's no soap in it, sure there's not?" said Mary, with her face down in the steam to make sure, and reaching for the soap box.

"No," Alice said, removing the soap box to the far end of the shelf. That was a different lesson, one she had learned. "That's the point of it. You want to rinse off the soap."

Even then Mary might not have been persuaded if she had not noticed that the dishes, taken from the boiling water and put on the rack, were often dry before she could get at them with the towel. This, she explained to Alice, was because "the hot water is so thin it can't stick."

128

"Yes," Alice said, thinking that the proper explanation was not far away.

There was little temptation, though, to think that Mary was a born physicist. When the "soft-boiled" eggs appeared with solid yolks, she said, "It's a terrible fast fire. The water was scalding," and when the potatoes came to the table in a puddle of water, "It's terrible wet steam today," she said, shaking her head at the terrible unpredictability of things.

Maybe she had been too eager to get out of the kitchen, Alice thought, and if she would just spend a little time with the girl she could give her some idea of order, of the natural progression from cause to effect. Perhaps, if she put Mary in the role of teacher, the lesson would stick, as she had learned in *Methods* at Oakley. She tried to get the girl to show her how to make Irish bread, which was a thing she had been wondering about for some time.

"It's just bread, the *or*dinary bread," Mary said.

"I know, but it's new to me."

"Ah, no, it's the *or*dinary bread."

"Can you make it?"

"I can," she admitted.

"Would you teach me?"

"You could do better yourself."

And so it went. Eventually she convinced Mary that though it was the ordinary bread, served in every hotel and restaurant, made, in a pinch, in every kitchen in Ireland, it was not the ordinary bread Alice knew, which was more like what Mary called a "small pan," and though she could make that ("Ah, you couldn't, sure you couldn't.") she had no idea at all of how to make a proper cake of bread.

So Mary showed her. It turned out to be simply a mound of soda dough, an outsized muffin with a cross slashed on top.

"Oh, why do you do that?"

"There's no reason. It's just a cross, like."

129

Alice moved ahead of her, imagined a muffin that size. "I suppose if you didn't cut the cross, the loaf would rise in a peak and crack."

"Ah, no. There's no harm in not doing it."

At the moment it seemed to Alice that this was the place to prove that things did not happen in an inexplicable, haphazard fashion, that cause did lead to effect. So she left the ball of dough smooth and uncut.

When she took the uncrossed cake of bread from the oven, it was peaked, and three gullies ran down the sides. She showed it to Mary.

"A terrible shame," the girl said.

"Now," Alice said, coming in with the lesson, "that happened because I left off the cross."

"And why would you be wanting to do that?" asked Mary. "There's no harm in doing it, sure there's not."

Whatever she had proved, it wasn't that there was any physical connection between cause and effect.

Mary Flaherty hadn't been there long before they took the bed and wardrobe out of the drawing room and began carrying the furniture up from the first floor. They had carried up quite a bit of it before it was apparent that all the furniture in both the library and the music room wasn't going to have any effect in that space until they had a carpet at least twice as big as any in the house.

"We'll get the carpet just as soon as the weaving gets going," Rafferty said, taking a good look down the length of the bare floorboards.

"It's a little cold anyway, right now," she said. The grate was never intended to hold a small fire, and the coal was nearly forty dollars a ton—which seemed a lot more than when they said it cost fourteen pounds. "Of course, that's a long ton," she added.

"What's that?"

"Twenty-two hundred and forty pounds."

"Even so," Rafferty said, after a minute or two.

The view disappeared with the daylight anyway, unless you sat in the dark to appreciate the lighthouses or the moon on the sea. One by one the chairs were returned downstairs, as they were needed.

"We'll have to get that rug before warm weather," Rafferty said, "just as soon as we get going."

"Yes."

"It won't be long now."

"No."

CONSIDERING THE WAY THEY WERE GOING TO DEPOPULATE THE WEST, it was odd that his ads hadn't pulled in a single reply. He hadn't even received the bill, which, in itself, meant nothing, billing practices were erratic; but when two papers were erratic together it made him wonder . . . if perhaps someone else hadn't paid the bill and picked up the replies.

He would give the civil servant a week more, until after Christmas. He crossed the room and put a big black X on the twenty-sixth of December. That day he would get in the car and drive to the West, and not come back until he had someone to teach his men. And if he didn't do it, the X would be there, accusing him of cowardice every time he entered the room. Too bad it had to be a one-sided deadline, exerting its pressure only on himself.

"You marking the holidays?" asked Brian, when he saw the calendar.

"Holidays?"

"St. Stephen's Day," he said, stretching to put a finger on the twenty-sixth. "Most places they have St. John's Day too." He moved the finger to the twenty-seventh.

"We'll see." Why not. Once Willie had finished there would be nothing for Brian to do except keep the fires and make his own tea. And Willie was nearly done. He kept going only by working

131

for an hour or two at a time and then leaving until the next day.

"He's waiting on his Christmas box," Brian had explained.

"Poor Willie. I'll get him a bottle of whiskey."

"You'd best not. He's a Pioneer."

"Well, I'll think of something else," Rafferty said.

"Pioneer Total Abstinence," Fogarty explained. "They wear that little medal up here. Lot of them around," he said, fingering his lapel and looking around the bar without finding one to point out.

Now Brian, standing by the calendar, said, "About Willie, you'd want to get him the bottle, I'd say."

"I thought you said he was a Pioneer."

"Yes, but he says he gives up the Pioneers for Christmas. And then he gives up the drink for Lent."

"I see."

"It's a great saving for most of the year that way, and you're not stuck with it, so as to find it inconvenient." Brian was nodding with his frightening old-man look. There was no doubt that this year was a mistake for him. It was growing harder to imagine him back in school.

"And you didn't mark Christmas," he said, still at the calendar. "Should I do it?"

"It's a red figure. It's all right as it is."

IT WASN'T UNTIL SOMEONE MENTIONED THANKSGIVING IN A LETTER that she realized it had come and gone. They talked about "harvest" here, but they didn't have the feverish gathering into barns and sheds against the morning when the sun would rise and strike the frosted chrysanthemums a wilted black.

The gardener continued to bring curly kale and Savoy cabbages to the kitchen door. One day he dug the potatoes and brought them in, a bagful in which the proportion of clay was abnormally

132

high, Alice thought. Stella and Vanessa said they had seen the gardener carry "bags and bags" down to the gate lodge.

"It seems there should be more than one bag of potatoes out of that big patch, Mr. Molloy," Alice said the next time she saw him.

"It was a bad year. Mr. Hamilton, he lets me have the small ones for me dinner. They was a bag, maybe two, of them."

"That's fine," she said. "And how are the Brussels sprouts?"

"Ah, they're coming along, any day now."

"Fine," she said, and went into the house with her string bag full of the fruits and vegetables she had brought up the hill from the greengrocer's.

It was too warm for December. The football season would be over at Oakley, and the first snow had fallen there. They were farther north here, which was very hard to believe when you saw the gardens and the green hedges, but the Gulf Stream made the difference. They got up in the dark and breakfasted in the dark. The sun rose only to nick off a corner of the sky, sliding behind the clouds, southeast to southwest, and by mid-afternoon it was slipping away.

Now that Mary could watch the girls, Alice often kept her shopping until late in the day, and then she would find herself coming back up the hill in the dark, moving toward the black mouth of the lane. There were three street lamps beyond the first gate, but what with overhanging trees and fog, the light stayed close to the poles. Rats, tinkers, anything could be in the bushes, dark against the walls, and once you had entered the passage, there was no way out before you reached their own gate, except, set into the wall at about the midpoint, a green door without knob or handle, only a keyhole. She understood what Mrs. Redmond meant about a girl's not wanting to come up there late at night.

She was coming home late one afternoon, from Dublin, where she had been Christmas shopping and had stayed in hopes of finishing everything, until now dinner would be delayed—unless

Mary had thought to start the potatoes, a possibility since she did like a big plate of potatoes with her own meal. Her feet found their way up the dark lane, moving cautiously in the thin-soled town shoes that let her feel too well the knobbly pebbles. Suddenly, just as she was about to turn into the inner gateway, she struck a pile of soft dirt, stumbled and caught herself.

A little fuzzy light came from the gate lodge, enough to let her see that something had been at work on the road, and between the wraiths of mist she could make out a hump of freshly disturbed earth, running across from the grassy verge into the edge of their driveway. Her own footsteps seemed muffled, and a fog-horn, which must have been down in the bay, sounded straight over her head. Ghosts, ghouls, graves—she cut off the thought and hurried toward the door of the gate lodge, where she knocked, impatient for the sight of the gardener.

He opened the door cautiously. She had never come to the lodge before, and even now she was curious to see what it was like. The door, however, opened into a tiny square hall, with curtained doorways at each side and a wall of flowered pink wallpaper just behind the gardener. He was still wearing his beret and had a dish towel tied around his waist over his raincoat. "What's been going on in the driveway, Mr. Molloy?" she asked.

"The driveway, you say?"

He came out through the gate with her and looked at the hump. Cautiously he rooted into it with his boot and said, "Digging."

"Yes, I thought you might have seen what did it."

He shook his head. "I was in the garden all afternoon."

She left him there, looking at the hump. It was odd, she thought, considering how well he was able to keep tabs on the IRA or the ESB.

After that there didn't seem much point in asking Mary, who would have been in the kitchen, as far removed as possible from the front gate, but she did anyway.

"The girls were in all the time," said Mary.

134

"Oh, they couldn't have done it. It's a foot high anyway. You'd better be careful when you leave," Alice said, impatiently. The potatoes had been put on to cook, and in the steamer too. Unfortunately the pan beneath had boiled dry in the terrible heat of the stove. The potatoes looked all right, but they had a peculiar flavor, remotely scorched, like Scotch whisky. Rafferty would certainly not overlook it. Perhaps they could cook just a small second batch for him. "Oh, if we could only get the gas stove," she said.

"Oh!" said Mary.

"What now?"

"The gas man was here. I was about to tell you."

"To see the gas pipe?" She looked over at it, but saw no change.

"Oh, no. He wanted me to boil the water, and I thought it would be all right."

"You mean he wanted to see how slow the electricity is?" That would be their way, to find out just how desperate the situation was before they acted.

"No. It was for the tea."

"The tea?"

"It was their tea break, like."

"And that's all."

Mary nodded.

Alice took the flashlight and went out to the lane again. The gas might have been shut off there at some time. But it did seem strange to start work without first seeing if the house pipes were sound. No smell of gas, anyway.

She crossed the lane to the beginning of the ridge. On a large, flat stone there she found some rings made by a milk bottle and nearby, a paper bag with a few biscuit crumbs inside. That was all, that and the ridge.

She went out to the gate several times the next day, but the gas men did not reappear. There was a fine rain, which might have been the reason, though she saw a railway crew working unconcernedly on the track. The next day was sunny, and when the men hadn't appeared by ten-thirty, she phoned the office. The man on the phone couldn't tell her exactly how far they had progressed with the installation. He could assure her, however, that they would be back on Monday, or certainly the day after that.

She was too busy to give it much thought until the day before Christmas, when the turkey was delivered and she saw that she would have to cut off the legs to get it into the oven—and it was a small turkey at that.

"We'll be sure the legs are done this time, anyway," said Rafferty, who ought to have left the house long before then. He had been getting edgy lately, and if the senior civil servant didn't produce a weaver pretty soon, she was afraid that Rafferty would feel he had to do *something* himself.

They weren't going to make a big thing of Christmas this year, he had said, just a simple tree, if they had a tree, and there was no point in buying 220-volt Christmas lights.

Then, that morning, they had been waked early by the little girls, who had been checking to see if *this* could be the day for Santa Claus and had found something disturbing. "Are you sure it's important?" she asked.

"You'd better come down now, Mama," Stella said.

"They won't let you alone until you go," Rafferty said, putting the pillow on top of his head.

So she followed them down to the library to see what it was that was too awful to describe, and found that her gingerbread men had softened in the damp air, and their bodies, pulled down by the weight of their silvered sugar clothes, lay on the floor and left the tree decorated with only their grinning heads. More heads than bodies, she could tell at a glance. She let that pass, considering the season, just as she did when Mary turned up half an hour late with presents still wrapped in grocer's paper for the little girls, tin boxes of toffee, which even Mary knew was forbidden.

The gardener had given them a few apples and pears, and a

beautifully packed chipful of Brussels sprouts, a week's supply at least, the little heads placed as carefully as cobblestones. "Oh, thank you, Mr. Molloy," she said, and handed him his envelope, his Christmas box—the word meant the money itself, she had been surprised to learn.

"Rafferty," she said, "Brian and Willie will be waiting for their Christmas boxes. Why don't you go in to town, now?"

"Yes," he said. "You know, if I put the radio on top of the bookcase, then we could bring the lamp holder with the double adapter down from the ceiling light and run both the radio and the tree off of that."

"You could, except that you'd need another double adapter."

"I wouldn't."

"Where would you put the pink lamp then?"

"Oh."

Double adapters were an illusion. The first made two outlets of one, but two made three outlets, and seven made only eight. Besides, each one cost four shillings, and one string of lights on the tree wasn't going to make Christmas.

"Why don't you go in to town and look at the lights first? Then you can buy the double adapter, if you want to."

"Yes, but I thought I'd wait until the mail came."

"He hasn't made it here before noon this week."

Rafferty looked indecisive.

"If you go you might meet him on the hill."

So he left, but two hours later he was on the phone, asking, "Any mail?"

There was. They had several cards, one from Dr. Steichen, a stiff, heavy envelope, returned for additional postage, which he had paid. They had heard nothing from him since Rafferty had sent off his little note, the one in Brian's inky envelope. The card was a winter scene of Old Main and the elm trees, and her stomach had tightened at the sight of the snow. Inside was a printed greeting and the name, with a line drawn through it, *Dr. & Mrs.*

Steichen replaced by a scrawl: Louise and Henry. Not a word about Rafferty's leave, she was sorry to tell him.

"Oh, well," he said, and she knew that something was up. "I was just called over to the ministry."

"Any hope?"

"I've got two weavers. They'll start the twenty-eighth."

"Where'd he find them?"

"Oh, around somewhere," said Rafferty, and she let it pass.

12.

"THEY'LL BE HERE IN A MINUTE," SAID BRIAN.

"Yes," Rafferty said. He went out and looked up and down the mews and wondered whether he ought to call the civil servant or just get into his car and head West. Then he saw them coming beneath the arch, the small man frisking from side to side like a rat terrier and the large one coming on as though the mechanism of his stride had been adjusted for some smoother and drier terrain.

"That'd be your nine there, and this'd be your ten," he heard the small man say as they neared him. "There, right there, Raftery's Woollens."

"You're the weavers?" Rafferty said, stepping forward.

The small, grey-skinned man was Thady, and the large pink one, Ned. They were older than he was, Rafferty thought, somewhere between forty and fifty.

As soon as Brian had made the tea, they sat down to what Rafferty had billed in his mind as a conference.

139

Some conference.

"Just say what you'd like, Mr. Raftery."

"Rafferty," he said.

"It's all up to yourself, Mr. Raftery."

"Rafferty."

And so there was nothing to do but bring out his own half-developed ideas, one after another. "Ah, that's a grand idea, Mr. Raftery."

"Oh, you've a real gift for thinking, Mr. Raftery."

Ned kept nodding quietly, but Thady nodded with a *ss-ss-ss*, something to do with the man's teeth, he thought, and resolved not to let it get on his nerves.

Was it possible that the whole business of weaving was very simple after all, that he couldn't go far wrong whatever he did? It seemed that way.

He left the men to assemble a couple of the looms while he went upstairs to report the men's arrival to Frank. Brian followed him with a basket of turf.

"I shoulda kicked him in the gob," he said, banging down the turf basket.

"Who?" Rafferty asked. He wasn't ready for a feud within his staff. City vs. country, was that it?

"The little one. Did you not hear what he was saying, Mr. Rafferty?"

"No. What was he saying?"

" 'It's useless.' That's what he said. Every time you'd open your mouth—' 'S useless.' There's no respect there."

So that was the hissing noise. "But I *asked* them to tell me if anything was wrong."

"Ah, you wouldn't talk back at the boss, Mr. Rafferty."

It could have been sabotage, too, he thought later. He didn't know where the men had come from, didn't want to know. So he would have to play it by ear. Get the looms assembled, bring an apprentice weaver or two into the shop, and keep his eyes open.

140

In the afternoon Willie dropped by to pick up his tools and found some of them in use. Rafferty jumped at the chance to re-hire him to work on the looms and on devices for filling the beams and the bobbins. He felt better when he went back upstairs. He had never expected to find a feeling of security in having Willie Ryan around.

By the next morning they had one of the looms nearly ready for work. "You can put the warp on it," Thady said. "And you'll be wanting the men to fill the beams and the bobbins. You'd want to get going with them now."

"All right, I'll take care of that this morning." He had gone into it with the civil servant, and he knew what to do.

"You know, I was just thinking here that if we was to move now, we might get me cousin Mick before he goes back to England."

"I didn't know they did this kind of work in England," Rafferty said. It would be a break to get a trained man.

"Ah, no, but he's a cute lad all the same. You wouldn't want to be telling him anything but the once."

"Is that so?" said Rafferty, beginning to get the picture. He had to watch his step. At the moment his success depended on the good will of Thady and Ned, but now that he had met all his weavers and would-be weavers, he knew that the two shop men were his only chance to get executive material into the project. Someone, more than just an accountant, had to be ready to take charge when he went back to Oakley.

Thady was going on with a long anecdote about Mick's remark-able start as a driver. Some of the detail: ". . . just showed him your startin' lever and your stoppin' lever . . ." was clearly apoc-ryphal, but, after a couple of months on the roads here, Rafferty was ready to believe that with no preparation at all, he had "just alligated down the road as if he were on the old bike."

"And then there's me friend, John Hennessy," Thady was say-

141

ing, about to go into another anecdote, it seemed. "He's—oh, Janey, these heddles'd drive a man mad," he said, suddenly brought up short by the task at hand.

Rafferty, freed none too soon, hurried out the door. "Hey, watch it with that bike, will you!" He had seen it through the window, Ned dismounting as though he had been on a horse and expected it to keep on its own legs.

Rafferty picked up the bike. The car seemed to be unscathed, but there was a scratch on the bike that hadn't been there before, he was sure. He gave it a rub with his handkerchief.

Ned, who had taken the bike to get dowels, just looked at him, as though he were out of his mind.

"If there's one thing that makes me mad," Rafferty said, "it's mistreatment of tools."

"Ah, it's only a bike," said Ned, looking embarrassed, to his credit, and hurrying into the building.

Rafferty moved the handlebars back and forth to see that they hadn't been knocked out of true, and then dropped down the forked stand and settled the bike carefully on the cobbles.

He didn't like the turn things were taking. The week before, he had seen men, some hardly more than boys, coming off the boat trains with their cheap clothes and paper suitcases and stopping in Dublin for a meal before they went home to the West for Christmas. Three mailboats a day, and into every port they were streaming by the thousands, Fogarty had told him.

"But what's happening in England, now, where they're supposed to be working, I mean?"

"When you hire a Mick, you expect that," Fogarty said, "and you wouldn't get an Englishman to be a navvy anyway."

"Too bad they can't work in Ireland," Rafferty said. He couldn't expect to create more than fifteen jobs, and indirectly, a few more in the supporting industries.

"Oh, I don't know," Fogarty said, looking pointedly at the raucous group standing at the bar. "You don't know whether to shoot the English for taking the cream, or thank them for taking the scum."

He didn't want to reject Thady's cousin, but there was no reason why he should take up the slack of the system. A pair of lads as eager as Brian, a bit bigger, to handle the heavy beams, that was what he needed. He could say that they were not his qualifications, but Frank's, beyond appeal.

He went back into the shop where Brian was heading for the stairs with a cup of tea. "I'll take it down here, Brian," he said and walked over to the men. Ned was undoing the newspaper from around a sandwich, a big, loose thing made head to toe, the mushrooming top crust of one slice against the narrow bottom crust of the other.

"Now, about these men for the shop work," Rafferty began.

Thady frowned, as though he didn't want to discuss the subject. "There's me cousin Mick, as we agreed," he said quickly, "and me friend John Hennessy. So that's the two, right there."

Ned was waving his sandwich, hooting through his nose, but otherwise silenced by a gob full of bread.

"Take your time," said Rafferty, knowing now why Thady had dropped the subject just as the bike appeared.

Ned swallowed, choked. "Wait," he said and sluiced his throat with a gulp of tea. "I've all but promised one of them to Malachy Dillon, and Tommy's put in for the other."

"They've been doing this kind of work, then?" Rafferty asked.

"No, but you won't find a cuter pair in Dublin."

Rafferty nodded, and took a company-issue biscuit from the bag, Mariettas, Brian's choice of the week and not one of his own favorites. At any moment Brian or Willie might speak up for their candidates. "The men at the ministry have arranged for the head of one of the vocational schools to recommend—"

"Ohmegod," Thady said, "that crowd'll skin you."

143

"There are some, mind you—" began Ned.

Willie cut him off. "Ah, you wouldn't go *there,* Your Honour."

Brian had nothing to say, or perhaps he was too absorbed in the consumption of biscuits to follow the conversation. No breakfast again.

"All right, gentlemen," he said, as he did when a class began to forget themselves. "I have no objection to *considering* your candidates, providing they fulfill the qualifications—"

"Oh, they do," Thady broke in.

"All of them things," said Ned.

"You don't even know what they are," he said, not hiding his annoyance. "Either we're serious about this, or we're not going to discuss it at all."

That quieted them.

"The job requires a certain amount of brawn for handling the beams and quite a bit of brains for doing the job right. I'm looking for a craftsman, not a navvy."

What may have been significant glances were exchanged around the room.

"I want young men, say twenty, and unmarried." He had to get them before they had caught the going attitude toward work.

"Ohmegod! They don't know what work is. You'd have a pack of flighty eejits."

"You'd want a man that's been trained to work before the war, Your Honour. Now it's nothing but tea breaks and overtime."

Rafferty shook his head. "I want young men on an apprentice basis. If they can pull us through the first two years, they can expect the job to last forty or fifty years. Twenty-five is the absolute top. So if Thady and Ned want to nominate one man each, I'll see them tomorrow, and if they seem okay, we'll give them a trial."

He walked back to the pantry and was draining a last cup of tea from the pot when Brian walked in. "I'll make a fresh pot, Mr. Rafferty."

144

"No, I didn't want to throw this out. And I've got a question for you, sir: what did you have for breakfast?"

"Ah, well," Brian said, hesitating, "there wasn't much time. The clock—"

"I thought so," Rafferty broke in to save Brian from producing further "details." "Here, go buy a shilling's worth of oranges and eat them, right now."

"On the company's time?"

"That's right. I might as well run the car without oil as run you without breakfast. Tank up on biscuits that way and you'll lose your teeth." Brian laughed. "You'll get spots," he added, trying for something that Brian cared about.

He laughed harder at that. "Thank you, Mr. Rafferty," he said and left the room.

Why couldn't he just hire people and they would do their work and he would pay them, instead of having to put them together and zip them into their skins with all the toes in the proper holes? He could hardly wait to see what Thady and Ned were going to bring in.

IT HAD GROWN COLDER AFTER CHRISTMAS, THOUGH THE DAYS WERE now noticeably longer. There were exhaustive conversations on the subject in the shops, where the clerks had piled on sweaters until their smocks fit them like the stuffed skins of rag dolls, and they could hardly bend at the elbows.

For all the talk about weather, it was surprising that the official reports were printed inconspicuously on an inside page of the paper. After following them for a while Alice understood why. "The temperature was 40° at 10 A.M., had risen to 42° by midday. By later afternoon it was 43°." Day after day the figures remained much the same, a crisp fall day, it would be in Oakley, or a balmy one in spring.

But forty degrees at Prisma, in the hall, in the bedrooms, in the

145

bath, with a nonstop forty-degree wind that raised the library carpet and made a joke of Rafferty's weatherstripping around the windows, that was winter.

She had bought blankets at the after-Christmas sales because they were a bargain, something to take home when they left Ireland. And one particularly wild night, she put them on the beds to see if they would make a difference. Heavy as sand dunes, they remained there, while she wove fantasies of sunlit beaches. And when the sun did come out she would sit in the window and feel the heat soak down to her backbone, until a cloud sent her shivering back to the fire. Eighteen hours of sunshine in the entire month of January, said the final report.

The gardener had less to do than ever. The hedges had been clipped to perfection, and the mowing had to stop, for the rains had softened the lawns until not even the little girls could walk on them without leaving holes. More than once on a bad day she had seen the gardener go on for hours mechanically scratching his weeding hook along the driveway as though someone had forgotten to bring him in out of the rain.

"You know, Mr. Molloy," she said finally, "these days, when there's so little to do outside, it doesn't make much sense your standing in the rain like this. Maybe if you worked just a little longer on the fine days and stayed indoors on these days . . ."

"Ah, I don't feel the cold like the way you would," he said and broke into a rasping cough.

"Well, until you're through with that cold, I'll have to insist that you get in out of the rain. There must be something you could do in the greenhouse."

"I could paint the benches maybe."

So he took the three or four park benches from around the grounds into the greenhouse and holed up with them there. It galled her to have to pay him for not working, but granting winter and a full-time gardener, what could she do?

146

It snowed twice. The first time it lay on the ground for two days. The gardener remained under cover, the smoke pouring from his chimney and a bare round on his step marking the spot from which his milk bottle had been taken. Mary phoned late the first day to say that she was suffering an attack of flu. She had managed to make it out to the chemist's, and she was going right back to bed.

A week or so later they woke to find the ground snow-covered again, but by ten an unexpectedly bright sun began to melt it. And then Mary phoned. She had waked feeling "terrible weak" but it had passed, and now she felt quite well. Should she come up for the rest of the day? Alice told her to stay home in case it should be something catching, and hoped that the unnecessary loss of a day's wages would teach her a lesson.

Back in the kitchen with the dishes, Alice discovered incrustations of dirt near the sink and the stove. She would point them out. Sweeping the floors, she found in each corner a triangle left untouched by the rounding swoops of the mop; she would mention that too. On the top shelf of the larder she came upon two bowls so hairy with mold that there was no guessing what was beneath it. The girl dearly loved a mess, you could see. Let one thing remain where it didn't belong and watch everything silt up behind it. The window sill was packed, and there was hardly a shelf that didn't have its little corner of wasteland, if it was only a cracked cup holding a cork and a broken candle.

At first she planned to leave it all until she could point it out to Mary, but then she weakened. There was a certain satisfaction in removing a ragged, greasy newspaper full of crumbs and bottle caps from a drawer or shelf and dropping it all into the fire.

She kept at it, without stopping to go out to the shops, and dinner was a simple meal. Rafferty, whose standard response to a disappointing meal was: "Why don't you just serve bacon and eggs?" looked at them and said, "Ah, breakfast," and didn't seem as pleased as he ought to have.

147

"You know," she said, "Mary does like the girls and the girls do like her. And she's honest anyway."

Rafferty nodded.

"What I mean to say is that she's a mess, but she's better than nothing."

"Quite a bit, I'd say."

In the morning she delivered a short homily on mess, but made no threats. It took two women to run that house.

That night Rafferty came up the hill humping a heavy bundle. Alice let him in and, seeing the brown-paper-covered shape, thought of the drawing room rug. Heavy as it seemed to be, though, the bundle wasn't big enough for a full-sized rug.

"You'll see," he said.

Whatever it was, he seemed well satisfied with himself. Perhaps he had found a pair of matching rugs and had brought up only one of them.

After dinner he undid the wrappings. It wasn't a rug. It wasn't clear at first glance just what it was, and then she knew. "Oh, Rafferty!"

"First fruits," he said, smiling. "We're in business." He unreeled a length, draped it over a chair, and rearranged the lights. "There."

"It's beautiful," she said, feeling it and thinking that he had carried all that weight up the hill just for her to see it.

"You don't like it," he said, puzzled.

"I do. I do," she said.

"You don't like it," he said again. "I can tell."

"Oh, I do, Rafferty." But she couldn't find words to fit this wiry, furzy, rumpled thing. And Rafferty was waiting. "I'd just thought it was going to be more—well—you know—crisp." It was like heather, really heather, as it grew on the hills, beautiful, but hardly the thing to make up into a suit.

Rafferty was laughing. "It's not *finished*, you goose. It has to be

148

shrunk and stretched and a dozen more things. I wouldn't expect to sell a thing like *that*."

"They won't take the smell out, will they?" she asked, hoping to undo some of the damage of her earlier mistake.

Rafferty didn't seem to have heard. He kept stroking the cloth and holding it this way and that way in the light. He pulled out a small piece of something. "Thorn," he said. "Quite a few of those in this lot. I'm going to have to talk to the woolman."

"You know," he said a bit later, "sometimes I think that this will be the only worthwhile thing I'll ever do."

"Oh, Rafferty. Teaching, the way you do it, is a wonderful thing."

"I don't know. When I can get across the decline of Rome so that even one of the football boys'll say, 'Gee, that's a lot like to-day,' it ought to have some *effect*."

"Even so, he's a better person than—"

"Hogwash," Rafferty cut in. "But take the weavers, ten men who've been living on uneconomic holdings, doomed to poverty, emigration, or the factories of Dublin. Not one of them could write a paper on the Industrial Revolution, but they're putting it back in its box."

"Yes." More than once she had thought they would never make it this far.

"A couple of months ago that man," he said, pointing to the tweed, "couldn't do much more than slop the hogs, win turf, and dig potatoes. And now he's got a different life. He can buy a radio if he wants it. His wife can have running water."

"I thought he'd put the Industrial Revolution back in its box."

"We're using it, not letting it use us," he said, "and we've got the cloth."

It had warmed in the heat of the fire and was giving off an ancient reek of sheep and turf smoke, still holding something of the moment when man had first realized he could shear the sheep instead of killing them for their skins.

149

And Rafferty had dreamed these colors. He had found the loom and found the weaver and trained him to weave this tweed. The man would go on, weaving length after length of it. Rafferty had done what he had come to Ireland to do.

13.

Downstairs in the shop there was a sound like creaking oar-locks—the stove door. But why would it be opened again and again? There were a lot of these mysteries since the men below had learned that he could hear their voices up in the office. By the time he had crossed the squeaky floor and come down the stairs, they would have been able to conceal the Ark and everything in it.

He went over to the window, opened it, and leaned out into the drizzle. Even if the wind had been right he couldn't have been sure of picking burned wool from the other smells of the neighborhood. And what would it prove anyway? Only what he already knew, that Thady and Ned were still busy covering up for their pair of protégés, Tommy and Mick, the shop men.

They had been hard enough on the weavers and had had only one failure, a little man with ten left thumbs, who had lasted a week. But for the shop men, Thady's cousin and Ned's friend, they had a different manner. It made him think of generals whose own families went to hell because they wouldn't read the riot act at home. After nearly three months Tommy still had to be told what to do, while Mick, the know-it-all, just kept on talking down there, about the weather, about people no one else knew, about soccer, and, at wearing length, about his girl's father's greyhounds, Blossom and Harry, or Bottom and Hardy, he never had time to enunciate. (Ugly animals, greyhounds, Rafferty often met a pair of them being exercised on leads up and down the hill, not grey at all, but a splotched, liverish color, and with narrow, stupid heads. They had torn a cat to bits one afternoon in front of the little girls. "It looked like an old rag," Stella told him, but Vanessa woke screaming several times.)

Brian knocked and came in with a cup of tea.

"What's going on down there, Brian?"

"Oh, nothing, Mr. Rafferty."

"Brian," he said, "I can tell when something's up."

"They was just two grey threads together, Mr. Rafferty. It's all right now."

"Fine," Rafferty said and let him go. It wouldn't be fair to Brian to push him into a full-fledged informer's role.

A mistake like that on the beam would render seventy yards of tweed substandard. He could just imagine Ned down there (it was his week's turn in the shop), whispering about "Mr. Raftery" and working himself into a lather to undo the damage. He didn't see how there could be any progress until Thady and Ned had finished with the weavers and gone back to their own little farms, leaving the two shop men propped up on their own feet.

They would have a few rough weeks then, he knew, but he could see that Brian already had a good grasp of the beam and bobbin end of the business, and together they would get Tommy and Mick in line.

Brian was the wild deuce in the game, and there were a dozen spots where he could have played him: Brian in beam and bob-

152

bin, Brian at the now redundant loom, Brian who was already run off his feet with the fires and the tea and the washing up and "Yarn, Brian," and "Would you ever get ten Woodbines, Brian?" But he had already played Brian's card—back to school. It would be six, seven, eight years before Brian would be free again.

He didn't see any way to leave Ireland in the fall. He had written Dr. Steichen again, explaining the situation. Across the room the little mahogany box was already turned to the third month. Beneath it, a strip of wood tallied production, map pins for single pieces and a red drawing pin to mark the completion of each five, a kindergarten device that now amused even Brian, as the line marked *Projected Monthly Output* had as much relevance to the situation as the markings on a fancy desk thermometer he had seen in a Grafton Street window, with an arrow marked *Boiling Point*.

Downstairs the oarlocks began to creak again. Rafferty crossed the room to the door and put on his rubbers. He had hoped it wouldn't come to this, just walking around Dublin on a rainy day. His rubbers were wearing out, and he couldn't find another pair in the half-dozen shops he had tried. No call for them at all, he was told—and there was food for thought. He wore rubber Wellington boots when he went out to see the weavers, but he would be damned if he would appear on the streets looking like some farmer in from Cavan.

The window downstairs was open, and the door too. The sickening sweet smell of singed wool lingered, however. "What's that awful smell?" he asked.

Tommy's and Ned's faces were set in masks of unblinking innocence. Mick sniffed, sampling the air. "Must be the sweepings Brian put in the stove."

The other two nodded. Brian was not there, probably in back, washing up tea things.

Rafferty just shook his head and went out the door. He couldn't

153

very well say, *All right, class, let's have five hundred words on that by tomorrow.*

THE GAS MEN HAD NOT RETURNED IN JANUARY AT ALL, AND AS THERE was not enough traffic in the lane to pack down the ridge, the rain carried off the loose soil. By February the ridge had been flattened completely, and by March a deep seam had been washed out, clear across the road.

"Ten minutes more work and they could have put it back the right way," Rafferty said one morning.

"Yes," she said and wondered whether he considered her and her stove as the real cause of the damage. "But one more bump isn't going to make much difference in that road."

"That's right. And that's how it got that way—generations of people thinking that one more bump wouldn't matter. Gas, water, sewer, to say nothing of the master surveyor who put the poles right down the middle."

"That is pretty bad."

"They'll kill you in the end. Smile and take a tea break and let you die inch by inch."

She nodded and understood that they weren't talking about the gas men as much as about the shop and the weavers. But before he went to work she saw Rafferty head out the gate with the bucket of coal ashes from the stove—as if this were one thing he could do something about.

Later, when she went out with her basket she found the gardener looking at the road. "Do you see that? There's been someone tipping their ashes right in our doorway."

"Oh, no. That was Mr. Rafferty. He was just trying to do something about the rut that the gas men left."

The gardener shook his head. "It'd take five hundred pounds to put that road right. The County Council told Mr. Hamilton. And they wouldn't put it on the rates. You'd have to pay it yourself,

154

you and them two ladies below, and they haven't got it. And I don't wonder."

"Oh?" She had yet to see Prisma's only neighbors.

"Time was, before the war, you couldn't stand here be the gate without someone passing with a parcel for them below. Frocks and hats and the butcher twice a day. You'd be trying to cut the hedge and they'd be jawing at you till you didn't know what you was doing. And at night—the hooting and the coming home from parties in the morning. I'd have to keep me window closed if I was to get the good of me sleep."

"You wouldn't think it now."

"Oh, it's a grand place now, the peace and the quiet."

"It is," she said, and hurried off, hoping to get to the fishmonger before the cod was gone.

As luck would have it, she was out the day the gas men returned. She came home to find the road rucked up again and, beside the flat stone, a brazier, one of those iron cylinders punched full of holes through which she could see the coals, still glowing red.

"Yes," Mary said. "They wanted a can of water."

"For the tea."

"I asked should I bile it, but the man said they had a fire."

The next morning there was a penetrating drizzle, and when she went out shopping the deserted brazier was orange with rust.

She was surprised later when Mary said that she had been asked for water at mid-afternoon. By that time it was already dusk, and the rain had come on strong, so there seemed little point in going to investigate. Then the bell rang. "I'll go," she said.

The man at the door was sheltering a partly filled cement bag with his rubber raincoat. "Do you have a dry shed where we could leave this?" he asked.

It was a long, wet way around to the sheds, and the gardener

155

tended to be proprietorial about them. She hesitated a moment and then showed the man into the unused music room.

"That's a grand room," he said. "You wouldn't want this in here."

"It won't hurt the tile hearth," she said. "Are you nearly through with the job?"

"We'll finish tomorrow, please God."

The day dawned fine. After breakfast she would go out and make sure the right stove was being sent, and then she would stay right here until the gas men had finished and tamped down the loose soil properly.

She knocked at the library door with her elbow, trying not to shake the heavy tray. Rafferty threw open the door, and barked, "Well, I hope you're happy now." What could she have done? Made some terrible mistake in the accounts?

"Trust the Irish," Rafferty was saying.

She had never known his nerves to be this raw. "Listen, Rafferty, I'll see that they fix the road today—" or had he seen the cement sack?—"whatever they've done. It was just for overnight."

"I didn't know we had more trouble there too," he said. Now he would check. "Look at that." He held out the morning's paper. "Here, give me the tray."

The murky picture—police in shiny raincoats and holding flashlights—was the border post after the explosion. The "B" Special had been out at the time, but his wife and infant son were dead. An "illegal organization" was suspected.

"The IRA," said Rafferty. "My God, I've half a mind to go find your Mr. O'Connor and give him a talking to that he'll never forget."

"He couldn't have had anything to do with it, I'm sure. He wouldn't hurt a fly." She couldn't explain what he was doing in the organization, though.

"You know we really ought to ring up the Guards right now and give them his name. He may not have been there, but I bet he knows who was."

They ate in silence. There was nothing she could say that wouldn't make it worse. He knew what he would be opening up if he phoned the Guards. O'Connor, Mary, O'Reilley—who had Dr. Steichen's ear.

When he was leaving the house, Rafferty said, "You'd better get those checks out today, and the accounts to Frank. And while you're at the desk you can write a letter to O'Reilley. Tell him what his boys are up to."

"All right," she said, not too happy about the letter, but relieved that it was all the action he seemed about to take.

It wasn't a bad job, doing Rafferty's books, and once she got going, she liked adding pounds, shillings, and pence, feeling herself in touch with history, a scrivener to some Egbert or Ethelred, fingering through the archaic numbers, thinking now in twelves and now in twenties. Too often, though, her reward for redoing two or three columns of figures would be the discovery that they owed more than they had been billed for.

Once the figures were checked they had to be put into dollars and sent on to Frank. He had written in his last letter:

Watch that Mscl Col, Al. No objection here to total expenditure, just deplore unbusinesslike usage. Production here up 63%, and the new looms (just arriving) will show everyone our dust. Seems we ought to be seeing something of the tweed soon. Can you expedite?

Expedite. Why didn't Rafferty just send off what he had? He didn't want to let it go—some attitude for a manufacturer.

She went down to the village when she finished the accounts. It would be a lot easier to write to O'Reilley if she could find a newspaper story that would say everything for her. The news had come too late for an editorial, and just to state the facts, as their

157

paper did, might not make the right impression. O'Reilley might be one of those people who thought that publicity was everything, and there was plenty of that.

She bought a quarter of bull's-eyes from Mrs. Redmond, who no longer tried to speak of maids, and managed to get a look at the other morning papers: bigger, blacker headlines and a tone that verged on the gleeful. So much for that. (And where were the gas men, she wondered in the lane. The ridge had been obliterated in the night's rain. She wouldn't have known they had been there at all, except for the bag.)

She got through the letter, told O'Reilley he had a sense of chivalry, and then appealed to it against these hit-and-run, women-and-children-killed-first tactics, and so convinced herself of the inhumanity of the organization that she thought it well to add:

> If you decide you want to pull out of this group, please don't mention us at all, as I would not like a close-up of one of their explosions.

"Not exactly the way I'd have gone at it," Rafferty said, "but it'll do."

"And what shall I tell Frank?"

"Frank? Tell him anything you want to. I don't want to read his letter."

"Oh, Rafferty." She got the letter and pushed it into his hand, so that all he had to do was look down.

He did, his eyes sliding down in a diagonal line, top left to bottom right, then returning to the top to read it properly. "*Can you expedite?* I'd like to see *him* expedite this lot. Know what I had to do today?"

"No."

"One of the weavers, hadn't thrown a shuttle all week, said he'd been sitting out in the cow byre five days. So I took this sick calf to the vet in the back of the car. The damn thing kept licking my head. I wouldn't be surprised if it just needed salt."

158

"Oh, Rafferty."

"I washed my head at the shop and Brian cleaned the car."

"Why don't you let Frank have what you've got?"

"I'm waiting until I have enough to get a better rate at the finishers."

"I know, but just to let Frank see it. Tell him it's just a sample, not a shipment."

"All right. I'll take it over to the finishers tomorrow, and we'll see what it looks like."

14.

"TO GET BACK TO THE THORNS—" SAID RAFFERTY, TRYING TO PIN
that problem onto the woolman, which was where the finishers
said it belonged.

"A thorn is it? I'll show you a thorn." The woolman pulled
Rafferty through the little-used back door out into the squelching
grass of the overgrown garden beyond. "There," he said and
pointed to a lethal piece of horny vegetable matter two inches
long, "we call *that* a thorn."

"Well, burrs, then."

"Burrs, I'll show you burrs," he said and fastened himself on
Rafferty's elbow to lead him off.

"No." Rafferty pulled away. "There's *something* in the wool,
something that shouldn't be there. I don't care what you call
them, I just don't want them in the wool. Prickers, let's say, not
that they are prickers, but just for the sake of this discussion."

"Prickers, is it?" the woolman said, nodding, and explained:
what Rafferty thought were "prickers" was just the "natural

160

strength of the wool itself." The Irish—he said "Oirish"—sheep lived in the mountains in places where an American sheep would starve to death. (Rafferty couldn't get in a word about the Navaho sheep in the New Mexico desert.) The Oirish sheep at great inconvenience to itself was producing the best wool in the world by sticking to a diet of limestone and gorse. As for the rest— Rafferty having extracted an inch of wiry twig from the wool then and there—the Oirish sheep, leading the life he did, couldn't be expected to keep himself like some New York jackeen. That the washer, the carder, the dyer, the spinner, *somebody* ought to remove the *things*, was met by a further barrage of words behind which the woolman retired to his position of the "natural strength of the wool." He would not be drawn out a second time, though he did promise to bring Rafferty's problem, nonexistent as it was, to the attention of all the innocent workmen.

The woolman left, and Rafferty resigned himself to a continuing job on the finished cloth with tweezers. Oh, they were a grand bunch of lads, great boys for detail, like Tommy and Mick. All *they* had to do was alternate the threads in the warp: A-B-A-B, Stella and Vanessa could have done it. Tommy could have done it alone, he thought, but not with Mick there, jawing.

And to think of all the hogwash he had given them about "responsible adults and common sense," when what he should have had was a full set of rules, like the back of the steamship ticket, covering every possibility that a fertile imagination could conceive. Then he could have just pointed to: *No jewelry permitted,* instead of having to argue with Mick about the ring.

"Aw, have a heart. It's from me girl," Mick said, and aligned the sharp tin Arms of the City of Blackpool on his finger.

"You were given the choice of covering it every morning with elastoplast," Rafferty reminded him.

"I forgot. It was just the once."

He gave him another chance (the fourth). The bandage was applied and his voice rose up through the floor: "You'd think I was some stupid horse, getting ready for the Grand National."

A rug might kill the noise, Rafferty thought, but he knew how much that would cost, and Alice would rightly expect the drawing room rug to come first.

Before the week was out it was: "I forgot, Mr. Rafferty."

"All right. Off it comes. Now." He stood there waiting. "You can tie it on a string around your neck—under your shirt."

"It's like an engagement ring. There's such a thing as human rights."

"That's right. Rafferty's Woollens has a right to see that your wearing apparel doesn't cut up the yarn. And if you don't like that, you have a right to get a job somewhere else." He waited. He would have given fifty pounds to have had Mick walk out the door then.

Mick pulled the ring from his finger, crushed it in his fist, and tossed it into the waste barrel.

"Great," Rafferty said, and went upstairs.

Was there any hope that the loss of the ring would lead to a breakup with the girl, her father, and his damned greyhounds?

The word a few days later was that the wedding would be moving forward from the four or five years originally planned. When he had a job like this, said Mick below, what was the point in waiting?

My God, for his own protection Mick ought to be given the sack. He might go out and buy a house with a forty-year mortgage on the strength of the job.

If it hadn't been for Brian the whole department would have collapsed the day that Thady and Ned stopped coming in. And Tommy and Mick didn't even seem to suspect that he was using Brian as overseer, or to notice that the really big foul-ups always got going while Brian was out doing the messages.

After the next big tangle he tried to put everything into perspective for Tommy and Mick. Did they realize that they were still on probation? His own departure, which might be forced on him at any moment, would bring a change in management. They might find themselves under some hardheaded accountant, who would expect the whole beam and bobbin division to run like clockwork. Just one mess like *this* and they would be finished. Even if their work was perfect, the business might have to go under the wing of one of the other weaving firms, who would probably choose to fill the beams with their own men.

They both looked chastened by that, a steamship-ticket type of eventuality that had occurred to him as he spoke. In short, he concluded, the job was never to be considered certain beyond their week's notice.

Mick, breaking a record silence, said, "You'd think Thady would have made that clear before I chucked a good job for this."

"Too bad," Rafferty said and went upstairs.

The next week it was announced through the floorboards that the marriage was to take place right after Easter. "You'd want to be mad to wait now," said Mick, "the way it's all gone uncertain here."

"Any mail?"

"Up here," Alice called, coming out of the drawing room, where he was finding her more and more.

"Who from?"

"Dr. Steichen. We've got the first semester for sure, maybe the second."

It would be just like the man to bleed it out, a good thing they didn't have trimesters at Oakley. It might not be a bad idea to suggest that a third year was a possibility and give the man a chance to refuse them *something*.

"And that's not all," Alice said, as he reached the room. "Here, read it yourself."

I'll be able to give you my answer on the second semester when I see you in August, he read. "August? You mean he's coming here?" She nodded. *Mrs. S. and I have a marvelous opportunity to*

163

*do Europe this summer. We'll stop in Dublin, and Louise insists
on going out to the house to see Alice and those dear little boys.*
He looked at Alice, who must have guessed where he was, and
made a face.

*We'll be in London from the nineteenth to the twenty-sixth and
will land in Dun Laoghaire (how do you say that?) on the morning of the twenty-seventh.* "Wait a minute." Nineteenth to twenty-
sixth. "Where's that London *Times* I brought home yesterday?"

She headed for the pile of papers beneath the windowseat and
fumbled through the top ones. "Here."

He skimmed through the Personals. "It could have been the
Telegraph." He had a picture of it on the front page, though.

She went back to the pile. "If I knew what you were looking
for—the *Guardian,* maybe?"

"No. It has to be London. How about the *Times* for the day
before?"

"You certainly read a lot of newspapers."

"It's about the only thing I can do at the shop, with those crit-
ters downstairs."

"Here it is."

"Ah," he said. "Here it is." He reread it over her shoulder: *Ex-
panding U.S. College requires Lecturers and Assistant Professors,
History, English, Sociology & Journalism. Scenic old mid-
Western campus. Forward-looking administration. £1500 to
£1800 per annum. Fare (one-way) paid. Interviews London August 20–26. Box . . .*

"Those poor bastards, I said to myself, they could find themselves in some place like Oakley. But I thought it was just standard second-rate waffling. I should have recognized the hand of
our own forward-looking administration."

"Yes, but what are we going to do when he comes here with
Mrs. S.?"

"Do. Why, I'll say, 'Won't you sit down in our magnificent
eighteenth-century drawing room?'" He extended a hand into the

room, toward the two chairs that they hadn't thought worth carrying back downstairs. Their webbing was rotten, and the springs rested on the floor, so that from the side they looked like a pair of setting hens.

"We'll have the rug by then, won't we?"

She was really worried about that. "Of course we will. I meant to say, 'our *really* magnificent eighteenth-century drawing room.' And we'll have a glass of sherry. I'll see if I can get our man Molloy to hand them around. And then our maid will appear in her quaint old-world black and white uniform and show us down to the dining room, where we'll dine on a haunch of venison."

"Oh, stop it, Rafferty," she said, laughing. He knew he was being silly, a bit dizzy and unbalanced by the sudden removal of one of his worries.

"You know what we'll do. We'll come up here, and we'll have a rug on the floor, and with that view no one's going to notice that the rest of the furnishings are pretty tatty. We can have a turf fire and they can talk about how we're burning 'peat,' and you can serve something or other. Cold ham and potato salad up here, if you're afraid the dining room table's going to collapse."

"Oh, it won't."

"All right, it's settled then."

ALICE HAD NEVER IMAGINED A VISIT FROM OAKLEY. SHE WONDERED if she had perhaps been a bit more fulsome in her descriptions of Prisma and its location than she should have been.

But, as she stood up in the drawing room and looked down at the sea, she could truthfully say that she had exaggerated nothing. Even at this season the gardener had the place in perfect condition, the grass short, thick, and green. The hedges looked a little scalped, perhaps, but soon the fresh growth would be upholstering their spare frames.

Oh, the grounds were all right, she thought, turning her back

165

to the window; the room was the problem. Cleared of the dismal bedroom fittings, it was a blank, waiting for her to act: white walls and white woodwork, and the bleached patch on the floor that you couldn't cover with anything smaller than twenty-two by twelve.

She had more in mind than just giving the Steichens something to tell them in Oakley. Sometime, if only for the little girls' sake, Dr. Steichen must be made to see what Rafferty was all about. Oakley had produced few scholars, half a dozen or so who were doing their best to conceal the connection, and Rafferty. After his years in grad school he had turned down three or four really good offers in order to come back to Oakley.

The school had been drifting then under President Simmers, who had never thought of much more than staying afloat, until Rafferty came along and talked of making Oakley, with its lovely little nineteenth-century campus and its modest endowment, into one of the few small schools that mattered. Carleton, Grinnell, Reed, Kenyon, Oakley.

Mr. Simmers was impressed. He talked of making Rafferty his assistant, a position that would put him in the natural succession to the presidency. And then the old man went to Chicago for a summer weekend, was run over by a bus, and died.

The fall term began a month later, with Dr. Steichen already installed in the president's office. The trustees said they had snapped at the chance to get a man of his caliber on such short notice.

Alice, on the staff of the newspaper that year, had been sent round to get Dr. Steichen's story for the September issue. Still smarting from the affair, he told her far more than was necessary, and prudently she wrote only that he had come to Oakley "after a successful career in the political sphere." But many times since then she had regretted, almost as much as he, that he had been denied the endorsement that would have put him on the ballot

166

that fall, a shoo-in for State Railroad and Warehouse Commissioner.

If Dr. Steichen dreamed, it was only of an expanded Oakley, fat with government grants, government loans (if it came to that), and government-aided students.

What cash there was went on planners' fees, while even the best faculty salaries were a disgrace. Their friends were leaving Oakley one by one, but Rafferty, offered one of the last and smallest raises, took it and stayed. Even now he seemed to believe that Dr. Steichen was only a temporary trial, a bullfrog trying to be a bull and about to burst and leave Oakley, somehow, what it was before.

No hope of that. Dr. Steichen had to come to Prisma and walk into that room and be simply bowled over, dumfounded by the thought that a man who could live in a Georgian gentleman's house, with a thirty-foot drawing room overlooking the Irish Sea, should intend to return to Oakley. And if he could not be made to see Rafferty as a man with a mission—whose mission could not be denied—then Rafferty had to be made to see *him* clearly, the man who valued the entire liberal arts faculty at less than the tile bathrooms in the new dormitory, and had set the school on a road from which there could be no easy turning. Otherwise there could be nothing but frustration for Rafferty, and for her, never a house of her own.

ASIDE FROM THE THORNS, THE FINISHERS HAD WORKED WONDERS with the tweed. Even Alice, who had shaken him a little with her doubts about the first piece of cloth, had asked if he could cut off enough for a skirt from one of the pieces. The shipment was too small as it was, but he promised to have some short runs made for her—and for himself—as soon as the men got into the rhythm of weaving.

167

It was hard to stop marveling at the very existence of the cloth. He was unexpectedly sad as each bundle was wrapped and sealed. Perhaps a painter, seeing his canvases go, would feel that way.

He didn't like to think of its leaving his hands and spending time on wharves, boats, and in dank storehouses, and he considered air freight until a phone call and a little arithmetic put that out of the question. So he booked cargo space on a passenger liner and engaged a freight forwarder with a good reputation. He gave them detailed instructions, but hadn't thought of everything the first time and so had to phone them again. And a third time as well. The man in the office was very polite, but Rafferty felt that he was on the verge of being considered a head case. Perhaps he might have trusted a little more to common sense, and yet . . .

The night before his shipment was scheduled to sail, the wind tore at the house, cracking the whip with the telephone wire. Fanned by a dozen draughts, the turf fire burned fast and red, and on the radio the meteorological office issued one gale warning after another: *Irish Sea, Fair Isles, Hebrides, Crommoty, Fisher, gales now imminent.* He wished he could remember what it was they called the seas off Cobh.

He turned down the radio. "They'll be going out on the tender."

"The play's coming on in a minute," Alice said, pointing a knitting needle at the radio. "What about the tender?"

"The tweed. They're going to transfer it from the tender to the boat in high seas."

"They're used to that, I suppose," she said, clearly not bothering to picture the scene, and impaling her ball of yarn on the knitting needles, she hurried over to the radio where she cut off the announcer in mid-syllable and tried to make a quick rundown to the other station. He heard her there, adrift among Spaniards and Scandinavians.

168

"Up at the end, under the P in Philips," he said, annoyed. In a way she was right, it was out of his hands.

"There are two p's."

He went over to the radio. No one could think of everything. He could just hear them explaining: *We knew how you were wanting it on that boat, Mr. Rafferty, and we thought they could stand off on the lee side long enough. . . . Just three seconds more and we would have made it, Mr. Rafferty, two seconds, even one. . . . Lost? Ah, no, Mr. Rafferty, they generally fetch up on Spike Island the first spring tide.*

There was a brisk wind in Cobh, but the tender rode smoothly out on a sea that was no more than choppy. He had had to explain himself: studying loading procedure with a view to perfecting packaging for future shipments. And he was doing that, though he doubted that his packaging could be improved.

There was more of a swell out in the bay where they met the steamship, but not enough to hamper the men with their loading. From the rail of the liner he watched two cars swung up through the air and into the hold. After that his cartons seemed pretty small stuff. They were thrown into the cargo nets with the trunks and other freight, a giant bag of mixed nuts. The roll of the boats sent one of the netfuls banging smartly against the plates of the ship. It bounced off with no apparent damage to his packages (though someone's trunk got a nasty-looking mark) and on the second try it came down neatly through the hatch. One of the other shippers with a sizable consignment of large, soft-looking boxes was dropping a light rain of his steel bands onto the deck of the tender. He wondered if he had a duty to inform the company —Glennabeg, whatever they were—but decided that they might even have figured it that way, a big gain on packing and a loss of a few packages. What a way to feel about your product! He had wrapped each bundle in damp-proof, rip-proof, laminated tarpaper, rolled them in corrugated material, sealed them in cardboard, triple steel-banded the boxes (once lengthwise, twice crosswise), and double-stenciled everything: consignor, consignee, and *Use no hooks.*

When he had counted all of his cartons in through the hatchway, he took a walk around the deck of the liner. It was a day of sun and salt wind, which the mewing frenzy of the gulls only made seem more peaceful. He thought of a long voyage, away from Tommy and Mick, the weavers, Prisma, even—if he could be certain of coming back to find them safe—Alice and the little girls.

Later, as they got into the real business of transferring the mailbags, he went into the lounge. There was a dancing lesson in progress: a brittle South American tune on the phonograph, and a pair of instructors, the dapper man and the hard woman who, for him anyway, would be only lengthening the time they were supposed to be whiling away. He felt the cold monotony of the voyage creeping up on him. He had to face the fact that his own departure could not be forever avoided.

It was hard to recall how he had expected the weaving to become self-sustaining, the weavers needing only a pick-up and delivery service, the men in the shop doing a routine job effortlessly. He would have been needed only as designer, working by mail, coming back for a summer or two, and willing to hand over even that job to the right man. In time, he had thought, the men could have purchased the shop out of production and as a co-op would have gone on supplying cloth to Frank, who would have remained only their wholesaler. It was still possible, barely, if he could find the right man to take his own place.

By fall, when Brian went back to school, he would have to find executive material somewhere, an Englishman, if it came to that, or perhaps a German, a Japanese. There might be one at Trinity, a young man thinking of taking an Irish wife, and perturbed about her life in Tokyo.

170

When the return of the tender was called, he hurried down the gangway with the women who had come out to sell their woolens to the passengers. Half an hour or so later the whistles sounded their farewells and the tender cut out for shore. Standing in the stern he saw the liner waiting until they were clear before she, too, began to move.

"It's only a hop and a jump these days, sure it is," said a voice at his elbow, one of the peddler women.

"Nothing like what it was," he said.

"Would it be your family?" she asked, with a nod toward the liner.

"No." At least he hadn't been waving. "I was just keeping an eye on a shipment of mine, making sure it got on the boat all right." He wasn't going to recite the piece about *studying loading procedure*.

"Ah, so," she said, but he saw her eyes turn toward the shipping clerk who was standing at the rail with his leather case.

No one could have told him what he had found out. It was only reasonable to suppose that the shipping business was run like most of the others he had come up against, with their touching belief in the elasticity of time and the dependability of Divine Providence.

He would just put the trip down to education, peace of mind. And how peaceful it was to stand at the rail with no more baggage than the newspaper in his coat pocket, nothing to do between the docking of the tender and the departure of the train, no need to bag an empty carriage for wife and children.

On the train back to Dublin, eating his favorite meal of rashers and eggs, tea and toast and jam for the second time that day, he drew up a timetable for the progress of the tweed, a minimum timetable, and another that allowed for missed connections, weekends on platforms, everything but a longshoremen's strike— which he calculated an unlikely risk in view of the last strike's having only recently been settled.

In a minimum of two weeks and a maximum of five he ought to have heard from Frank about the tweed.

JUST AS THERE HAD BEEN NO FALL AND NO WINTER, NOW THERE WAS no spring, none of the melting snow, breaking ice, flooding, nor the sudden change from a black and white landscape to a green one. The temperature rose degree by degree, the ground dried a little, and the gorse on the hill behind Prisma began to bloom, first one bush, then another, slowly turning the hill yellow-green.

The gardener was everywhere, spading, raking, burning. The last of the curly kale disappeared in a cloud of vile-smelling smoke. Only the cauliflower remained. For once the greengrocer offered little more than their own plot, cauliflower and root vegetables, carrots and parsnips that had gone limp, turnips more clay-like than ever—and lettuce, with beautiful green heads like blown roses, delicious, fragile, expensive, grown in other people's greenhouses.

"We'll have to have them next year," she said.

The gardener, down on his knees with a dibble, dropping peas into deep holes, nodded. "You might," he said, "if your tomato things'd leave you the room." Her seedlings, which were just getting their second leaves, filled two small wooden boxes at the moment, lots of little plants.

"I'm only going to transplant the strongest," she said.

"I see. That's what you're going to do." He looked a little amused. He would have done it some other way, she imagined, just as he was planting the peas a good eight inches deep.

"Why do you plant them so far down?"

He nodded. "If you was to put them up top they wouldn't have the strength, like. They'd come up too fast."

"I see."

Did he mean that delay in itself was a good thing? If she could train herself to think that way, she would be all right. The cement

172

bag, lying on the music room hearth week after week, could be taken not as the evidence of sloth and disorder, but of stored energy. And there would be few people, even in Ireland, who had such great stores of delay building up to their credit as Rafferty, if only you could look at it that way.

When you considered, as she often did, that both Thady and Ned were free to work their own looms, that all of the nine farmers were now weaving, and that the first of them had had time to pick up a little speed, then the very small gains that she had been booking for Rafferty's weekly pickups had to be reckoned as a man-for-man fall in production.

"I know they're supposed to be farmers," Rafferty said, "but how much time can you put in on six or seven acres?"

"A good man can spade an acre a day," she said, having read it just that afternoon.

"*Spade*, my God, no one's tilling the soil. They don't even cut the hay, just leave it there until the cow gets around to it."

"Well." She could counsel patience for Rafferty, but the carpet depended on the weavers too, and she didn't see how they could receive the Steichens in the drawing room without a carpet.

"It's a man with a telegram," Mary said, calling her to the phone. She came in from the garden, panting up the stairs to the phone on the landing, a highly central location, the house agent had called it.

"You shouldn't have hurried," said the man on the phone. She thought she recognized the voice of the village postmaster. "It's not bad news."

"That's good," she said, still trying to catch her breath.

"Would you be in the fillums, be any chance?"

"No," she said, wondering if he thought that only movie people got telegrams unconnected with birth or death.

"It's from a Mr. Francis Rafferty."

"Yes."

173

"Magnificent shipment get dozen more beavers immediately."

No.

"That's all it says," he said.

"Thank you. Do you think you could mail it out so that my husband can see it?"

"I'll do that, of course. But there's one thing you'd want to know."

"Yes."

"There are no beavers here, you know. What he means is otters. You'd want to get them in England."

"Oh, I think he means *weavers*."

"Ah, you're all right then," said the man in the post office.

15.

Rafferty left the shop. It wasn't good to stay around there too much, not good for them and not good for him. It was possible to get heart trouble just from frustration, he understood.

There were probably other devices for measuring the yarn, ones that wouldn't require those two to count. But once set on that road, where could he stop, short of the monster that Frank was getting: the engineer reading a detective story in a glass booth while the yarn wove itself, until the thread broke and a couple million dollars' worth of machinery stood idle, dinging its bell for help?

Within ten years, Frank said, they would have perfected the yarn. It would never break. He hadn't seemed perturbed to hear that in producing the perfectly weavable thread they were going a long way toward eliminating all the qualities that made a yarn comfortable, and he would be producing almost unlimited quantities of a hard-wearing, if unwearable, cloth.

"You don't know what labor trouble is like," Frank had said.

"I'm not talking about making the cloth, not right now. I'm talking about wearing it; you certainly can't get machines for that."

Frank laughed. "The trouble with you, Pat, is that you can't think of anything but clothes. What about curtains, upholstery, window shades, awnings, towels, sheets? Where do you think the wear comes on a hotel sheet? Not on the beds. It's those washing machines, bleach, detergents, driers, and two-ton mangles."

He was beginning to understand Frank better. He could see why management had gone for the idea of bringing the outworkers in under the factory roof, and, once they had them there, why they had wanted to replace them with machinery. It didn't make it right, but he could understand the temptation. Some of the workers who had lost their jobs to the spinning jenny may have been no more innocent and ill-used than Mick.

Mick's marriage was blackmail. He couldn't very well have sacked the bridegroom on the eve of the wedding. And then, feeling sorry for the girl, after all she was getting Mick, he had given him Easter week off, four and a half days extra, with pay, for the honeymoon. And how they had been hearing of Douglas, Isle of Man, since. He had to wait a few weeks more, a decent, and interminable, interval, before he could give Mick his notice.

There would never be enough work for three men in the shop, particularly with Brian being worked like Gunga Din. As for getting a dozen more weavers, it might as well have been beavers. He had run another ad, not in the Gaeltacht, not after his promise, and he had got the predictable nothing. The tenth loom still stood unused in the shop, with the men's trial runs untouched on the beam. (Someday he would have to see if there were any usable lengths there for Alice or the girls.) He couldn't face training another man and see him begin to make the grade and then lose his drive.

The farm, they said. He had thought of calling their bluff, of buying a tractor and letting the weavers take turns using it. None of them had more than a half day's ploughing. But it would be a

176

full-time job working out who got it when, and who had credit for rainy days, and who delivered it, and who put in petrol and inflated the tires. He had part of an eighteenth-century book in which the unidentifiable, but obviously English, author tells gleefully of three Irish farmers who had together owned one horse, and how none of the three would deign to shoe the fourth leg, and so the horse had gone hopelessly lame. Too bad he hadn't been around then. What they had needed was another man, someone to shoe the other leg before he discovered that there wasn't room for a fourth man on the horse.

He had reached the sidewalk table in front of the bookstore: 3d., 6d., 9d. There was a lot of junk, textbooks and old devotional drivel, but he had found quite a few books, usually part of some old set of histories, the backs broken or gone down to the strings, the boards covered with a brittle, dry leather, and inside, the pages beautiful still, white rag paper and crisp black ink: *ftill a pleafure to fee.*

He would make an afternoon of it, go on to the museum for another look at the medieval tweed found in the bogs and the Egyptian linen woven by men so long dead that there was simply no way to take hold of the idea. And then he would buy a block of shortbread to take home to the little girls and go see if Fogarty was around.

ALICE HAD CALLED THE RATHDOWN GAS COMPANY AND FOUND THEM closed for the day. She didn't like to use the night number—was this an emergency?—without asking Rafferty first. He had gone out early in the afternoon, said Brian, who was just closing the shop. "But he'll be back for the car. Should I put a message in it?"

"No, just leave it, Brian."

After two months, a few minutes more wouldn't make much difference. And she might do well to let him eat first, too.

177

When he had finished eating, Rafferty took a package of short-bread from his briefcase, got out his pocket knife and stropped it on his trouser leg—not honing it, as she had once thought, but removing the traces of his tobacco which he sliced with the knife. He cut four pieces, two large and two small. "I'll call the girls in for these now," he said.

"Why not wait a minute?"

He looked at her.

"You know that cement sack the gas men left here? In the music room. I thought I'd take a tablespoon of it and—"

"What *are* you trying to say?"

She had only wanted to explain how it happened. "Well, I don't know what dynamite looks like, but there's a piece of paper in with it, *Explosives, store apart from detonating devices.*"

"Great," Rafferty said, standing up. "Where's it now?"

"I didn't want to move it."

"Stay here," he said, and went out the door.

When he returned he asked how long it had been there.

"I don't know for sure, maybe two months. It was raining and one of the gas men brought it to the door and asked if he could put it in the shed. I told him to put it in the music room because it was raining. I thought it was cement."

"How do you know it was a gas man?"

"Obviously he was a gas man. They'd been digging out in the road."

"Was he wearing a uniform?"

"He had one of those big raincoats over everything."

"Did he say he was a gas man?"

"Yes. I mean I asked when he was going to finish and he said, 'Tomorrow, please God.' I remember because I was going to go over there the next day and make sure the right stove was being sent, and then I didn't be— I didn't." Let sleeping dogs lie.

178

"Why?"

"Well, because you were so annoyed about that IRA raid in the paper that I thought it would be better to stay home."

"It was precisely the day before that?"

"I suppose if we looked in the old papers we could find the exact date." She didn't see what difference it made.

"Do you know where I can find your friend, Mr. O'Connor?"

"O'Connor?"

"O'Connor."

"I've got his address upstairs, but I don't see—"

"Obviously."

"Rafferty, I thought it was cement. I thought the man was coming back the next day."

"I'm not blaming you, Alice. I'm blaming O'Connor and O'Reilley, and maybe Mistress Mary."

"The IRA?" He couldn't mean that.

"Right."

"Not Mary."

"We'll think about that later, tomorrow, when she's here. Right now we have to do something about the bag."

"We just call the Guards and they'll take it away in just a few minutes." She started for the door.

"My God, Alice. They'd be asking questions for weeks, you and me and Mary and Molloy. It wouldn't end until your friend O'Connor is in the clink, and the FBI and Interpol are knocking on O'Reilley's door."

"And that would serve him right, too."

"All right. Save your indignation, just get me O'Connor's address."

RAFFERTY WALKED DOWN THE DESERTED LANE WITH THE BAG AT arm's length, keeping his eyes on his feet and his ears alert. He

179

had the idea that there would be some preliminary noise if the bag were going to explode, a hissing perhaps. Gelignite, he thought it was, on no greater evidence than the color of the covering, which he thought should have been red for dynamite, and because it was what the IRA used, according to the newspapers, which said too that if gelignite was left in a damp atmosphere it became "unstable."

At the outer gate he pulled the bag in to his side. A dozen or so of the villagers passed, carrying their burdens up the hill, a hedge clippers, a ladder, a lawnmower. Nothing remarkable about a bag in that company. "Grand evening." "Grand evening," he agreed four, five, six, seven times before he made it to the garage. The car had been loaded for his next day's rounds, and he made a bed for the bag at the very back with a pair of Wellingtons and several pieces of mackintosh sheeting, a red rubber-coated cloth that he used to protect the beams on a bad day. The weavers' beams themselves, heavy, wooden, padded with yarn, would deflect the explosion backwards, away from the driver, possibly.

His decision to take the bag to O'Connor, rather than have him send someone to get it, had almost nothing in its favor, only speed. Let O'Connor keep it in his own shed, let the delays and litany of excuses be his worry. But now, locked in the stream of idiot drivers, with his load of unstable gelignite, he wondered if he might have dismissed the alternatives a little too quickly. He could have driven in with an ultimatum, six hours, say, and then he would call the Guards. But would he? Was he an informer?

Why not? What did he owe the IRA? A broken travel iron. A maid who might be anything. (Alice was always saying that she didn't see how anyone with experience could do things the way Mary did.) Or was he doing this for O'Reilley, and if so, why? The best thing for him would be to let the FBI come asking questions. Let him see that what he had been doing wasn't the same thing as sending a check to CARE.

He turned into the street where O'Connor was said to live and took his foot off the gas. The engine died. Georgian, past decay, and moving into dissolution, it looked as though one good cannon cracker would bring the whole street down. The road teemed with children. He wouldn't leave the bag there, and he would have to make sure that O'Connor didn't either. He started the car again, nosed up to the proper number, stopped, and got out.

Half a dozen filthy urchins converged on him. "Mind your car, Mister?"

He was still safe, with an Irish registration on the car and all his clothes Dublin bought; it was only his accent he had to fear. "Mr. O'Connor live here?" he asked brusquely, jerking his head toward the open doorway. Even out in the street the smell was something. "Old man? White hair?" Some of the boys nodded. "Go get him." The boy nearest the door slipped inside, into the hall, dodged around a couple of prams, and ran up the stairs.

"Give us a copper?" asked one of the others.

He shook his head, and they moved off to the next of the crumbling stoops to watch. He leaned against the car and waited.

Three or four minutes passed, and the boy did not reappear. Rafferty did not intend to follow him. If O'Connor chose to lie low, he would go to the Guards, give them the disposal problem, and do what he could to keep O'Connor's name out of it. The boy returned. "He'll come now."

Rafferty took out a single penny and gave it to the boy, who ran off to join the others. If he had given him more, they would have been all over him again. He preferred to be identified, if it came to that, as just another stingy Englishman. *Mr. Fogarty, for the defence, cross-examined the witness.* Was Fogarty any good? They had never gone much into his business. Rafferty had seen his name mentioned a few times in newspaper accounts—disputed codicils, defamation of character—one of a platoon of lawyers at the end of the story.

181

Someone was coming down the stairs, a man tucking his white hair into a black beret. "Mr. O'Connor?" Rafferty said when he came out the door. The man did not deny it.

"Get in," Rafferty said and went around to the far side of the car. O'Connor got in.

"Rafferty's the name. I've got your bag here."

"Me bag?"

"Let's get out of here." He pulled away from the curb. There seemed to be a head in every window, and a clock struck the hour as they made their getaway.

O'Connor denied everything, denied that Mary was working with him, denied giving the address to anyone, denied sending anyone out with the gelignite, denied working for the IRA, denied the IRA itself. "Ah, it's all a cod for the Teds. There's nothing in it, only talk."

"What about the border post they blew up last winter?"

"Ah, you'll find your wild men in everything."

"They killed a woman and child."

"Shocking," said O'Connor. "Shocking."

"And what about that charge of explosives under my own children's bedroom?"

"A bad job, Mr. Rafferty."

They drove along in silence for a while. Rafferty didn't like to hand the bag back to the IRA, but disposing of it otherwise would not be easy. There were wastelands where it could be safely detonated, if O'Connor could be persuaded to do that. Or they could deposit it in some out-of-the-way spot and then phone the Guards from a place like Amiens Street Station. Or better, phone a newspaper, tell them to tell the police to pick it up. They would be less able to trace the call. He had listened to too many installments of Gang Busters. Doubtlessly woolen fibers from his car would cling to the bag. The woolman would be questioned.

"Oh, it's ours all right. You can tell be the thorns."

182

"Thorns, Mr. Carmody?"

"Thorns, burrs, prickers, whatever you want to call them."

"And would your records tell you where you sold this particular lot?"

"No need of that, it was a special order, always a fuss about his colors. Rafferty's Woollens."

They were at the edges of Dublin now, cruising through streets of semi-detached houses where office workers mowed their lawns and clipped their hedges. "Well, what about it? We can't go on driving all night."

"Up to the mountains," said O'Connor, decisively.

"Which ones? Dublin? Wicklow?"

"Just keep going. I'll tell you later." O'Connor looked out the window. After a while he said, "It's like going in a tunnel, so it is?"

"What is?" They hadn't reached the high walls yet.

"The motorcar. It's that low."

"You don't often ride in a car?"

"I've been in the bus all right, and in a van too, but I was in a motorcar only the once, and that was a funeral. You couldn't enjoy it, like. They was too much going on."

Rafferty nodded. That was probably why he hadn't hesitated when ordered into the car. "I need it in my work."

"Ah, you would. You would."

Soon they were in the uplands, with the suburbs behind them, and only the odd house now and then. "Which way?"

"Keep going," O'Connor said, peering out. "There," he said after a while, "up above, there's a lane be the side."

After a few more of O'Connors directions Rafferty began to get the picture. O'Connor was directing him around in circles, hoping to confuse him before he ordered him to one of the drops, if that was the word they used. Or was he waiting for dark? The blue of the sky was purpling, but they had more than an hour of light left.

"Would you look at that, he must know a shorter way," O'Connor said to distract him as they passed the same red-jerseyed cyclist the second time.

"Turn right," said O'Connor, sending them in a new direction, and after a while, "Left there."

It was a bog road, and at the sides, the sods which had just been lifted were standing, tripoded to catch the wind. A hundred yards in, O'Connor said, "You can stop now."

As a drop it had everything wrong with it. Anyone on the bog road was visible for miles, and the bog itself looked impassable. They got out of the car. The emptiness and silence were heavy in the air—too late for birds and too early for whatever it was that made the night noises. Rafferty could see nowhere to leave the bag, just the raised road and a ditch with a bit of water in it.

"Grand," said O'Connor, "we'll drop your man in the water there, and no one will ever find him."

Rafferty shook his head. "Now, you listen to me. Do you or do you not know someone who will come and pick up this bag after we've dropped it?"

"Who would I know?"

"Your friends in the IRA."

"I told you. I don't know the IRA. I swear to God I don't know the IRA."

"You bring me up here to a working bog, one that may have a dozen people in it tomorrow, little boys, women maybe, and you ask me to drop that bag, which may go off at any moment, not twelve inches from the road."

"I didn't know they was working here."

"In other words, we're just driving around, looking for a place, any place, to get rid of this stuff."

"That's right," said O'Connor, pleased with himself, as though he had finally managed to make himself clear.

"All right. Now I understand. I know these hills, and there's no place where we can drop this bag and be sure that some child

184

won't come on it sometime and run the risk of being blown up."
He looked O'Connor in the eye, a bloodshot eye, the blue held
uncertainly, as in the white of an underdone egg.

O'Connor didn't flinch.

"You understand?" Rafferty asked.

He nodded and said, in a voice that was surprisingly childlike,
"What will you be doing then, Mr. Rafferty?"

MARY HAD HAD NOTHING TO DO WITH IT, ALICE WAS CERTAIN OF
that. She might have been wrong about O'Connor, but then she
hardly knew him and, anyway, his connection with the bag was
still unproved.

The real villain might well be O'Reilley. In the library she dug
through the drift of correspondence at the back of the desk for his
letter, the one in answer to her objections. She had read it once,
quickly. Now she wondered if its meaning was as clear as she had
thought.

> . . . I wonder if you aren't being too hard on our "friends,"
> you know you can't make an omelette without breaking a few
> eggs. Much as I regret this incident I don't feel I can with-
> draw my support on its account. I have, however, warned
> them to be "more careful in the future."
>
> Yours for Ireland,
> "Pat" O'Reilley

Warned them to be more careful of *what?* Of the Raffertys,
who could no longer be considered "safe"? And so they had been
afraid to return to Prisma for the bag.

Supposing it were possible that they had some kind of leverage,
some hold on Mary, she wouldn't have allowed the bag to remain
in the house—in the shed, perhaps, but not in the house.

She remembered the day she tried to prove to Mary that yeast
bread could be made at home and, driven almost to despair by

185

the unfamiliar yeast, grey and smelling of kerosene, she put the crockery hot water jars around the bowl and swaddled it all in towels, while Mary gawped and she explained that yeast was a living being and took a lot of care. And then she hurried off to do her shopping and came back to find Mary waiting at the inner gate. "Oh, hurry, Mrs. Rafferty, they're trying to get out of the kitchen!"

They ran downstairs where she found that the dough had lifted the towels and was streeling down over the edge of the table onto the grey flags.

"Thank God the girls are outside with Danny," she heard Mary say, and she turned to see her standing there with drawn broom, ready to defend them both.

Whatever you made of that, it was not the act of someone who would calmly allow a bag of explosives to remain in the house.

She was so certain of that that she intended never to mention the matter to Mary—as long as Rafferty got home safely.

RAFFERTY ROWED, HEADING THE BOAT DEAD OUT TO SEA AGAIN, AND wondered why they kept veering toward Howth. The boat was almost too deep and heavy for one man to row alone, but O'Connor had kept splattering them both with his shallow strokes until at last he dug in deep—and brought the boat to a shuddering stop. Rafferty had to send him back to the stern before they could make it out of the harbor.

He had mentioned the sea himself, a wits'-end thought that O'Connor had seized, saying he knew where they could get a boat, and so they had driven down out of the hills in the last light of day. He hadn't understood then that the old man meant to rent a boat at a public landing which, even at that hour, was crammed with fishermen, loungers, and other witnesses, not excluding a Guard, one who was just watching, with his hands crossed behind his back. Compounding a felony? Accessory after the fact? Aiding and abetting? There was a word for what he was doing.

However, no one seemed to think it odd that two men and a bag should be requiring a boat at dusk. One of the loungers who helped them *hoick* the boat down from the shingle said only that in his opinion there would be too much moon that night, but pollack had been taken earlier. Rafferty had the feeling that the man was fishing for information of the smaller sort: what they were after and what kind of bait and tackle they were carrying in the bag.

He wouldn't care to have that man see him landing with neither fish nor bag. Better to give him and everybody else at the pier plenty of time to get tired and go home.

The farther he rowed, the better. Trawlers, tides, currents, things he had met on the periphery of his newspaper reading, all would have been considered in any orderly undertaking. His plan was only to keep going as long as he could, unless they began to see lights from the Welsh side.

He was still trying to find an easy rhythm with the oars. He had never been much for boats, he hadn't wanted to think about what might be at the bottom of the lake. What might be beneath him here simply didn't bear thought—sharks, giant squid, the whales he had been hoping to see from a distance.

"Do you go boating often, Mr. Rafferty?" O'Connor's dark clothes blended with the night, so that a disembodied face floated above the stern.

"No, hardly ever," Rafferty said.

"You do very well, all the same."

Rafferty grunted. Two waves had caught them, and he hoped they were not representative of what was to be found in the deeper water.

A commotion broke out in the stern, a wordless scuffle. "Good God, what's going on?"

187

"Ah, it's only a fish," said O'Connor, "I'm trying to get me hands on him. It's a plaice, I think."

"Well, throw it overboard."

"Overboard? I'll have him for me breakfast."

"See if you can keep it quiet then."

They went on in silence. The broken facets of the waves began to pick up a silver sheen. He turned to see the moon rising—past full anyway, a gibbous moon. The sea was the color of lead; it felt like lead.

There was another ruckus in the back. "Can't you keep that damned fish quiet?"

"It's all right. I'll put him in me vest."

"No, don't do that. Just do what you can."

"You won't hear him again."

He did though, and said nothing, just listened to the old man talking it down, the way you would a dog, in whispered anxiety. There probably wasn't much in the old guy's life if a fish for breakfast could be an event. No telling what he did for a living, or why he had wanted to get mixed up with the IRA.

"It's all right, just let him flop."

"Thank you, Mr. Rafferty."

How long had he been rowing? An hour, two hours? He had to save something for the trip back. He couldn't turn to O'Connor. A pull like this could kill the old man. He would give it another hundred strokes.

Twenty more, and this time he wouldn't stop to consider how close the shore lights still seemed.

He shipped the oars.

"Stay there," he said to O'Connor. "Never stand up in a row-boat."

He felt in the bows for the bag and caught the short rope with which he had tied it shut. He lifted it carefully over the side, lowered it, and let it go.

188

"Oh, my God."

"What's the matter there?" O'Connor asked.

"Stay there. It's floating."

"That's grand, the tide'll carry it out to sea."

"Great," said Rafferty, leaning over as far as he dared. The bows of the boat were built high above the water. The bag was wave-colored; if once he took his eyes off it, he would never see it again. He leaned over, stretching the laws of gravity to the limit, snagged the bag, and pulled it down to where the sides were lower. The canvas was repelling the moisture, and the air inside had turned the bag into a float. He sloshed it up and down, trying to force the water in. At this rate it might take hours to sink, floating in the track of the coasters and the mailboat. The rope was a hairy manila, wet and inflexible as wood. He could saw through it with his knife, but it would be too short to retie, and the stuff might very well float free of an open bag.

"I don't suppose you've got any rope on you?"

"I have," said O'Connor.

"You have? Enough to tie this sack?"

"Oh, it would that, all right."

"Well, give it to me then." He reached into his pocket for his knife.

O'Connor didn't move. "Well?" Rafferty said, sawing at the knot.

"The rope—it's holding me trousers."

"Is that all? I'll find you something just as soon as we get back to the car."

O'Connor was silent. He was making no move to undo the rope.

"Here, I'll give you my belt." Working with one hand, he got it unbuckled and slipped it from the loops.

"Ah, you didn't have to do that," said O'Connor, creeping forward. The deserted plaice drummed on the planks.

Rafferty cut through the last strand and, holding his head well

189

back, opened the bag. No telling what fumes might be released by the action of the salt water. He pushed the outside lip of the bag under the water. Bubbles, probably ordinary air bubbles, came up. The canvas, wet from both sides, darkened. He tied the bag with O'Connor's rope.

The bag was pulling away from him. He held the end of the rope, the bag wanted to go straight down. He let it go.

"AND HE KEPT ON DENYING IT, RIGHT UP TO THE TIME I LEFT HIM AT his door, with his plaice."

A grey fish with orange spots, she thought, but disappointing to taste.

"There was only once when he even looked disturbed."

"When was that?"

"When I said, 'Mr. O'Reilley will be hearing of this.'"

"I suppose it was the idea of wasting supplies, dumping them in the sea."

"Something like that," he said and poured out the rest of his Guinness.

The sun was well up, though the little girls were still sleeping, and he was having a lunch before he went to bed. Brian would expect him to have gone straight out to the weavers; the weavers could wait.

"What about your belt?"

"I don't see how I could ask for it. I'd feel foolish, offering to buy him a new rope."

"And so?"

He looked a little embarrassed. "I said that I had another belt."

"In Oakley."

"That's about the size of it."

"Well, you'd better go out and buy yourself a new rope."

Rafferty nodded. "I'm going to bed now, just don't let anybody leave anything here until I get up."

"I can't find the tray, is it upstairs?" Mary asked.

"No, I ate with the girls, and Mr. Rafferty won't be eating until later. He was up working most of the night." She hesitated. "Mary?"

"Yes."

"How well do you know Mr. O'Connor?"

Mary shook her head. "I don't know him very well, but if I'd think who he was, I could tell you better."

"He sent you here."

"Oh, that one. He's a friend of me father's. I never saw him but the once."

A close friend? She wouldn't ask it.

"Why do you want to know?"

"I was just wondering."

Mary nodded, as though that were a perfectly reasonable explanation. She was a lot easier than Rafferty to deal with.

That was the end of it then. She would say no more to Mary, and they would say nothing to O'Reilley either. When Rafferty had considered the possible results of his night's work becoming common knowledge, he would agree that silence was best. And as for O'Connor, just let him try to show his face at that house again.

She was ready for sleep herself, after a night of worry. First, though, she would go out and make sure the greenhouse windows were open. The gardener had forgotten to open them the day before, and when she had gone out during his lunchtime to water the plants she had found them wilting in the heat. She had intended to tell him in the afternoon, but she hadn't happened to see him before the discovery of the bag had put everything else out of her mind.

Now, as she approached the greenhouse, she saw that the windows were opened only a crack, exactly as she had left them in the evening when she brought in the little girls. Ten-thirty, he had

191

had plenty of time to open them. He was not in the kitchen garden and both shed doors were shut, so he must have been in the front. She opened the windows first, and then walked around the house, looking into the empty orchard as she passed. He was nowhere in sight. He was not on the lane side of the hedge either. She knocked at the door of the lodge. There was no answer. His morning bottle of milk was not on the step, so he had been out. But where was he now?

She went around to the back again, calling, "Mr. Molloy," until she came to the kitchen door.

Mary and the two girls were in the scullery, blowing soap bubbles in the webs of their fingers with the wash water. "Do you know where the gardener is?"

Mary dried her hands on her apron. "He's not here now."

"I can see that. I don't think he was around much yesterday either."

"Ah, no."

"Is he sick then, do you know?"

"Ah, no. He's not here now."

"What do you mean?" That he had two jobs in the summer? That he worked only half-time, because it was just a half-time job?

"You see, he asked me would I get his stamp card so he could leave."

Alice looked over at the stillroom door, where his and Mary's cards had been hanging from a clip, and saw only one.

"When was that?"

"Saturday. It was his half day."

"And today's Tuesday. Why didn't you tell me before?"

"Ah, you might have been distressed, like, and I knew you'd be asking me, all the same."

"And what about the gatehouse? Is he still staying there?"

"No. There's the keys."

There was just one more thing. She took the watering can out to

192

the greenhouse and had a good look. He had hauled down the striped shirt, and for the first time that she could remember all the lines were absolutely empty. She had undisputed possession of the greenhouse. Damn.

16.

"WHY EXPLOSIVES?" RAFFERTY ASKED, LOOKING AT ALICE FOR THE answer. "Why not guns? Or if they just want to destroy property, why aren't they more careful about people?"

She could see that it would be a while before they would be able to talk about the gardener. "I think they're just trying to cause as much trouble as they can."

"Yes, but I don't want to be told only that 'the world's in a state of chassis,' I want to know who's doing it and why. Why O'Connor?"

"I don't know." And why had Rafferty been ready to give back the bag? She didn't want to talk about it ever again. "The problem now is the gardener. I'm trying to make you appreciate the fact that he's quit."

"I know. Why are you looking so glum about it?"

"I *am* glum, why shouldn't I be?"

"I took it that you didn't want a full-time gardener."

"Well, it's one thing to have a full-time gardener in January and February, and it's another to have one now."

"That's the thing about a full-time gardener, he's full time."

"Yes, but I keep coming back in my mind to how could he stay the whole winter and leave just when everything is about to get out of hand?"

"I'm sorry. I really am. I always liked the idea of a gardener."

"You did?"

"Why don't you see what you can get out of Mary?"

Mary knew nothing, she said. She was obviously eager to finish with the subject. "It was just a little thing."

"Then you do know why he left?" Alice said.

"Ah, no," she said and disappeared into the larder.

Alice waited for her. "What's the little thing, then?"

"Ah, it wasn't anything at all, just calling him Mr. Molloy."

"Wasn't that his name? It was on his card," she said, nodding toward the door where it no longer hung.

"Yes. But *Danny* would be more friendly, like."

"But, Mary, he was older than my father. How could I call him *Danny?*" That would have been presumption, practically Imperialism, like calling the natives *boy.*

Mary looked solemn, nodding, seeing the problem, and at last she said, "You could say *Old Danny.*"

She took the gardener's bunch of keys and went out with them. The garden tools hadn't been on the inventory. Maybe they had belonged to the gardener and she would find the toolshed bare. Or maybe she would find it bare anyway. He hadn't left a forwarding address or anything. What if he had mail? Or visitors?

She opened the door of the toolshed and looked in at the jumble of handles. When her eyes adjusted to the dark she saw that they seemed to be mostly hoes, or hoe-like implements. She should have been paying more attention to what the gardener had

195

been working with. That thing like a stirrup was what he used to scratch at the driveway. And next to it was some kind of edging tool. She could see the hedge clippers, secateurs, a pruning hook, a sickle, and the thing she had come for, the lawn mower. Just watching him with it, she had never realized how small it was. Even so, it was hard enough getting it down the precipitous path down to the orchard.

Danny. Old Danny. Mr. Molloy. To be annoyed because you were being given more dignity than you wanted, that hardly seemed reasonable. It was the kind of excuse that a child, one who had already made up his mind to act, would settle upon.

After an hour or so with the mower, she went into the house. She was hot and tired, and the glass of unrefrigerated ale wasn't what she had had in mind when she opened the bottle. "You know," she said to Mary, "it seems such a paltry excuse for quitting."

"Ah, you never know. There's people who take things different than they was intended."

"Just calling him Mr. Molloy."

"Well . . . yes." The word had an experimental ring, as though Mary had just stumbled on the possibility of not telling the truth.

And so it came out that the gardener hadn't liked being sent into the greenhouse on rainy days. It made him feel that he was being kept on as a charity.

"But he was coughing all the time. He might have had pneumonia."

"He was a bit chesty."

"So if I'd left him out it might have killed him, and when I brought him in, he was offended."

"Mr. Hamilton had him paint the kitchen, was what he said."

Alice nodded. They were moving onto familiar ground. Once, perhaps, he had painted the kitchen. Even Mary ought to remember what the kitchen had been like in the winter: the little girls

196

playing, clotheslines everywhere, smuts flying from the Imperial Iron at every stoking. Think of the reasonable complaints of a painter in that situation, and of everyone else.

No, she couldn't have held onto him, whatever she had done. But he might have left in a different way. He could have given her a few pointers at least. Just how did you cover the ground with this lawn mower? The reel couldn't be more than ten inches across, and with the way the grass bent out away from it, she wasn't gaining much more than six inches on every lap. And what about the kitchen garden? Would things just grow where they were, or would they need transplanting?

He probably objected to her tomatoes too.

"Ah, no," Mary said, when she mentioned it. "He said he might be coming back in August to see how they grow. But"—Mary hesitated a moment—"he did speak of the little girls."

"Oh, now, Mary. They didn't bother him. I know that for a fact. I warned them dozens of times."

"Oh, he said you did. 'Come on out of that, she says, and don't be aggerating *Mr.* Molloy,' he says. 'You'd think I had a disease,' he says."

"You mean he wanted to be bothered?"

"Ah, he was an old man, and his grandchildren's all in England. 'It's too quiet here,' he says, 'days would go by and you wouldn't see a car in the lane.'"

"But he said he liked the peace and quiet."

"You know how it is."

She shook her head. She didn't know how it was. She didn't even know where she stood with Mary. "You wouldn't just take your card and leave without saying anything, would you, Mary?"

"Oh, no. I wouldn't leave the girls."

"I was only trying to be decent," she told Rafferty.

"I know, but you are a bit of a hairpin sometimes."

197

"What does that mean?"

"Nothing," he said and squeezed her hand so that she winced at the pain of her broken blisters.

There were two rooms in the gate lodge, a large one and a small bedroom. The furnishings were somebody's cast-offs, and included no overlooked antiques. A fine sawdust shimmered in the empty drawers. "Woodworm," said Mary, who had come along since there had been no telling what they might find. But the only thing, besides the furniture, was a huge pile of newspapers in one corner of the bedroom, a pile almost as big as the bed itself.

There was no kitchen, just a small scullery—sink and shelves and a shaving mirror over the sink. The toilet was in its own room, so small that the window had set the plumber a problem and he had had to place the tank at right angles, high on the side wall. There was no room for a hand basin, to say nothing of a bathtub.

There was no stove either. "He'd use the fire," said Mary, pointing to the blackened kettle on one of the little swing grates.

"Let's get it cleaned out for the new man then."

"Should I wash the curtains?"

Alice looked at them. "No, don't touch them." One good shake might finish them off, and they were damask so starch would be useless. Perhaps she would be able to get new curtains for the drawing room before the Steichens came, and then she would bring those faded chintz strips out here.

Alice left Mary and the girls there and went back to the orchard. She had to keep the grass down until they found a new gardener, and there would be more to that than just getting the lodge dusted. ". . . £3–10–0 per week to the gardener as furnished by the owner . . ." was what the lease said, and so she had written to Mr. Hamilton, telling him that his man had just picked up his card and walked out.

She wasn't going to Mrs. Redmond for a gardener. In fact, she

198

wasn't sure that Mrs. Redmond was unconnected with the man's departure. There was nothing that she could put a finger on, except that, as she remembered it later, there had been something *funny* about the way Mrs. Redmond had asked, "How are you keeping?" on the Monday morning when she should have known that the gardener had gone.

Unless Mr. Hamilton produced another gardener, she would have to run an ad. She couldn't ask O'Connor to help, not after the bag. Mary had said that she would ask around, but they wouldn't count on that.

Mary was hurrying across the lawn now with the two little girls. Something was up, she guessed, and they all wanted to tell her. Mary easily outdistanced the others.

"They was a bathtub," she said, triumphantly.

"We found a bathtub," said Stella, panting up like a fat puppy.

"I saw it first," said Vanessa, coming up last. "Come and see it, Mama."

So she went back to the lodge with them, and there, in the corner of the bedroom, enough of the newspapers had been removed to disclose a boxed-in fir base and the top of a bathtub, and on the wall above, a single faucet, giving it a one-eyed look. A cold bath in a cold room, no wonder it had been used as a box for old newspapers. Poor old Danny.

Alice had waked at four, at five, at six, permanently that time. Before seven she got up as quietly as she could, afraid that the girls would hear her and start banging doors and thumping on the stairs. Rafferty had been sleeping badly, with his forehead drawn into a frown. She had noticed it even before the night he disposed of the bag.

She tiptoed past the little girls' room where they were lying twisted in their sheets, while the blankets lay on the floor. In the drawing room, already warm with the morning sun, she dressed.

At that time of the day the room was almost furnished by the sunshine. A rug would have been enough to finish it, the right rug, oriental, a rug with a life of its own.

It wasn't impossible: you bought one from an auctioneer and had him sell it again when you left. Frank might be persuaded to advance them their passage home and they could invest it in the rug. They would have it all summer, not just for the Steichens.

The view was best in the morning, too. Twice, once for certain, in the sidelong rays of the sun she had seen a furry purple line at the horizon, almost certainly the mountains of Wales. She hadn't wanted to wake Rafferty, whose eyes were much better at distances.

This morning there was only the mailboat, closing in on the harbor, its sound lost in the distance. What she heard was the rattle of the milk float, harness and empty bottles jangling as the milkman hurried in the streets and lanes below theirs. There would be no shops to supply this morning, and once the full bottles were on the front steps he would have the rest of the holiday to himself.

Closer to the house, the hedges were softening, growing almost visibly hour by hour. She liked it better than the shaved precision of a few weeks before. If the fine weather continued, though, she would soon have yards and yards of hedge to cut, a good furlong of hedge, she figured, and most of it a ladder job. Even the grass was getting ahead of her. She should have left the hand clipping until she had finished the mowing. The grass was almost too high for the mower, and she didn't know how you went about finding a man with a scythe—though that might be one of those things, like chimney sweeping or seaweed, for which there was a regular demand. It was something she should have found out before this interminable holiday weekend began.

At least Rafferty would be home for the day, and if he did the mowing, and she carried on with the hand clipping, they might finish the worst part of the job, the front and side lawns, those big stretches where it was mostly a question of marching back and forth, cutting six-inch swathes, a kind of cross-country typing.

No POINT IN LOOKING FOR WHALES TODAY, RAFFERTY THOUGHT, standing in the drawing room window. The holiday makers were already out below, tiny dots in the boats, which veered around the bay as landlubbers fought with the oars. Fogarty didn't think he would ever see a whale. Porpoise, he said, when Rafferty said they had been seen.

Just beneath him the front lawn rippled in the wind. That was going to be his holiday, pushing the mower. Alice was no good, trimming around the tree trunks with a pair of shears when they needed a four-horse reaper to get going on the lawns. It was too bad about the gardener, but she had resented the man from the beginning and had simply resented him out of their lives. No one could tell her, and he wouldn't try.

Still holding his last cup of the breakfast tea and the morning papers, he moved to the chair and sat down cautiously.

The paper seemed thin. He was probably lucky to have one at all, considering the way holidays were getting out of hand. People no longer seemed to be celebrating anything, except another day off the shrinking work week: Columbus Day, Labor Day, and here bank holidays like this one, Whit *Monday*—as though you needed two days for Pentecost, the Holy Ghost descending, like volcanic ash, for forty-eight hours. How many of them down there even knew they were celebrating the fiftieth day of Easter?

Saturday a man in the hotel game had told him that he liked an early Whit. "A late Easter and an early Whit, that would be the perfect year for us."

"You don't get too many of them," Rafferty said.

"No," said the hotel man, and *he* wasn't being funny, "not more than one in fifteen years, I'd say."

He could hardly bear to think of the tweed that was being lost today, two hundred and some yards that could have been woven if each man had been working at anything like his best rate. He had thought that he could have made his own rounds at least, but everywhere he was told, "Oh, Monday's *Whit*, Mr. Rafferty." He wasn't asking them to weave, just to hand over a piece of tweed and take in a fresh beam.

Now he would have to put in a double day tomorrow, or copy the laundry man, who ordinarily picked up their work on Monday and had left notice that he would skip them entirely the coming week. There had been very little pick-up and delivery in his own rounds lately. Traveling pep sessions was more like it. He would dust off the lay, blow the grit out of the warp, and try to leave the men sitting at the loom. They remembered too well how he had sold them the job, telling them that a weaver's work was something they could pick up and put down.

Sometimes he blamed the bogs, where the men kept playing around with what looked a lot like block forts. *Turn-foots, castles, rickles, lumps, clamps,* Fogarty said they were, traditional piles for wind drying and curing the fuel. Be that as it may, he didn't think they would be built in quite as leisurely a fashion if the men had to work in the rain.

Already May had set some kind of record for sun. "We'll pay for it later, you'll see," people said. But Fogarty had been telling him something hopelessly technical about the Azores anti-cyclone. "It wouldn't surprise me if this went right on up to the equinox."

September, Rafferty thought, May, June, July, August. The summer of the decade, of the century, after everyone had told him he was a fool to go to Ireland where he wouldn't see the sun for weeks at a time.

He looked for the bright side and tried to think of traveling around to all the places he had promised himself and Alice, seeing Tara in the sunshine, Inishmore and Inishmaan in the sunshine, Coole and Kilfenora and the Macgillycuddy's Reeks while the sun shone, and all his bright plans went glimmering. He wasn't losing two hundred yards just today. He was losing two hundred yards every day the sun shone.

He thought of Frank's last letter. *From where I sit, it looks like production there is actually falling.* That was what he got for having the figures sent on with no comment and hoping that Frank might not compare them with the last.

Barring a miracle, a monsoon, say, there was going to be a further fall. Tweed, it seemed, was a seasonal product, and they were moving into the off season. (But when was the "on" season?) He would point out to Frank how they were cutting expenses: fuel and electric light, and, when he changed his rounds to alternate weeks, petrol too. It would be impossible to keep Mick on, new wife or not. Production would continue at a slower pace, he could tell Frank, and in the fall, with a season's experience behind them, the men would really get cracking.

He had done everything he could—within reason. He would be a fool to think that just because something had to be done, he must do it himself, willy-nilly.

But perhaps he would be a bigger fool to think that one man could do nothing.

"WHAT TIME WILL YOU BE HOME?" SHE CALLED TO RAFFERTY, AS HE loped down to the gate.

"Oh, I don't know," he said, turning back to her. "About dinnertime." And he was gone.

Damn. Could he have forgotten he had offered to help with the lawn today? Nobody would be at the shop, and the weavers didn't want him to come around. What was he going to do? Brood and smoke and drink tea? Plan some vast campaign? NRA blue eagles, a big thermometer in front of the shop, Captain Midnight pins for the kiddies whose daddies turned out the yardage, and a weekend in Blackpool for the champion weaver and his wife?

What about the boss and his wife? She could just hear herself talking about her trip to Ireland. The Emerald Isle. That's the grass, lush green grass. It grows chiefly in lawns, front lawns, side lawns, and orchards, also between herbaceous borders and graveled walks in narrow strips where the gravel plays hell with the blades of the lawn mower. (Can we have that slide of the mower now?)

Sometimes she wondered if she still understood Rafferty. She had always thought that the weaving was secondary, a means of getting to Ireland, away from Oakley. Now here he was, spending the pleasantest day of the year in that rundown alley of his, as if the price of the trip to Ireland were to see nothing of Ireland.

ALL WINTER LONG HE HAD WATCHED WHILE THE MEN WERE BEING trained and had never thought of weaving himself. It hadn't looked particularly difficult, mostly a matter of keeping your wits about you, he thought as he drove toward town.

He had his half of the road to himself, with nothing ahead but an empty bus, barreling along to the beginning of its run back out the crowded half of the road, where the queues were long and still cheerful, family groups with folding prams and bagfuls of seaside gear.

He didn't have a clear picture of what he was going to do: weave, of course, but he was counting on more than his own production to make it worthwhile, intangible things like his example to the men in the shop (to Tommy, that is; Mick was getting his notice in the morning), his closer rapport with the weavers.

It was too bad he hadn't had the idea a few days earlier. He might have already spent Saturday afternoon and all day Sunday on the job. As it was, he had a hard day in front of him if he wasn't to sit down to the loom amid a chorus of guffaws the next morning.

After the first few minutes at the loom, his confidence began to sag a little. If he didn't pull the shuttle cord hard enough, the shuttle would die before it reached the edge, and he would have to reach in and pull it out. And if he gave it a real jerk, a greater temptation for him, the shuttle would hit the stone so hard that it bounced back a few inches into the warp, from which it had to be retrieved, the slack rewound on the bobbin, and then sent properly on its way, remembering, of course, to switch the heddles. No, to pull the lay forward, and then change the heddles. It reminded him a lot of a humiliating day he had once spent with a rod and reel. (And he still didn't see what was so unspeakable about catching a black bass by the tail, especially since neither of his two instructors had caught anything, by either end.)

At the first really noticeable mistake he decided to unweave a thread or two, and found himself in serious trouble. By the time he decided to move on, he had aggravated the original wayward thread into a sizable flaw, one he wouldn't care to have Tommy or Mick come upon in the morning, assuming they noticed anything. Fortunately, he had a lot of time. The important thing was not to panic and rush at the work—remembering, of course, not to relax so much that the shuttle wasn't sent hard enough.

By late afternoon the original flaw had been carried down onto the beam and out of sight. As far as you could see now the entire length of the tweed was his own work. He didn't think that any man last winter could have done as well on his first day. But they had had Thady or Ned standing right behind them, to catch them with a shout of "lay" or "heddles," or to help them pull out a thread or two without scrabbling up the whole surface. This might not occur to anyone just looking at his finished piece of tweed, nor would they be sure to notice that he had been doing almost successive runs of twelve, fifteen, or even twenty perfect threads.

He went to the pantry and made himself a pot of tea and found a few of Brian's ginger nuts in the cupboard. He drank the tea slowly, standing there beside the sink. Out the window the thorn tree, which had bloomed, was in full leaf, hiding the bedsprings

205

and broken sink which had dominated the view all winter long. He had never seen those houses from the front. From the back it required resolute imagination to see the one-time elegance. Small wooden rooms, jutting out like opened drawers, had been added on, probably for bathrooms. Two of the houses were buttressed—propped, in fact—by enormous beams flying well out into the gardens. Their window sills were their larders. He didn't want to know any more.

He felt much better after the tea and he left the pantry, telling himself to look at the over-all effect and forget about the individual faults. A mistake. The individual faults were minor, the over-all effect was awful.

He sat down again and began to work, very slowly, very carefully. His right arm, raised to pull the shuttle cord, made him think of Joshua, who had kept the Lord on his side as long as he had held his shield aloft, but hadn't he had someone to help hold his arm for him after the first few hours?

At ten o'clock he quit. His efficiency was declining fast. He had no choice but to cut off his cloth, together with the fifty yards or so that remained from the other men's lessons. As soon as it was off the loom he realized that he had no place in the shop to put it. He threw the tweed, beam and all, into the back of the car, and drove off, feeling more tired than he could remember. His long row with the bag had been only a pleasant outing compared to this.

As he drove home, against the traffic again, he saw that he had solved nothing by removing the beam. If he left it in the car, he would just be bringing it back to the shop in time, doubly interesting for being out of its proper place. The garage in the village was hopeless, rusty corrugated sheeting and a mud floor, and he certainly couldn't carry the cloth and beam up the hill in his present condition. Even the walk up unladen was almost too much to think of.

He had to take the chance of running up the lane with the car, straddling a rut and hoping for the best. At least it was dry.

ALICE HAD A LOT OF QUESTIONS TO ASK RAFFERTY AT BREAKFAST. When she had heard a car, coming up the lane and right into the forecourt, she naturally hadn't thought of their own car, only of the Guards with bad news about Rafferty or even the IRA coming to get their bag, O'Connor's not having wanted to tell them how they had lost it—while the gatehouse lay unmanned. Rafferty hadn't explained anything, just said, "Is there anything to eat?" and started to fix himself a drink while she went down to the kitchen.

As she dished up the vegetables she felt they underlined the situation better than words, the long wait for his late arrival. He made her feel a little guilty about that though, when he just pushed the potatoes and carrots to one side without saying anything. He looked tired—not that she wasn't tired herself after a day with the lawn mower.

"How about a nice, fresh omelette for dessert?" she asked him. "You have to eat something. Or did you have a big lunch?"

"No. No lunch. No omelette, thank you, and don't bother about the coffee," he said and went up to bed without even asking her to lock up.

She was giving him plenty of time to bring up the matter himself this morning.

"Wasn't it wonderful yesterday?" she said. "There must have been fourteen hours of sunshine, at least."

Rafferty nodded.

"More than the whole month of December."

"I don't doubt it," he said bitterly. She hadn't known he had been that hurt by the dark winter.

"I finished the mowing."

"Good."

He was moving stiffly, as though he were bruised, or had a hangover, but she was positive that he hadn't been drinking before he came home. He was often brusque in the morning, not naturally an early riser. She had learned to take care with his breakfast, and by his second cup of tea, he was usually himself. It was going to take longer this morning. She waited for him.

And then, when he should have been pouring himself a third cup to take upstairs with the newspaper, he just rose and said good-by.

He went out the door, and she went downstairs with the breakfast tray. Perhaps he would be in a better mood when he came home. In the kitchen she was surprised to hear footsteps above, in the music room, it seemed, and a minute later the car drove off. On her way upstairs she opened the door and looked inside. With only the couch and the piano remaining there, it didn't take her long to find the other object, a weaver's beam, a full one.

So Rafferty had gone on his rounds after all. But why bring the beam in here? The cloth didn't look right, she thought; even unfinished tweed ought to have been smoother. She unrolled a few feet for a better look. Poor Rafferty. If that was what he was getting from the weavers it was no wonder he didn't want to talk about it.

She went down the hill to the shops then. The double holiday had left her pantry almost bare. Even someone with a refrigerator and no mouse problem would have found it difficult to stock ahead. Most women were shopping meal by meal, so whenever you ordered two or three of anything it was usually assumed that you meant one. But in a place where any mention of the future was always accompanied by a "God willing" or "Please God," improvidence might be no more than a knock on wood.

When she returned home she found a truck up in the forecourt of the house. It was an ancient, high-riding model, with a home-

208

made box cobbled onto the back, at about the height of some fresh gouges in the sandy concrete of Mr. Hamilton's balusters.

She glanced into the almost empty box and then ran up the steps to the house. The door of the music room was shut. She opened it and looked in, crossed the hall and looked into the dining room, even though she now knew where she had to look.

Rafferty was up in the drawing room with a little man in a beret, and on the floor lay the dismantled loom. The room looked like an attic.

"It's only for a little while," Rafferty said when he saw her, "just until production picks up. It's not permanent."

17.

RAFFERTY HAD COME CLOSE TO ABANDONING THE WHOLE PROJECT IN the morning. His back ached, his arms, even his jaw ached, from the tension. He considered not shaving, thought better of it, and after a few swipes, wondered what Alice would say if he asked her to finish the job. With every movement of his arms he felt the muscles of his back rend apart, layer by layer. He should have been bleeding somewhere. He thought of St. Blaise, his back flayed by a carding comb, and therefore the patron of wool workers—a logical development, considering that St. Catherine was the patron of wheelwrights and St. Sebastian the patron of archers.

He had been insane, he told himself. What difference could one man make? If anyone noticed the empty loom he would say that he had taken the cloth to see if he could salvage enough to make skirts for his wife and the little girls.

After breakfast he carried the beam quietly into the music room to leave until he had time to examine it. He didn't want to explain anything. He left then, without stopping to read the paper. If he couldn't weave himself, at least he could give Mick his notice. Now that he was certain he had to do it, the sooner he did it the better, and for Mick too. Now, at the beginning of the summer, was the time to start looking for a new job. The first thing they knew they would be hearing that he was expecting to become a father.

He acted as soon as he reached the shop, unable to help himself —and gave Tommy his notice. A few minutes later Mick's complacent tones of commiseration carried upstairs to Rafferty. He felt the utter folly of what he had done and saw the summer stretching ahead with Mick lounging in the room below, thinking he had pulled it off, that talking was, after all, everything.

Good Lord, the man should be told that merit hadn't entered into it. Social justice perhaps (producing injustice), pity.

He went downstairs then, determined that if Mick said a single word he would have his notice as well. But no one said anything, and he turned and walked out the door in an unnatural silence, his spine prickling, as though he expected a spear from behind.

He found a man who would take his van anywhere for three pounds, and they brought the loom home. He hadn't been back to the shop a dozen times since. Once a day he gave Brian a ring, and Saturday morning he went in (or sent Alice) to deliver the pay packets and to check on the week's progress, mostly "Maintenance," since very few of the beams were being finished these days.

Most of the yarn had been packed away in brown paper and paradichlorobenzine, this after he had given chase to a pair of clothes moths. (They holed up in a crack, which he set Brian to watch while he went out and found that a Flit gun was called a *syringe.*)

They were painting now, whitewash on the walls and ceilings and white enamel on the bins and other woodwork. That took care of the overlaps, and the solid white was least likely to affect

211

the appearance of colored yarns. The stove had been removed from the room, to keep it clean, he had said, thinking of explosions. Brian was to stay fifteen minutes after Mick every night and put all the combustibles into closed biscuit tins. Still it wasn't possible to think of everything, and he daily expected to hear of some unforeseen catastrophe.

Alice had looked a little shocked when she had first seen the loom in the drawing room, but they hadn't been using the room for anything else. It was an ideal place for weaving. In some of the cottages the loom took up most of the one room they had for sitting, eating, and cooking; he wasn't surprised that the wives were sometimes snappish about the arrangement. Here, instead of appearing cluttered, the room seemed to be furnished by the presence of the loom, and Alice now spent her evenings there, knitting or sewing quietly in one of the windowseats. The loom made just enough noise to inhibit normal conversation.

"Do you know there are hundreds of little apples and pears down there?" she asked when he paused to change the bobbin.

"Let's hope they get ripe." This weather should be good for that anyway.

"Do you think they should be sprayed?"

"I don't think so." Too much would be involved in that. "I think it's supposed to be done when they're in the blossom."

"We'll leave it then."

He wasn't sure that so much gardening was a good thing. She was getting leathery from the sun. And he wished she would finish the sweater she was knitting, one of those fisherman's jerseys, twelve different stitches in it, with names like ear-of-wheat, blackberries, and honeycomb, a real *tour de force,* as overdone as a baroque suit of armor. It crept toward completion, unmistakably his size. Could anyone be sufficiently grateful? An impartial observer, looking at the two of them there, would have to conclude that weaving was the superior way of making a fabric.

He was a damned good weaver, even if he said so himself.

212

Sheer, dogged persistence had carried him through the first painful weeks, but he had been a good basketball player, and as he mastered the moves that went into the job, he found a flare for it, putting in the extra fraction of an inch that turned his movements into a relaxed glide, instead of a tense bit of mincing. Some men would never learn that. The work was hard on them and hard on the looms.

He could keep at it for twelve hours a day and was already turning out his two pieces a week, the only man in the business on full production. He made his rounds on Sundays, telling the men why it was the only time of the week he was free. He picked up a piece now and then. Even Thady and Ned weren't turning out much. As far as inspiration and example went, his weaving was a failure. But as long as the sun shone and kept the others from their looms, he would go on weaving, an action that might count for a lot more than was immediately apparent.

MR. HAMILTON'S ANSWER HAD COME WITH JUST ENOUGH DELAY TO have given him time to inquire into the situation, she guessed. "As I am unable to arrange my affairs to come over during the next few months, I expect you'll be in a much better position to pick up a man," he wrote. And then he went on for a while about the leak around the skylight. "Are you quite sure that the window is *closed?* The catch there is a bit dicky." The "catch" had been a brown string, wrapped around two nails until Rafferty had fixed that with a threepenny hook and eyescrew. As long as it didn't rain everything was fine. At the end of his letter he returned to the other problem. "If you should prove unable, for any reason, to find a gardener, we'll have to ask that you add what would have been his wages (£45–10–0 per quarter) to the rent to offset the depreciation of the grounds."

He could *ask* all right, but that was as far as he would get. "Gardener, as furnished by the landlord," was what the lease said.

213

He had outfoxed himself there, protecting himself against their replacing his first-class man with some cut-rate substitute, wanting a finger in the pie if it ever came to replacement. He had just forgotten to notice the date on the calendar, the century. Bluff—and the visit to Ireland was more bluff.

She had given up on the ad. Maybe at the end of summer, when things slackened, she could get a gardener to come in and clean up the place, clip the hedges. Next year she would advertise ahead of the rush, in February (if they didn't have to return for the second semester). She couldn't carry it alone for another year.

It had been an exceptional June. You heard it everywhere, a wonderful year for hay—but not for someone who just wanted to get the grass cut and carried back to the compost heap. The hedge was a fog of green, darkening the lower half of the house. The kitchen garden, despite the vigor of the weeds, was doing wonderfully. Molloy had done a good job of planting it. The peas came up, climbed the peasticks, bloomed, and bore. The scarlet runners emerged just at the edge of the wire mesh, which was now a picture in red and green.

"There should be strawberry netting," Mary said one day, and they rummaged in the steds until they found it. The blackbirds kept up a patrol at the edges, finding any loose spot to crawl under. Once in, they raised hell with the berries and forgot where they had come in. More than once she was able to free a bird only by cutting the net, which then had to be sewn again. A couple of the birds had been so badly wounded by the time they were discovered that she got Mary to kill them. She buried them herself and said nothing to Rafferty, since you couldn't see the back garden from the drawing room.

Upstairs all day the loom pounded, as the brassbound shuttle slammed across between blocks of Connemara marble in a rhythm so regular that she now noticed it only when Rafferty stopped to drop in a new bobbin. Occasionally she would be

214

aware of a vague uneasiness in the air, and then she would realize that she was waiting to hear the loom, and that Rafferty must have been tying on a new warp.

They ate upstairs in the drawing room. She had suggested it herself, although it made two flights of stairs to carry the trays. It was easier than making ready in the dining room and then going up to persuade Rafferty to come down and eat. She was sorry not to be using the dining room, now that heat was no problem. With the drawing room a complete shambles, the dining room was all that was left of what the house had once been.

In six weeks the Steichens would come, and there was no sign as yet that Rafferty's temporary use of the drawing room would ever end. It was impossible to imagine his stopping as he had started. There was no reason, though, why the loom couldn't go down into the music room. There would be plenty of room for it if they just got the couch out. They could take it out while they had men in the house to move the loom. A big piece like the couch would help the drawing room a lot. If they couldn't get the oriental rug (she had mentioned the matter of advancing them their return fare to Frank without going into it with Rafferty, but had had no answer yet), she had seen some very nice jute carpeting. A dark brown would go well with all the white. They might buy it with what they were saving on expenses: the gardener's wages, on coal, on the vegetables and fruits from the garden.

The curtains would be more of a problem than the rug, they would take something over thirty yards of cloth. But Rafferty could weave them in a day and a half easily, even if he had to tie off and on a new warp. Gold curtains. At the moment she didn't care to suggest it.

There were times when she believed that he thought he could do the work of the dozen weavers. There was no end to his day. The little girls were lulled by the sound of the loom and fell asleep earlier than they had done in the lengthening days of spring. After

215

her day in the yard only her knitting kept her awake, a complicated pattern that you couldn't relax with. Long after it was dark in the hedge-smothered lawns below, the room with its white walls and the three huge windows remained lighted by the bright sky. Rafferty wove until she could hardly see him. He wouldn't have a light. It drew the bugs, he said, and the bats. There were no screens and, with the windows shut, the room would have been stiffling from the heat of the slates above. Sometimes it would be eleven before he dropped the last empty bobbin in the box and came over beside her.

They would stand together, looking out at the lighthouses and the fires which had started in the bracken and gorse beside the railroad tracks.

"Poor Alice," he said, "it's not quite what I promised you."

"I'm all right, but you ought to go outside into the sun for a while. You're getting to look peculiar." At first she had been happy to see the fat melting. Some had turned to muscle, some just went, leaving the bones.

"You've got to watch the sun," he said, "you'll get cancer of the skin. And why don't you wear gloves when you work in the garden?"

"It makes everything take longer. Listen, Rafferty, come outside tomorrow, right after breakfast, just for half an hour. It's beautiful then."

"It's turning brown, drying up. Two, three more weeks and it'll look like New Mexico."

"Oh, now."

"These people don't know what to do about the sunshine. They just lie around like lizards. It never occurred to anyone here to come out of the sun."

"Shall I get your beer?" she asked to change the subject.

"All right," he said and went to put a few blocks of turf on his fire, another thing he wasn't going to be logical about.

216

Every night, after dinner she would set the beer in the larder window, in a shallow pan of water, with a damp cloth wrapped around the bottles. It didn't work as well as the theory behind it, but it was cooler than the air.

He would go down and sit in the library for an hour or two, reading the morning papers, drinking the beer, smoking, listening to the singers on the German radio stations after the BBC had closed down for the night. She went to bed. He might insist on outstaying the sun at night, but it quietly got a four- or five-hour start on him every morning.

It was now officially a drought, thirty days without rainfall, according to the morning paper. Somewhere in Cavan, the rails, heated beyond the expectations of a hundred years' experience, had expanded, buckled, and thrown a locomotive over into the bog, where it was photographed lying like an upturned hippo.

She almost hated to see the papers coming, with stories headed: HOTTEST SUMMER EVER? or a picture captioned: *Not the Riviera, but the scene at Killiney Strand in yesterday's record sunshine.* Could Rafferty's reaction be any worse if he were to find a neatly scissored hole instead? Once she picked up a copy of Bede's *Ecclesiastical History* that Rafferty had bought, and coming on his description of the languid Irish climate, stuffed the book out of sight in the pile of newspapers beneath the windowseat.

For days now she had been watering the vegetables, laboriously, with a pair of Peter Rabbit watering cans, one filling beneath the tap while she carried the other. She might have bought a hose, if hoses had been available and if there had been a faucet with a threaded tap. Fortunately the lawns had stopped growing or she would never have had the time and energy for the watering. At the moment the mowing seemed to have been the easier job.

The gorse fires burnt day and night, and one by one the mountains turned black, while upstairs Rafferty's fire still burnt, a few live coals in the orange ash. "Keeps out the damp," he said, and she didn't bother to answer that.

"There's one of my weavers," he said, "his fire's been burning for over a hundred years, ever since the Famine."

She could see the point in that, the desire to keep any series unbroken, even a tradition like the drawing room fire that was only a few months old. (But what a place for it. You couldn't keep a turf fire in a basket grate, so he had built it on the floor, beneath the grate.)

She saw no reason, however, to keep the Imperial Iron going, and there would have been some point to that for it was their only source of hot water. She found herself thinking of the gas again, the stove and a small gas hot water heater, too.

She got on the phone, waited for the free line (a wait she now believed had no purpose beyond discouraging callers), got her man, and stayed quiet until the end of the usual assurances, and then said simply that if the stove wasn't in before the week was out, the whole thing was off. She didn't care how American she sounded.

THE SUN HAD BEEN SHINING EVERY DAY FOR TWO WEEKS, THIRTY-ONE days without rain, an official drought, the papers assured him. It seemed to Rafferty that no one else thought the situation was worth worrying about. On Sunday he had gone a full round of the weavers, who were all smiling their heads off at the weather, and didn't have a single piece of cloth for him. His own two and a fourth pieces were Rafferty's Woollens entire production for the week.

It was no longer a question of a finger in the dike. He was holding back the full force of the flood. If his loom were to stop, then every loom in Leinster would be silent—silent as the harp

218

that once through Tara's halls? He couldn't believe it wouldn't be significant.

It wasn't the passing of manpower that he would regret, not the pull that sent the shuttle in front of him some four hundred times a yard. He wasn't prepared to fall in behind every banner that said *Handmade*. Things like the flail and the winnowing basket, the laborious, itchy process of hand threshing, could disappear with his blessing. But the tweed, this wiry, heathery mist, or the checks as subtle as the pattern of the hill fields, it was worth fighting for.

It made sense too. He could produce, economically, as little as a ten-yard length to order, while Frank would have hundreds of yards tied up in the innards of his monster before the first yard emerged at the end of the line.

They were hearing less from Frank lately about the new machinery, as though he realized that his talk of how many yards an hour they would be producing wasn't encouraging anyone to greater production. He shouldn't be too hard on Frank, though. Without Frank there would have been no Irish venture, and even the American mill owed its life to him.

There had been a time when the mill could have been bought for back taxes. The only business left for Frank and his father had been carding quilt batts, mostly for farmers. They had gone around the state to drum up business, taking chickens and pigs, anything in payment, once a bushel of navy beans, bags of hazel nuts, sour cream butter.

In the middle of those bad years he had graduated from high school. Oakley had offered him a scholarship: books, tuition, and a table-waiting job that fed him and gave him enough cash to buy an overcoat.

There were maybe two hundred in the school then, including the girls. Football had been strictly amateur, and it took a doctor's certificate to stay off the squad, the Oaks. They worked at basket-

219

ball, though, and weren't too bad at it. (That, rather than scholastic standing, had been behind his own scholarship.)

He took the required Freshman History, and one day that first autumn, a smoky, red and gold day when class attention was low, Mr. Booth said, "Your father is a weaver, is he not, Mr. Rafferty?"

"He owns a run-down, shut-down mill, if that's what you mean," said the young Rafferty, who knew only one thing for sure —that he was going to have nothing to do with wool or milling.

"Weaving," said Mr. Booth, paying no attention to the reply, "is the second oldest form of manufacture."

Weapon Maker, he wrote on the blackboard. "Hammers, axes, spears, knives, skin scrapers. You carry on from there." He drew a line then. Rafferty could still see him holding the chalk sideways to make the line as broad as possible. "Up there we have the first man who is not ape, the toolmaker, and below is civilized man." *Weaver,* he wrote.

There was a hand waving over near the window, one of those self-sufficient girls he had never liked. When she got Mr. Booth's attention she asked, "And what about the potter?"

"Ah, yes," he said. "The potter and the ubiquitous potsherd, the means by which we date almost all archaeological finds."

She nodded, wooden beads tinkling.

"I think you'll find that the origins of pottery lie in basketry, which is, in fact, weaving."

One for our side, thought the young Rafferty, before he remembered that it wasn't his side.

There was a lot to it, although he wouldn't pretend now that the classification would hold water. And it was possible that its real purpose had been to snare him, a substitute for Old Booth's son who was perfectly happy selling shoes somewhere. It was never clear whether Booth's interest in weaving had come before or after Rafferty had signed on as a history major.

For four years he had followed the old man, through the regular courses, and through others in the upper division that had seldom appeared outside the catalogue, just the two of them sitting there some afternoons, hours past all bells and nowhere near the advertised matter of the course.

The history of the weaver—what else could have turned over so many furrows in the whole field of history? Once clothes meant more than the unassimilated skins of animals and leaves of plants, society was unavoidable. The first weaver of wool had had to become a nomadic herdsman with a tribal organization large enough to assure grazing rights and protection from pillage, a life such as Abraham knew. The weaver of cotton and linen presupposed the farmer, with fixed abode and laws of land tenure and inheritance, even irrigation, a people like the Egyptians. And after that Booth found the weaver's hand in everything: in Joseph's coat of many colors, Penelope at her loom, Solomon's valiant woman weaving her fine linen; in the swaddling clothes and the Holy Shroud; the candidate in his white toga, the archbishop in his lambswool pallium; silk from the Orient, the Woolsack in England, the Field of Gold Cloth, the weavers carrying heresy from the Low Countries, the *Drapier's Letters*. And then the spinning jenny, the power loom, the cotton gin, and the cotton towns of Lancashire, houses back to back and black with soot; a wilderness despoiled for Hudson's Bay blankets; a continent where cotton cloth bought ivory and slaves (to grow more cotton); the islands where the missionaries came with God and the Mother Hubbard and laid waste a stable society. Savagery to savagery, with the weavers in the van. And if Booth had the cart before the horse now and then, at least he got where he was going.

For a while then Rafferty thought that he would go on into the mill after all, work with his father and brother on the kind of woolens that his grandfather had made, but even before Frank had landed the first of the army contracts that had set them on their feet again, he knew that he had no choice but to be an historian.

He was never hooked on the past itself, though Booth had ten-

221

dencies that way—his goose-quill pens, cut with his own penknife, real ink sprayers. It was their only disagreement. For Rafferty history was the idea of continuity, the ebb and flow of a tidal river, the progression from cause to effect, the order that appeared, finally, in the retelling of the events.

He wasn't the only one at the University who had come from what some of the others called Cow Colleges. He was the only one of them, though, who was still speaking of his origins after the Thanksgiving vacation. And in his last year there he had taken pleasure in turning away feelers from the sort of school that didn't have to be pointed out on the map for anyone.

He went back to Oakley full of plans. He had been reading his old journal shortly before they sailed, and had been surprised at the recollection of that first winter: he and Booth and Miss Bacon from the English Department and Mrs. Foley from Modern Languages, all of them burning with enthusiasm for their coordinated plan, a four-year course that would send the graduates out knowing who they were and where they came in—a corrective to the undergraduate conviction that this was *it*, the time and the place the whole world had been heading for all along.

Even President Simmers came close to enthusiasm. He told them to go ahead and bring him a new catalogue in the fall. Rafferty's journal, colored by his conviction that these burblings in the grass were the spring from which a mighty river would flow, trumpeted the news. And all the while, just beyond the next hillock lay Dr. Steichen.

And yet, perhaps he had been right, and when they were all far enough off, they would see that Dr. Steichen was not the mainstream, but one of those freak surges of water upstream, like the Great Severn Bore.

He still believed in Oakley, that the education he had received there by chance could be given by plan to hundreds more, even now. And in any case, he belonged there. There was no hope for

222

the world until men were again choosing to live where their grandfathers had lived.

One man could do anything. Here, out of his field, he was already weaving more cloth than Thady and Ned said was possible, but at a cost, he thought, looking out at the bright morning, that they would never consider paying.

Good Lord, what was that? It sounded like a horse on the stairs, with Alice's voice. After a point, outdoor work had a coarsening effect.

18.

The palm tree ought to have been flourishing. This was its kind of weather: dry, tropical air that didn't seem to depend on the strange orange sun daily looping around the horizon. The greenhouse stood open, doors and windows; Mary had climbed up into the cupola and forced open the vents there. The drooping tomatoes revived, but the tree, already crisp and brittle, continued to fade. Its water supply, between the floor of the greenhouse and the rock of the mountain, must have failed, and the tree's fat ironbound trunk left little room for water in the octagonal pot.

The vegetable garden, its very soil reconstructed through the years for easy drainage, cried for water too. The hedge, however, was growing like something in the jungles of Ceylon. The years of close clipping had left the root system to grow unchecked, storing its energy, biding its time, which had come.

She topped up the few ounces of water at the base of the palm tree. If it died Mr. Hamilton would blame it on the absence of a full-time gardener. How much compensation would he ask for it?

224

Ever since he had stumbled on the idea of claiming forty-five pounds and ten shillings per quarter for "depreciation," she had had her hands full. She assured him that she was putting in four to six hours a day on the garden and had everything under control, except the hedge, and she was getting a man for that. (He wasn't lined up yet. The ironmonger said that the only man he could think of had gone to Coventry and taken a job in the car plant there. The butcher suggested that she try Mrs. Redmond.) A *full-time gardener*, Mr. Hamilton kept writing. He must have found out that she would almost certainly have to offer five pounds a week, so that horticultural chaos and forty-five pounds ten for him would save her nearly twenty pounds a quarter, and who, in his view, would choose otherwise?

Well, if it came to an exchange of solicitor's letters, he wouldn't have a leg to stand on. But there was something he hadn't thought of yet, and when he did—The loose rattling noises that could only mean a car or a truck in the lane, pushed through into her consciousness. She dropped her watering can and hurried in to wash her hands. This time she would stay right there, making their tea if necessary. Today there would be no mysterious departure with only a badly filled trench and a few glowing coals in the brazier to show that they had come and gone.

The doorbell rang. "I'll get it, Mary."

She ran up from the basement and down the hallway toward the open door.

"Grand morning," said the man there. He was unmistakably wearing his gasman's uniform this time. "I've come for me bag."

She left him standing there and turned up the stairs, running, shouting, *"Rafferty!"*

"AND SO," RAFFERTY SAID, "WE'VE SEVERED OUR CONNECTION WITH the gas company. No supply, no bill."

"Ah, you was cute there, all right," said O'Connor.

"I wouldn't mention it to anyone else, you understand, we might have been a little out of line in our disposal methods too." O'Connor nodded. "I thought I owed it to you to tell you the whole story. I'm sorry for dragging you along that night."

"It was a grand outing, all the same."

"The question now is O'Reilley." He had no reason now to believe that O'Connor was in the IRA. "Where does O'Reilley fit in?"

"Mr. O'Reilley is me patron," said O'Connor.

"And what does that mean?"

"He sends me a bit every week."

"And do you pass it on to anyone else?"

"Well, there's the landlord and that crowd in Moore Street where I get me puddings and potatoes and cabbages." He paused. "And the public house, though there's not much left for that, mind you."

Rafferty believed that. O'Connor was drinking his pint like a man accustomed to making it last—or perhaps he thought he would have to buy a round if he finished it. "Drink up, I'll buy you another."

"That's kind of you."

"I owe you something for your help with the bag."

O'Connor shook his head. "I forgot the belt. Come around be the house and I'll give it to you."

"No, it's yours. I told you that." He hadn't got around to buying another, though, and he was wearing braces, a bad fit with that particular pair of trousers.

"The question is still the same," Rafferty said when they had fresh pints in front of them. "Why does O'Reilley send you the money?"

"Many's the time I've asked meself that very question. It could be for his sins."

Rafferty sighed. "How long has he been doing it?"

"It would be . . . five years now, since Tom Casey went to live

226

with the daughter in America. It's Tom's patron he was the first."

"Who's Tom Casey?"

"He's another man, same's meself. And he says to me, 'Johnnie, you've been good to me'—and I had, too."

"Yes, of course."

"Well, your man in America had been sending Tom a bit every week, and as Tom was going to America himself, he said he'd see that your man'd send it to me."

"Didn't it seem odd, though, that he wouldn't have the money sent on to his American address?"

"That's the very thing I said to him, not that I wasn't in need of the money meself, being on the dole, as it happened. And he says that the money has to go to Ireland. Your man doesn't care who he sends it to as long as he knows it's helping Ireland."

"And so this Tom Casey sent O'Reilley your address, and ever since then he's been sending the money to you every week, and that's all there is to it?" And O'Reilley would be hiding his charity under the guise of helping the IRA?

"Ah, no. There's the letters. There's quite a trick to the letters."

"His letters?"

"Me own letters to the man. You wouldn't want to say I, you'd want to say we, like the Pope. And you'd want to say how much Ireland thanked him for his help."

"I see," Rafferty said, but he was still in the dark.

"It's a queer class of letter he writes himself," O'Connor said, and took an envelope from his inner pocket. He removed a folded American bill from it and handed the envelope to Rafferty. "He always sends the same. The bank gives me three pounds ten for it." So it was a ten, quite a sum over the years.

It was a plain white dime-store envelope with Air Mail scrawled on it and no return address, probably O'Reilley's idea of secrecy, for the paper inside was his personal stationery, name, address, and shamrocks printed in green ink.

God Bless Ireland! he began. Then followed a stanza from

227

something: "Oh, the strangers came and tried to teach us their ways. . . ." *Galway Bay*, he would rather not have remembered the sound and sight of O'Reilley's singing that. That was all, just the stanza and the comment: *How true, but we must not relax under the so-called Free State.* Rafferty looked at the envelope again. *Irish Free State*, he hadn't noticed that. Did O'Reilley ever need a history lesson. *Yours for Ireland, "Pat" O'Reilley. Enc. 1.*

Out of his mind. "Always the same?"

"Same class of thing," said O'Connor. "Sometimes he puts in a lot of history. There was a long thing about Oliver Cromwell once. He'd have found it in some book, you could be sure, but I told him that he had a grand gift for speaking his ideas. It doesn't hurt a man to be decent."

"But he's never said *why* he's sending the money?"

"No. But he did say a queer thing last winter. He says he wasn't sending the money so that the Irish could lose in one generation the reputation for chivalry they'd had down through the ages. That's his exact, prejudicial words."

"And what did you say to that?"

"I didn't know what to say—not knowing what your man meant at all—so I told him that it was always the wild types that got into the newspapers and the most of us was as full of chivalry as ever."

"Sounds like a good answer."

"Oh, it was. He wrote that he was happy to hear that. But you know the man yourself."

"I think we have to believe him," he said to Alice. "If he'd known what the game was he wouldn't have been so quick to deny the IRA to O'Reilley's friends, which is what he thinks we are."

"And Mary had nothing to do with it at all."

"That goes without saying."

He looked down at his dinner, stew again, and the temperature couldn't be less than eighty. Iced tea and cucumber sandwiches, that was what he would have liked. He tried to remember when he had last seen an ice cube.

It was much worse in Dublin. The poorest people, who had no clothes closets but their own backs, unbuttoned and untied layer after layer, and moved in masses of tatters and in utter misery. The Liffey stank, the houses stank, and the dirt of the city was no longer endearing. It would take a week of rain, if not a frost, to restore the city.

"I'd like to know how it got started," Alice said, pouring him some tea. "O'Reilley and the IRA, I mean."

"It's not too hard to imagine," Rafferty said. He had given it quite a bit of thought on the way back from town. "Just think of him in Chicago or New York on one of his buying trips. If there's an Irish bar he'd be in it, and he'd get going on the six counties and wishing *he* could help. All you need is someone, maybe Casey's son-in-law, to get a bright idea and with a lot of hush-hush give him the 'secret' address of the IRA in Dublin where he can send them a dollar or two—and tip off the old man, in case O'Reilley remembered to do it in the morning. And then Casey somehow got him to put it on a regular basis."

"Serves him right—if he only knew that he's really doing good." Alice laughed.

"I don't like it."

"You don't like it? I can see not liking it when you think he's sending it to a pack of fanatics, but it's different when it's just a harmless old man."

"Different on this end. O'Reilley hasn't become a humanitarian. He's still what he thinks he is: a man who's paying to have a job done, whatever the means."

"All right, but you can't tell him he's not blowing up border posts because he'll stop sending the money, and O'Connor won't have anything to live on."

"Slow down," he said. Why couldn't she take an idea just as an idea? "I didn't say I was going to do anything."

229

"Well, there's just one thing I know for sure," Alice said, putting the dishes on the tray as though she were punishing them, "and I don't think I'd better say it."

He waited for her to say it, and when she didn't, said, "Go ahead."

"It's just that I won't have that dirty old man working around in my garden." She headed for the door with the tray.

"For God's sake, Alice, where did you get that idea?"

"From you."

"Me?" He tried to backtrack through everything he had said since he got home. "I said nothing, absolutely nothing like that."

"You said three pounds ten, and if that doesn't make you think of the gardener, I'd like to know what does."

He didn't dare laugh. "It doesn't. Not at all." He opened the door for her. "We're wired differently," he said and let her go out with the tray.

He shut the door and went over to the loom, thinking that there might be something in it, all the same.

After a few minutes at the loom he could see that there was no hope of making up for lost time; he wasn't even moving at his normal pace.

There was a lot of plain slog in weaving now that he had passed through the excitement of learning. Still it was nothing like drilling quarter-inch holes all day or fitting the left fender to an endless stream of automobiles, which was the kind of alternative that most of the weavers had. There was nothing ignoble about this, working with the old wood of the machine and the clean, wiry wool, joining the crisp colors into a tweed that was no expendable novelty, but a cloth that might outwear a man. But, oh God, how tired he was.

At the hearth he found the teapot still warm, and he poured out the last of it, the tea slowly draining from the leaves into the white cup: yellow, gold, deep orange, brown, as the cup filled, the same

230

way as the yarn turned in the dye bath. The tea, pure tannin, tightened his tongue like claret, and went on down to do unknown damage to his stomach—or perhaps it formed a protective coating. Something was keeping him from getting ulcers.

The weavers, Dr. Steichen, and now that ass, O'Reilley, they were the sore spots, the places where other people's messed-up lives touched his. He couldn't take on O'Reilley too, he would have to forget him.

Time worked wonders. He remembered how the problem of Mick had haunted him. Yet, a week ago he had paid him off, given him a week's wages, and sent him on his way, with no more agony than he had felt when he had paid off Willie Ryan. Mick himself, seeing the way things were going, had not expected to be kept on. Brian said that he had been becoming restless to get on the mailboat and take some of the big money that the navvies, the Irish pick-and-shovel men, were writing was to be had in England.

It might be lonely for Brian, alone in the shop, except when Rafferty came in to help him with the beams. But soon Brian would have more than enough to do. He would be going to school every evening and could spend whatever spare time he had in studying.

Rafferty had investigated the school, talked with the men who taught there, and found that the difference between the night course and the day course was only that the night school people didn't have time for homework. He would see that Brian had two or three hours a day for his lessons, a much better arrangement for him than trying to study at home, where his mother, father, and five children younger than himself all lived in two rooms.

They might get a second boy for the beams when the weavers began to produce again, or perhaps he would go on working with the beams himself, cut down on his own weaving.

He heard footsteps at the door, and he resisted an urge to drop

231

the empty cup and dash back to the loom. Alice came in, looking even redder than she usually did when she had been out in the garden.

"What's wrong now?"

"I just wanted to say that it's all right," she said.

"All right?"

"I mean if you've got to be your brother's keeper, and *you* have to be, then I'll have the old man in the garden."

"If he'll come, you mean."

"Yes."

"I knew you'd see the light," he said. "I'll go in and see him tomorrow."

She nodded and an explosion shook the air. He hurried to the window and saw the boats wheeling toward the shore.

"It *is*—" The second thunderclap drowned the rest of her words.

The rain came from behind the house, sizzling down the chimney into the fire a second or two before it reached the windows. The boats wouldn't make it in time. Poor devils, he thought, watching the oarsmen, and then the rain blotted out everything beyond the hedges.

"Oh," said Alice, "the greenhouse is open."

He laughed and stood by the open window smelling the rain-washed air, reaching out for the fine spray that broke from the eaves above. All over Ireland the weavers would be leaving their sodden fields and bogs and going back to their looms.

IT HAD NOT BEEN ENTIRELY A MATTER OF SEEING THE LIGHT, ALICE admitted to herself, at least not the pure light of Christian charity. It was only a matter of time before Mr. Hamilton thought of renting out the vacant gardener's lodge—if she saw the possibility, he could too. O'Connor, with no wife, no dog, no children, had advantages as a neighbor.

232

As for Rafferty's concern about O'Reilley: "Couldn't we leave him with his illusions," she asked, "just send back his unopened letters marked *Address Unknown?*"

"Good Lord, Alice. His illusions are the thing we have to destroy. He isn't a big man in the IRA. He hasn't been blowing up British installations, dismembering women and children. He's been performing a simple act of charity, whether he likes it or not. He has to be told he hasn't got blood on his hands."

"You mean he might even decide to keep on sending the money?"

"I didn't mean that, but I suppose there is a chance."

O'Connor was convinced there was a chance. "You know yourself, your man couldn't be thinking I was the IRA," he said. Standing up in the kitchen where he was having one of his tea breaks, he held out his hands to show that he concealed nothing. He looked a lot neater than she had remembered. Perhaps Rafferty had said something to him.

"*I* thought you were the IRA," she said.

"Ah, you didn't, sure you didn't?"

"What I mean to say is that I thought that for a member of the IRA, you certainly didn't look like the IRA."

"That's me exact words," he said. "There's thousands of people in Ireland getting money from America without being in the IRA."

"That's right, from their families. You're not related to O'Reilley, are you?"

"No, but he might have lost his own father, like, or his brother, in the war, maybe."

"I don't know," she said. "It's just that he told me he was sending money to the IRA. I suppose he might have felt embarrassed to admit that he was just doing good."

"That's the very thing I was about to think."

"Well, we'll know soon enough," she said.

233

They had agreed that O'Connor would keep his room in town and come out every day until he and the work proved compatible. Then he would move into the lodge and would write, explaining the situation, to O'Reilley.

"And I'll have the little house all to meself?"

"Of course, unless you have a wife hidden somewhere."

O'Connor laughed. "I could never afford one of them."

It was to have been at least a two weeks' trial, but after a few days O'Connor pronounced himself satisfied. "Me rent comes due on Friday, and it would be a great saving to us all if I was to move into me own little house tomorrow."

"And you're sure you want to be a gardener?"

"Oh, I do. It comes easy to me."

So Rafferty brought out his things as far as the lane, the bike on top of the car, a couple of tea chests, and, sitting on O'Connor's lap, an enormous marmalade cat. It was a good thirty-six inches from nose to tail, Alice guessed. She hadn't counted on a cat.

"What's his name?" she asked.

"Actually it's Red Eva," O'Connor said and Rafferty nodded. "Me own preference was for Red Hugh, but they was a misunderstanding, and when I got home I found I had Red Eva."

"Kitty, kitty," said Vanessa, and Red Eva leapt up onto the roof of the lodge.

She stayed there the rest of the morning and returned there every morning, for the roof caught the early sun. She wandered about restlessly in the afternoons and, on her second or third day, found the open back door and slid in beneath the Queen Anne legs of the cooker.

Alice, who was making dinner, informed her that cats were not allowed in her kitchen. Red Eva looked at Alice and said nothing. Alice made a threatening gesture with the broom and Red Eva, her tail held high, sauntered out the door.

234

When Alice came down to the kitchen the next afternoon she found that someone had been hard at work clearing out the old fireplace and had started a small coal fire in it.

"Johnnie says it would dry out the damp in here," Mary said quickly, anxious to absolve herself from blame, Alice thought.

"It looks nice," she said, suspending thought on the expense for the time being.

A few minutes later Red Eva came in and settled down like a hearth rug.

"Scat," said Alice and started looking for the broom.

"If you'd leave her, there'd be no more mice," said Mary.

Alice hesitated. With doors and windows open there was no way to keep the cat out. Better keep her friendly—and O'Connor too.

She was a magnificent cat, if you liked cats, fit to bear her name, the name of Strongbow's six-foot warrior wife. She seemed to do nothing but come in and lie down by the fire, and the mice quit the house, a bloodless coup. Even the nighttime noises in the walls upstairs ceased. No one would begrudge Red Eva the saucer of milk that someone (Mary? O'Connor?) kept replenished by the hearth.

O'Connor wrote the letter. She put him at the kitchen table with her own pen and paper. He usually wrote his letters at the GPO, he said, "The way you'd be sure of having a pin."

"A pin?"

"And the ink too. You couldn't be keeping everything you'd need for that class of work."

"I suppose not," she said. "Now be sure you tell him everything, starting with your friend Tom Casey."

"Oh, I will that. And the bag too."

"Well, I don't see—" she began, and he looked so disappointed that she said, "All right, if you want to." He had told Mary the

235

story twice, she understood, and Alice was afraid that he looked upon it as one of the high points of his life.

Poor old guy, he was the end of a dwindling line of respectability. His grandfather had worked in a bank, his father had been a clerk in a coal office with too many children to help them all find their rightful places at a desk somewhere. While waiting for his own chance, O'Connor had taken a number of temporary jobs, and by the time he realized that he would never make it, he was too old to learn a trade. With odd jobs and long spells of unemployment he had survived until he had come into O'Reilley's windfall. And now, at sixty, he had ten years to go to the old-age pension.

"It's a good clean job," he said about the gardening, and he really seemed to enjoy it. She had bought a couple of secondhand books and was trying to teach him what he had to learn if he was to stay on when they left. The books must have been written for gentlemen gardeners, though. They were obsessed with roses, and evaded detail with statements such as: *Have your man spread a well-rotted manure and fork it into the soil.* She had been able to show him Molloy's trick of swinging the rake to make those fish-scale marks in the driveway, which her observations had convinced her were the mark of a place with a resident gardener.

She hoped O'Connor understood that they weren't just playing God with him, cutting off his help from O'Reilley. How long could he have gone on saying the right things in his letters, playing on prejudices he didn't know existed? And how long would O'Reilley have chosen to go on remitting such a sum, and it not tax deductible? A bad season and he might decide to cut his contribution to the IRA.

"Ah, no," O'Connor said. "You've done the right thing. And you know that even if he does send the money, I wouldn't leave you."

"I know, Johnnie, you're a decent man."

"And it's a grand job too. There's only the one thing—" He hesitated.

236

"Yes?"

"I was thinking. It does be quiet out in me own little house, and would you think of keeping thirty bob from me wages and letting me take me lunch and tea with Mary and the girlies?"

Her instinct was to refuse—not refuse the meals—to refuse the payment. But wasn't that where she had made her mistake with Molloy? What she saw as Christian charity, a warm, rosy feeling, had been received as cold, blue Victorian charity, something for the unfortunate, and undeserving, poor. Of course, even at thirty shillings—or did he feed himself for that?

"Two quid then?" he said.

"Oh, no. No, the thirty shillings is fine. I was just thinking about your little house, how different it must seem from Dublin," she added, trying to excuse her slow reply.

"Ah, it's a grand little house, but you'd want a bit of noise, all the same."

"Yes," she said, remembering Molloy.

"You won't forget the hedge now, will you?"

"Ah, no. I was just about to be going out," O'Connor said, rising.

She didn't like her role, always the one to say, *back to work now.* If she didn't, though, O'Connor would sit and talk all afternoon, the habit of years. The unemployed had to get through the days somehow.

"It's not too bad, if you don't look closely," she said, standing at the drawing room window.

"It's a damned good job," Rafferty said, "when you consider it's the first time he's clipped a hedge."

"I know, but I was speaking absolutely"—the way Rafferty did. "It does undulate." *I cut me own hair,* O'Connor said, *and it'd be the same thing, only you'd be in a better position to see.*

"Who's going to see it besides you and me and half a dozen delivery boys?"

"The Steichens."

"Oh, God," Rafferty said. "Sit down and drink your tea. You'd think this was a State Visit the way you're going on about it."

"That's about what it is. We've got to make a real impression on him if we're not going to spend the rest of our lives living upstairs in somebody else's house."

"I intend to go into things with him when he's here."

"Salary?"

"That too."

"Oh, Rafferty. At least make sure he understands that you're to get the department after Booth. Once he starts bringing in these coolies, there's no telling where he'll stop."

Rafferty shook his head. "The man can't last. He's off his rocker, megalomania."

"You don't understand about the heating plant."

"It's too big for the college. That's my point."

"It's made to serve fifty buildings the size of the new science hall. There are now twelve buildings at Oakley."

"My name is Ozymandias, king of kings, look on my works ye mighty and beware."

"The point is, Rafferty, they got government money and approval for that monster, so they've got tacit approval for another thirty or so buildings." You couldn't just close your eyes and hope.

"If you're building on the premise that the U.S. government knows what it's doing, we might as well stop talking."

"Oh, Rafferty, I don't want to fight with you." He was so thin and tired looking. "I think it's going to rain again."

"Thank God." If it rained the weavers would weave, that was the premise *he* built on. They didn't need more rain. The gorse fires had long since been extinguished. The grass needed mowing, and if it rained O'Connor would have to stop clipping the hedge and probably wouldn't finish it in time. And if it did rain Rafferty would leave the loom and get an hour or two of rest. So she prayed that it would.

238

19.

Frank had never answered her request to have the return fare and invest it in a carpet. There had been no letter at all with his last check, just a page torn from a note pad: *Will write later, everything upside down here. Thank God you live in a cool climate.* It was a double disappointment, since Frank usually concluded with a few chatty paragraphs that were almost the only news they got from Oakley, as their own friends, busy with exam papers, beset by children, often took months to reply to a letter.

So she hadn't said anything to Rafferty about moving the loom down to the music room. As long as it remained in the drawing room you might think that *it* was the reason why the room was so informally furnished. They managed to get the couch upstairs at almost the last minute, she and Mary going ahead with Rafferty and O'Connor below, taking the weight of it, twenty-seven steps with a hundred-and-eighty-degree turn at the landing.

"Does a lot for the place," Rafferty said.

"Ah, it's a grand piece of work there. You can tell be the weight of it," said O'Connor.

The music room rug, nine by twelve, was unrolled in front of the couch, where it lay like a bathmat, though you could see that it couldn't have been much bigger without interfering with the loom. "Too bad we didn't think of it earlier," she said, "we could have had the cover dyed."

"No, I don't think so," Rafferty said. "You're better off this way. Old and patched *and* faded, it all goes together that way." He apparently meant it.

"Ah, you're right there, and the windows is a grand sight too."

"You did a good job there, Johnnie," said Mary.

"There's more glass there than you'd like to believe," he said.

Alice, who had done the inside while O'Connor had worked from the ladder outside, could agree. Unfortunately they could do nothing about the mist which was now obscuring the view much more effectively than the dirt had done.

"How's the dining room fire coming?" Rafferty asked.

"It's better now," said O'Connor. "I think we've burnt through the nest. You'd want to get up on the slates and see."

"No one's going up on the roof," Rafferty said. "If it keeps on smoking we'll just have to eat up here, buffet style." Alice and Mary looked at each other. "Johnnie can help carry the food."

"The brother was a waiter once," said O'Connor.

"That's settled then," Rafferty said.

Alice didn't think there was a nest. The chimney was damp, and once they had heated it through, it would draw properly. She went to the door with the other two and stood there a minute, looking back into the room, trying to imagine that she was seeing it for the first time. You were aware first of the space, and then of the loom in the middle, and finally of the grouping at the far side: the rug, the couch, three chairs, and a lamp table. It was reminiscent of something. Yes, all it needed was the velvet rope and the little sign requesting you not to enter the model rooms.

In the kitchen the little girls were playing "Dinner for Dr. Steichen," assembling a sizable meal of modeling clay. "I made fly pie and worm soup," said Vanessa.

"Try to keep clean, dear," Alice said.

"Have a slice of ham, Mama," said Stella, cutting off a piece of green plasticine with a hair in it.

"Later," she said, and went into the larder for a look at her pair of black bottom pies. Someone else had been looking at them and had left one of the dish covers askew.

Back in the kitchen she said, "When we're through eating, the four of you can have what's left of the pie, but don't touch them before that."

Mary and O'Connor nodded. She had come to see that the advantage of shopping every day was that it cut the likelihood of tomorrow's meals being eaten today.

"You'll remember to wear the clean apron, won't you, Mary?"

"Yes. I'll put it on as soon as we've had our tea."

"Good. Mr. Rafferty's gone to the station, and they'll be here any minute."

The trouble was that if you seldom had people in for a meal it was almost impossible to pull it off. She had had to buy a couple more plates and to make napkins and table mats, and Rafferty had bought some secondhand glassware. The whole house smelled of prawns. And then it had to rain. She could hardly wait until it was over.

HE HAD ALICE'S WELLINGTONS WITH HIM, AND WHEN HE HAD PARKED the car at the outer gate, he was supposed to hand Mrs. Steichen a pair of clean woolen socks and tell her to take off her shoes and put on the boots for the last stretch. He wondered if Alice had ever had a good look at Mrs. Steichen's feet.

She sat beside him, in the front of the car, and Dr. Steichen sat behind, an arrangement they had apparently agreed upon before

241

he met them at the station—at her insistence, he believed, though she had what was said to be the more dangerous spot. Perhaps she planned to wrest control from him in an emergency.

"You should just see the Italian drivers," she said.

"So I've heard." A handsome woman really. Put her in a chiton and sandals with her hair tied up in a fillet and a quiver on her back and she would make a damned good Artemis. In a transparent raincoat over a printed silk jacket dress, however, she wasn't at her best.

He could offer her his own Wellingtons, the heavy-duty pair he carried for farmyards and flooded boreens. If they were too small, though, it would be more than embarrassing. A woman with her problem might easily resent all mention of footgear, and they didn't need an enemy in the president's house.

He would have to make up his mind soon.

"It's marvelous," said Mrs. Steichen, speaking of their morning's look at Dublin, "but it's a little dirty, don't you think?"

"I've heard it said."

"It's not nearly as clean as London. But then London's cleaner than Paris."

"I've never been to either one."

"And Rome's worse than Paris."

"How would you say that Rome and Dublin compare, then?"

"Oh, Rome is dirtier," said Mrs. Steichen without hesitating.

"Louise didn't like Rome at all," Dr .Steichen said.

"There," Rafferty said, "that's the road that leads to our house. We have to go up the hill first and approach it from the top."

"That's the back alley?" said Mrs. Steichen.

"No, it's the only way in. The curve is banked the wrong way. The high side of the road should be on the outside, you know, like the Wall of Death at the county fair."

"Maybe we'd better walk."

"It's too wet," Rafferty said, swinging the car around the tiny loop at the top of the hill. He gave it its head going down the hill.

242

Mrs. Steichen braced her feet against the floor and gripped the dashboard with one gloved hand. He stepped on the gas, shot up and around the flank of scored concrete, and landed on the pocked and rutted surface of the lane, all momentum gone and the motor screaming in complaint.

"That's the worst part," he said, changing down the gears and fighting the wheel to keep the car up out of the ruts.

"There's a pole in the road!"

"Three of them." Rafferty swung around the first.

"Did you notice how he went to the right?" Mrs. Steichen said, turning back to Dr. Steichen, a subtle warning, or proving some point she had been making earlier?

"There's not enough room for this car on the left," Rafferty said.

"But if someone's coming the other way?"

"Two cars anywhere on this lane, and you'd be in trouble."

"But——"

"It's never happened yet." It was enough just driving down the lane without thinking of traffic, unnecessary besides, like carrying armor against falling meteors.

Luck was with him, and they made it safely up through the inner gate. They roared up the last incline and came to rest in the balustraded forecourt, kicking up O'Connor's patterned gravel. He would have to drive them down again, a much easier run, however, unless it was dark.

"And that's a loom. That's what you call it, isn't it?"

"That's right."

"And you do your weaving right here?" Mrs. Steichen seemed to be speaking to Alice.

"It's my loom, as a matter of fact," Rafferty said. "I have all male weavers."

"Oh, I didn't realize you were going to get in any practical experience," said Dr. Steichen.

"I try out the new patterns here, and it helps to understand how the men feel about their work." They had agreed that it would be best not to go into the full extent of his work.

"Do you think you could do a little for us?" Mrs. Steichen asked.

"Certainly." He sat down, and Dr. Steichen wandered away toward the windows. Maybe he should have demurred, waited to be begged. After a dozen or so threads he stopped.

"That really is quick. I'd always thought that weaving was sort of under-over, like darning."

"It's basically that, of course, but—"

"Say, do you folks know you've got quite a view over here?"

"Yes," Rafferty said, rising from the loom. "Too bad it's not a better day. You know they say you can see whales down there sometimes, playing in the bay." He noticed Alice giving him a very peculiar look. "Never saw them myself, of course." He didn't mean to imply that he had.

"The view was really the thing that decided us to take the house," Alice said.

"Say, why don't you two girls go and take the Grand Tour around the house? Everyone's going to be asking Louise what this Prisma looks like."

"If you'd like," Alice said, looking at Mrs. Steichen. "Come, I'll show you."

Rafferty let them out the door. *Take your time,* he mouthed at Alice, and she nodded. Obviously Dr. Steichen was about to get down to business.

He shut the door. Dr. Steichen gave a sigh and sank down in one of the chairs. "You know, this travel business isn't easy. London, Paris, Rome," he said. "At home they all think you're having a ball."

"It can be difficult all right." He thought of the trains and boats and hotels with Alice and the two little girls on top of everything else.

"What I mean to say is they've had a war over here, and you can't expect the hotels to be what they'd be in L.A., say. We put in

244

for room and bath everywhere, but if a hotel in Rome, say, doesn't have any private bathrooms, it's not going to do much good cabling back to the travel agent in Oakley."

"No, I see your point there." Had Mrs. Steichen actually made him cable? It was always being said that she was the power behind the throne, a risk that any woman larger than her husband had to take. "How's the hotel in Dublin?"

"All right, I think. Louise gave it the old bureau of standards, and she didn't say anything. She wasn't too happy about the place where we had lunch, though."

"There are some real darbs. I can tell you a few places where you can get a decent meal."

"Oh, the food was all right. I mean I'm not much for those French things they give you at the Hotel Oakley. I'm sort of a meat and potatoes man."

Rafferty nodded.

"What I mean to say is—we haven't had time to discuss it yet, so I don't know for sure what got Louise, but in the men's jakes there's this fancy wrought-iron hook, real Williamsburg stuff, holding up a little loop of string that's threaded through a whole block of sheets torn from a newspaper, you know, the usual size, it's just that it's newspaper."

"Yes, you find that sometimes."

"Well, now I don't care if they use corn cobs, but Louise does. And I happen to know that her Aunt Mary had the Sears catalogue in the outhouse. Of course, as I say, I don't know what it was like in the ladies'."

"No."

"I figure it'll do her good to spend a few hours with people of her own kind, let her relax a little."

"You've only got a few days more."

"There's the boat. I wish we were flying now."

"Greek?"

"No, British."

"You'll be all right then."

"I don't know. Louise had some unhappy meals in London."

Rafferty nodded, feeling sympathy for the man, he realized. Alice had some of that, the thing about boiled eggs in the beginning, and the kitchen here, the way she had almost let it damn the whole house.

"Say, I nearly forgot. Where'd I put that briefcase?"

Business at last.

Dr. Steichen opened the flap. "Stopped in one of your Off Sales here," he said and handed over a bottle wrapped in brown tissue paper.

"Thanks," Rafferty said, untwisting the top of the paper. Three to one it was sweet sherry. No, he had underestimated the man, or his expense account. "I haven't seen *that* for a long time. They charge enough for it here, too." He could have bought a straight malt Scotch for the price, too bad.

"It didn't seem so much until we translated it into dollars. Most expensive thing in the place. It goes to show you that Scotch drinking at home is just snobbery. When you get right down to it, there's nothing like good Kentucky corn liquor."

"That's right." The individuality of any true regional product was something he believed in. "Shall we open it now?"

"Might's well."

They had not, he then saw, thought of everything.

"Well," Dr. Steichen said when he had explained, "there's no need to apologize. Time was when Louise and I had to do with an old-fashioned icebox. You just go down and chip a little off the block. I used to do that, and Louise'd have a fit. 'You don't know where that ice has been,' she'd say."

"Yes," Rafferty said, "but we haven't got an icebox. I don't think there's one in Ireland, a few refrigerators, but no iceboxes. There's no ice."

"You'd think they'd build icehouses."

246

"What I mean is that it doesn't freeze for more than a few hours at a time. There just isn't any ice."

"Well, they've got a lot to learn from us, I guess. *Say,* I like that," he said, seeing the siphon. "Here, let me do it." He really did like it. Tasting the drink that Dr. Steichen had handed him Rafferty remembered a high school dance, a pint bottle emptied into the punch (for seventy).

"We went out to Oxford for an afternoon," Dr. Steichen said.

"You did? How'd you like it?" At least they were on the subject of colleges, however far from Oakley.

"They've got the name all right. Say you're from Oxford, and everybody knows where you mean."

"Yes." He understood Dr. Steichen all too well.

"Of course, their setup is quite a bit different from ours."

"Yes," Rafferty said. There was no reason, though, why a small place like Oakley couldn't assign tutors to the students and put education on a more personal plane, at least in the liberal arts.

"There's no general plan at all. It seems everyone was allowed to do pretty much what they wanted without regard to the over-all situation. I believe that they don't have a heating plant at all."

"From what I've heard that could very well be true." It could be that Dr. Steichen regarded himself as chiefly in charge of the physical plant at Oakley and would have been content if the academics had asserted themselves about the rest.

"Hear much from your brother these days?" Apparently he had said all there was to say about Oxford.

"No, he's pretty busy getting the new machinery into production."

"When we left it looked like there was going to be a little union trouble about those new machines."

"Bound to be," Rafferty said. "Too late, though. What the workman doesn't realize is that as soon as he puts one foot inside a factory he's on a greased slide to perdition."

247

"I don't think your brother'd be too happy to hear you say that."

"Oh, Frank knows what I think. You might say that we agree that the worker has to be taken out of the factory. My argument with Frank is that his product is crap."

"Well, I wouldn't know about that," said Dr. Steichen, who obviously wasn't going to be quoted as agreeing with that. "And I thought you came here to start a tweed factory."

"Oh, no. Not a factory. We have all outworkers with their looms at home. It's a different position entirely, they own their own means of production."

"I *see*," said Dr. Steichen, and Rafferty remembered the man's political background.

"You might say we've created a pack of little capitalists."

Dr. Steichen whipped a finger to his lips in a gesture of conspiracy. "I think I hear the girls coming, want to fill up?" he asked, rising with his glass.

"No, thanks. Go ahead."

An air of unease had entered the room with the women, he felt. Mrs. Steichen couldn't make up her mind what she wanted to drink. "Maybe you'd like an old-fashioned," he suggested. "I think there's an orange and lemon downstairs."

"There is," Alice said.

"No. No thank you. I'll just have the bourbon."

"Good idea," said Dr. Steichen, who had the siphon at the ready.

Alice was having sherry, probably with the idea of keeping herself fit to serve the meal, no need to look so glum about it, though. He looked at the clock. He should have brought up the subject himself, point-blank: what about the second semester, Dr. Steichen? What about the coordinated plan for the whole liberal arts side of the school? But not now, not with Mrs. Steichen sitting there looking aggrieved.

Perhaps after dinner he could get the women to withdraw,

pleading the custom of the house. He still had a few of his duty-free cigars from the boat, and Alice could serve Mrs. Steichen something in the drawing room. He would have to get a word to her in private.

The tour had begun well, in the bedrooms, where Mrs. steichen had been wild about the views and said, "I wish you'd call me *Louise.*" Then the landing, with the telephone, "A very central location was what the estate agent called it," Alice said. "It means that you always have to run for the phone, unless you're in the bathroom there, or the W.C. here. Spare bedroom there," she said, at the other side of the landing, and opened the door a few inches. The bed and the wardrobe from the drawing room had been shoved in there, as well as suitcases and empty boxes. "The hill cuts off the view from there," she said, and she clicked the door shut.

In the dining room they found the chimney drawing properly at last, though a heavy smell of turf smoke still hung in the room. "Oh, a peat fire!" said Louise.

"Yes." And they had a long talk about winning the turf from the bogs and the general lore of turf fires, hundred-year-old ones, and related topics.

"You know," said Louise, "you're really very informative. You should be doing tours somewhere."

Alice felt her face get hot. "Well, we'll be back here soon enough," she said. Looking at the table, she assured herself that, shined and polished as they were, the three or four patterns of silver and two of glassware weren't noticeable.

"I'm starved," said Louise. "I didn't want much breakfast after the boat, and I really didn't like the looks of the place where we had lunch."

"I know," said Alice, remembering how she had felt at first, "it takes a while to get used to the country."

249

They returned to the hall and Louise said, "I just can't figure out where the kitchen could be."

Alice laughed. "I'll show you in a minute. First I want you to see my pride and joy." If they went out to the greenhouse first, then they would approach the kitchen from the side, at ground level, and thus avoid the feeling of descent into the dungeons that the stairs gave you.

Louise couldn't get excited about the tomatoes, but she took to the palm tree the moment she saw it. "We really had a time with it," Alice said. She told Louise about Molloy and his camel remark, and how the tree had seemed to be dying in the drought, and how she had worked to water it.

"And now it's going to bloom!"

"Yes. I have to go out to the botanical gardens and talk to someone there. I'm afraid we'll have to pollinate it by hand."

They looped around the kitchen garden the long way so as to avoid the compost heap, which could be a little high on a damp day, and they came at last to the court where the ashpit was. Alice opened the scullery door, and they passed through, into the kitchen.

Prisma had never looked better: the dark, threatening skies outside, and now the warm, bright room. It was a lived-in room, with rows of Wellingtons and raincoats, a few children's toys, and lots of laughter. O'Connor had his fire in the old fireplace, one of those glowing red fires that he was so good with. ("You have to be poor to know how to get the most out of the coal," he had told her, and she might tell Louise later.) He rose from his chair beside the fire, sliding a laughing little girl down from each knee, while Mary pushed the crane with the black iron kettle back over the fire. Louise was taking it all in. Best, perhaps, to let it make its own impact, and later, if she mentioned it, Alice would point out that the fireplace had been in use when the Declaration of Independence had been signed, and the floor they believed was much older than that, the survival of some earlier house.

250

"Would you have a cup of tea?" Mary asked, her face flushed with excitement.

They had been having theirs, and the table was a homely clutter of cups and crumbs. At the far end a fresh cake of bread was on the rack beside a bowl of butter and the crock of water holding the wooden paddles with which Mary had been rolling the butter balls, a still life of old-fashioned domesticity.

Louise had not answered Mary, so Alice said, "I don't think we'd better have tea now, thank you, Mary. We'll be having dinner in a little while."

"Ah, you would," said Mary, looking over at the old pendulum clock. It was a little after six, so they had about ten minutes before it would make the sprung, digestive noise that was its mode of striking the hour.

As Alice neared the fire, Red Eva, who had been stretched out, orange and magnificent, on the hearthstone, rose and walked indolently to the back door, where she waited, without a sound, for Mary to spring over and open the door.

"We used to have mice," Alice said.

"You couldn't turn your back but they'd be up on the table," said Mary, "and then Johnnie came with his cat."

"Oh, it's a lovely cat," said Louise, in a voice that was just a bit cold, Alice thought.

"Should we join the men for a drink?" Rafferty should have had all the time he needed.

Louise nodded, and Alice led the way to the hall door. Now that they had seen the kitchen was no dungeon they didn't have to return the way they had come. The effect of going up the inner stairs was very different from coming down. She let Louise go ahead, and was informing her, "You just push on the door, there's no latch so that it's easier to pass through with a tray," when the light broke through from above and Louise lurched out into the hall. She had forgotten to mention that damned step.

"Are you all right?" Alice called, running up into the hall.

251

Louise was steadying herself, holding onto the hall rack with both hands. "I thought I'd lost a heel there."

"No, it's that top step. We're all so used to it that we never give it a thought any more."

It shouldn't have happened. The bloom was off the tour now, and they rejoined the men in silence. Dr. Steichen, who was certainly not on his first drink, didn't seem to notice that anything was wrong, but after a while Rafferty caught her eye and grimaced. *Smile,* was what he meant to say, as though she were the one who was exuding gloom. She fixed a smile on her face and took a sip of her sherry. What she had wanted was a good slug of Irish whiskey, but as Dr. Steichen must have brought the bourbon, she didn't like to ask for the Irish instead.

"We're getting plans ready for a new food and drink center," said Dr. Steichen.

"Drink?" asked Rafferty.

"Soda fountain. Soda fountain and cafeteria."

"For the commuters."

"Everyone. We're going to do away with the dining rooms in the dorms. It'd cost as much to convert them to cafeteria style as to put in a decent plant."

"Why do they have to be cafeteria style?"

"It's cheaper, and I have never liked the idea of students waiting on other students."

"Oh, I waited on table," Rafferty said. "We had a ball."

"Maybe it was all right wherever you went to school, but in a school like Oakley—"

"I went to Oakley, Dr. Steichen."

"You went to Oakley, Patrick?"

Alice turned to Rafferty, expecting something, she didn't know what, but he was just nodding. "And my wife went to Oakley, too."

"Yes, I know that. The little girl on the newspaper."

It would be interesting to know how much of that he remem-

252

bered. She stood up. "If it's all right with everyone I'll go down and see about getting the dinner up into the dining room."

"Great," said Dr. Steichen, "I could eat a horse."

She was on her way out when Louise said, "Oh, Alice, if you don't mind, I think I'd rather have just a boiled egg, *two* boiled eggs, if you have them, and leave them in the shell, I'd like to take off the top myself. They do it so well in London, and I've been trying to learn."

"Yes, I'll do that," she said and closed the door behind her.

She went down the stairs and strode along the lower hall, opened the basement door, and began to descend purposefully. Her foot came down hard on that first shallow step and the shock shot up bone by bone to the top, with a blow as though she had been hit on the head with a sledge hammer—from the inside. Shaking, she sat down on the steps for a minute.

There were any number of possible reasons for wanting a meal of boiled eggs: an upset stomach or a reducing diet, to mention only two. Of course, if your idea of a kitchen was a lot of chromium and tile, it might take a few minutes to adjust to a granite floor and whitewashed walls. And she could remember when even she had felt that a wooden drainboard was somehow "dirty." It had taken her a few weeks to appreciate how quiet it was, how easy on the dishes, and, with a good stiff brushing every few days, really a lot cleaner than some of the things you saw in Oakley.

Somebody was opening the kitchen door, so she stood up quickly. O'Connor, carrying the coal scuttle, peered up the dark stairs. "Are you all right there?"

"Yes. I just forgot about the step here."

"It's a bad one all right," he said. "You know, if you was to get a man to chip an inch off the stone—"

"—then the problem would be the second step. I've given some thought to the matter."

"Ah, you're right. You're right there." He bent down and began

253

to fill the scuttle at the open door of one of those dim cells that used to be servants' bedrooms.

When he had finished, she held the kitchen door open for him and said briskly, "Now, let's see the eggs, how many do we have?"

Mary started toward the larder, and O'Connor said, "There's four hin's eggs and one duck's egg."

Alice sniffed, she had never bought a duck's egg in her life. When Mary brought the bowl, however, there were four white eggs and one larger, pale green egg in it. She filled the bowl with water to test the eggs. There was more to it in Ireland, in the summer anyway, than just asking for boiled eggs. A malicious woman would serve the duck's egg and the small white one that was all but floating. A malicious woman with nothing at stake.

Louise was scraping around in the empty eggshells, looking for more. She didn't look like a sick woman. "Maybe you could take some toast," Alice said. "You could make it right there on the fire behind you."

"Yes," said Louise, lighting up. She would know that heat kills germs. "That would be nice."

"I'll get the toasting fork," Alice said and rose to go downstairs. Louise began trimming the crusts from a piece of bread.

She brought back something else too. "I've found a Dutch cheese. They're supposed to be easy to digest." Fortunately neither Mary nor O'Connor liked cheese. She put it on the table, round and untouched in its red wax coating. "From Holland, you know," where the housewives scrubbed their steps and, leaving their shoes outside, retired into spotless kitchens of Delft tiles.

"Mmmmm," said Louise and occupied herself toasting the bread and eating it with great wedges of the Dutch cheese.

"How about a little of this now?" Rafferty asked her when he had helped Dr. Steichen to his third portion of ham. "Limerick ham."

"Ah," said Louise. They were well into the center of the ham. "I

254

might have a little." When she had it on her plate, she cut off the fat on the outside and fell to.

Alice relaxed. She understood Louise perfectly. It took courage in a way. You heard of travelers, missionaries, envoys, who out of a misguided courtesy had eaten everything they were offered and had gone on to an early death or an old age of miserable ill-health brought on by alien germs.

Rafferty cut a few more slices of ham. "Be sure and save some room for the black bottom pie."

"Maybe," Louise said, "I'll have a tiny piece of pie."

"Good," said Alice. She stood up to press the bell and heard it ring faintly somewhere beneath her feet. They had tested the bell in anticipation of this moment, but she had never rung for Mary before.

Mary entered the room with the tray and took off the used plates. She seemed surprised by the sight of Louise's, piled with bread crusts, red wax cheese rinds, and strips of ham fat. She hesitated with the loaded tray, swaying on the high heels she had felt the occasion called for, and Alice realized that they hadn't thought to put a table beside the door to rest the tray while the door was opened. She hurried over, opened the door, and let Mary out. Rafferty was in the middle of one of his stories about the weavers, and no one seemed to have noticed that gap in their gracious living.

The pie was at her place, ready to cut and serve. She lifted the dish cover. There, on the nutmeg-dusted surface, were two black flies, bigger than raisins, as big as small prunes. Dazed by the sudden light, they ran and heaved their bodies, overladen with pie, dizzy with rum, and awkwardly took off and buzzed toward the window. She shot a glance down the table. The others were still looking at Rafferty.

Should she make some inane excuse about the crust's not being right and trek down to the kitchen with this pie and back up with the other? They were only flies, and flies stayed close to home,

255

their own flies from their own compost heap, and she kept a clean compost. Even if they had already laid eggs it would be days before they hatched into maggots. Besides you were always hearing of the delights of a maggoty Stilton cheese. Did you put the maggots neatly to one side, like cherry pits? Or did you actually eat them? Whole, like oysters, perhaps—she wondered as she cut the pie. She prized up the slice carefully; the crust was the weak point. She handed the plate to Louise.

"Thank you," she said, and, "will you excuse me a minute?"

Alice heard her heels going up the stairs.

"Say, this is great," said Dr. Steichen, tucking into the pie.

"Eat up, there's more."

"And then we'll have Irish coffee," Rafferty said, nodding at the equipment arranged on the sideboard.

After a few minutes she gave Dr. Steichen another piece, but Louise hadn't as yet reappeared. The neat triangle of pie stood untouched at her place. She had been right about the gelatin, half again as much when you don't have a refrigerator.

And then the dining room door opened. Alice looked up and saw Louise standing in the doorway with her plastic coat on. "I felt a bit tired," she said, "so I phoned for a cab." Of course she had seen, or maybe just heard, the flies.

"Why did you do that? I was going to take you back to the hotel," Rafferty said.

"It's all right. You can take my husband when he's ready to go."

"Oh, I'll go with you, dear," Dr. Steichen said, standing.

"It'll take him a while to get here. You'll have time to eat your pie and have a glass of Irish coffee too," Rafferty said.

Dr. Steichen sank back into his chair.

"I'd rather wait outside. The air will do me good. You might as well finish what you're eating," she added, looking at her husband.

"I won't be a minute," he said.

Alice went to the door with her. "I'm sorry you don't feel well.

256

Maybe if you had a glass of whiskey, it'd make you feel better."

"No, thank you. I think the fresh air would be the best thing for me." And at the door she said, "It's been lovely, thank you so much."

"I'm glad you came," Alice said, and Louise walked out the door.

Dr. Steichen bolted his pie and wouldn't consider the Irish coffee. "I'm sorry we have to rush off," he said. "Louise has been having a little trouble with the food lately."

"That's too bad," Alice said.

"I wish she'd let me drive you instead of phoning the cab."

"I suppose she didn't want to break up the party," Dr. Steichen said.

"Trouble is, the cab man may just turn back to town when he sees our lane."

"I wouldn't know," he said and looked a little disturbed.

They were standing at the door. Over Dr. Steichen's shoulder she could see Louise sitting sidesaddle on the balustrade. Alice had waved, but she hadn't seemed to notice.

"You know," Rafferty said, "we didn't get around to discussing the second semester at all."

Dr. Steichen turned to glance at his wife. "Well, I'll tell you, you might as well take the whole year." A dark man in a heavy sweater was panting up the driveway. "Take the next year, too, if that's what you want," he said, smiled, and hurried down, striding across the gravel to cut off the annoyed cab driver before he could reach Louise.

The three of them started down the drive together.

"Good-by," Alice called.

Dr. Steichen held up a hand in farewell.

20.

"THAT SHOULD BE WORTH A GOOD TWO HUNDRED YARDS, IF IT HOLDS," Rafferty said, taking his morning look at the weather. "It's a little thin down toward Bray Head, though."

"I wouldn't worry about that," Alice said.

There was nothing for it but to live with his superstition that bad weather made good weaving. It wasn't the weather that was letting him down. All day long she had to listen to the *ping* in the pan beneath the skylight, and the kitchen was a forest of dripping clothes.

O'Connor had put the clothesline at ceiling height and spoke of the retractable clothes rack that he would have installed if only the ceiling had been three feet higher. "You'd have found it a great convenience," he insisted.

"Oh, we would have, Johnnie," said Mary's voice from somewhere beyond the pillow slips.

"You'd have it up there, right out of the way."

"That would have been grand."

"And then when you wanted to take them down you'd just undo the rope and let the whole rack slide down. And when you had your things on the bars, you'd just pull the rope and there they'd be, right over your head, even if you was to walk as tall as Mr. Rafferty."

"Oh, it would have been a fine thing, Johnnie."

"All right," Alice said. "If you'll just take hold of that end of the table now, Johnnie, we'll move it so the socks don't drip on the bread."

There was no drying at all in the greenhouse. The palm tree, its roots drenched and its head in the damp, sunless air, remembered where it was, and appeared to have changed its mind about blooming, though she couldn't be sure without getting up on the ladder.

Fortunately the little girls were in school mornings. Mary took them at nine-thirty and got them at noon. O'Connor had suggested it, and though Alice thought they were a little young, the nuns intimated that she had left it rather late. Vanessa was put in the second class, Junior Infants, and Stella was up in Senior Infants.

Mary was not too happy about the arrangement, "It's not the same at all without them here."

"They're only gone for two and a half hours," Alice reminded her.

"It's Johnnie's cat. She put him up to it."

Red Eva, undisturbed on the hearth, ignored the accusation.

"Oh, well. They probably should have been going last year too," was all she could say.

The dinner with the Steichens had been almost too bad to discuss, that long walk down the rutted lane, and Louise in high heels.

Rafferty, of course, had wanted to understand what was wrong with Louise. "Says she's too sick to eat, and then eats enough for a couple of harvest hands and ends up, to everyone's surprise, sick. Pregnant, I suppose."

"I doubt it."

"Well, you'd know."

She was more interested in what Dr. Steichen had meant by telling them to take an extra year. It almost sounded as if he were trying to get rid of Rafferty.

"No. He was obviously embarrassed by his wife, wanted to make up for it some way. I feel sorry for him."

"So do I. But why should he offer you a third year?"

"Oh, that. I'd just mentioned it in a letter, the possibility of a third year. I thought we'd be more likely to get the full second year that way."

"I'm glad to hear that."

"I never thought he'd say yes, but I feel a lot better, having it in reserve."

"Oh, Rafferty, you'll have them working, as well as they'll ever work anyway, long before then."

He had already cut down on his own weaving in order to spend a day or two a week with Brian on the beams and another on his round of the outworkers. His return from the weavers was no longer the worst moment of the week. He would come in late, at eight or nine, and hang up his big waterproof coat in the kitchen and talk while she dished up his dinner.

"Heifers were up at the Blessington fair last week," he said, moving over to the fire where O'Connor was sitting in a straight chair reading the morning's paper beneath the dangling ceiling light.

"That's good news there," O'Connor said, lowering his paper.

"Depends on whether you're buying or selling," Rafferty said.

"Ah, it would. It would." His glasses, which he wore for reading, gave him an unwarranted look of wisdom. They had been his father's, he said, and she supposed it was possible. "There's a chair," he said to Rafferty.

260

"I'm going up in a minute anyway."

"You know," said O'Connor, "the thing you'd notice most, the difference between here and Dublin, like, you know what it is?"

"What?"

"The people. There's no people here."

"Basic premise," said Rafferty. "The density of population is higher in the cities than in the country."

"Ah, it's not just a cod. There's more houses and buses, and the smoke—you'd never need change your shirt here—but what you'd miss is the people."

"You could go down to the pub. Lots of people there."

"Yes, but I'd have been drowned the last time I had occasion to go out, only for me boots."

"You can't be too lonely then."

"Oh, I'm not. I'm only trying to explain the position to you, why I'm not out in me own little house."

Rafferty laughed. "It's all right, Johnnie," he said and winked at Red Eva.

Alice put a cup of tea on the table for O'Connor. "Don't forget to see the back's locked when you go, Johnnie," she said and handed the tray to Rafferty. Taking the teapot herself, she opened the kitchen door and followed Rafferty up the two flights of stairs to the drawing room. At night, even with the shutters closed, it looked a lot like a deserted railway waiting room, but she couldn't see keeping a fire in the library or the dining room just so they could eat there in some comfort.

"We got a letter from Dr. Steichen this afternoon," she said.

"Say anything?"

"He thanks us for a lovely afternoon and dinner. He says Louise sends her thanks but she's too busy giving dinners for the new faculty people to write."

"Did he say anything about next year?"

"You'd better eat while it's hot," she said. "I'll read that part to you." She took the letter from the mantel and read: "I've been

261

thinking about next year's leave, and on rereading your letter I see that you didn't actually ask for it. The picture here has changed quite a bit since I saw you in Ireland.

"I wouldn't want this to go any further, you understand—"

"That's right," Rafferty broke in, "put it in writing. The caution of the man overwhelms me."

"Well, how's he to tell us anything, if he doesn't?"

"Go on."

"We're beginning to wonder how this guy I picked up in London for the History Department is going to pan out here. After we went to a lot of trouble to find an apartment for him and his wife, he walks into Amos Hall the day before the boys came back and pinches one of the corner rooms, moves in bag and baggage.

"This guy claims that in England a teacher lives in his college during the week and goes home only on weekends. It isn't just the loss of the revenue on the room. Louise says that the girls in Faculty Wives are upset about it."

Rafferty certainly had an amused look on his face. It would be no joke. With only the library and the faculty offices to hide out in, some of the men never made it home before nine or ten, and girls who had married for intellectual companionship found themselves with nothing to do after the kids were in bed but to read ahead in *Charlotte's Web*.

She went on: "I don't see how we can keep this man in the school for another year, and it would save a lot of trouble if you could be back here next September."

"I can see how it would."

"It's worked out very well, I'd say," Alice said. "We don't have any reason to stay here, but he thinks we do, so now is the time to ask for the extra thousand."

"Of course, we don't have any reason to go back either." He said the words in an offhand way, as if he hoped the idea would pass into currency.

"What do you mean?"

262

"Did it ever occur to you that maybe I'm not cut out to be a teacher?"

She remembered the night he had brought home the first fruits of his weavers and how she had been careful to ignore his flirtation with that idea then. "You know you're a teacher."

"This is my chance to find out. By next year we'll have the weaving on the rails. Ten, twelve hours a week should take care of it, and I could spend the rest of the time in the National Library and Trinity. I could finish the book and see how I like that kind of life: research, writing, thinking."

"When somebody's as good a teacher as you are, it's selfish to deprive people of a chance to take your courses." And what were they supposed to live on?

"Oh, cut it out, Alice. Nobody gives a crap, and you know it."

"I certainly don't know anything like that."

"Look at it this way. I went on to college because I couldn't help myself. Every year I kept going it was like a drunk moving on to another bar. I should have been looking for a place in the real world, I thought, before I found myself twenty-two years old with nothing but a B.A. from Oakley, and all the good jobs nailed by the guys who'd been buttering up the boss and his daughter. I never thought I'd be able to make a living out of history."

"I know, Rafferty, and that's what makes you such a good teacher."

"I'm not through yet, Alice. How many of the kids at Oakley now would be there if they thought that their college education was going to *cut* their lifetime earnings? What do they care for history? Seventy-five per cent of my students are in required courses. Item three in the scavenger hunt for a degree, between Phys Ed One and Choice of Laboratory Science: Human History from Paleolithic Times to World War II. The trouble is that the course provides a certain amount of food for thought, and not only about Dr. Steichen and the Babylonian heating plant, but what about Patrick Rafferty? I've had only three real students in

263

the whole time I've been at Oakley. Two I had to send quietly along to other schools for their own good, and the other I married. So who's the prize booby? Dr. Steichen's got invincible ignorance on his side, but I know what I'm doing."

She tried to forget that speech, which was a little like trying to forget that you had had a leg amputated. She liked Ireland, she really did. She liked Mary, she liked O'Connor, even Red Eva. And yet . . .

It was October and still green, greener than it had been in the dry summer. Only if you looked carefully would you see that some of the leaves had begun to dry from the edges, and for months they would fall, she knew, one by one.

For weeks she managed not to think of home, driving the thought back and sandbagging her mind to keep it out. *This,* she told herself, was the autumn: the rain, the drop of a degree or two in temperature, the headlong rush toward darkness. To remember more was to court disappointment. This was the harvest: the greenhouse shelves filled with apples and pears, and a glut of tomatoes in an enamel bath.

She cut the tomatoes up for chili sauce, concentrating on their strangeness, small, firm, cherry-red tomatoes, lest she be seduced into remembering those soft, scarlet cushions of other falls and not be able to stop there. It simmered at the back of the stove while she went down to the shops, and she came home up the green boreen, to be ambushed by the smell which carried everything before it on a tide of nostalgia—for the birch trees with their small leaves of pale gold; the red oaks, their leaves a deep lacquered maroon, a little too perfect, like their precise acorns in neat berets, and the maples.

They would have turned now, that pair of them across the street from their old apartment, and for three weeks the whole street would be lit with the fire of those two trees. Even when they fell, the leaves lay burning beneath the bare branches, un-

264

touched until a wind came to whip the leaves from all the un-
fenced and unhedged yards through the bushes and out into the
streets where cars went clashing by, up to their hubcaps in leaves.

There would be no fall for her this year, or next, nor winter
either, the snow, falling lightly, the ringing shovels; no spring,
flowing in the gutters and the river—and in the maples. They
would miss June and its sudden green again, and even August
when the grass turned to straw and the sidewalks felt hotter than
the sun itself.

Ireland, coddled in the Gulf Stream, warmed in winter, cooled
in summer, had only the exaggerated behavior of the daylight to
carry the burden of the changing seasons. It would always be
green, grass green, hedge green, green lichen on the concrete
walls, mildew green, and mold green. Fog and bog.

This, she realized, was homesickness, the pain in the pit of the
stomach. (And that was the stomach, higher than you might
think.) Was this what Rafferty wanted, the seasons running
wrong and never the sight of a wooden house? Exile. They
wouldn't see the maples this year, or next year, and Dr. Steichen's
planners had their eyes on them, begrudging them their few feet
of ground, envisioning there an agora, a plaza, a strip of concrete,
embellished with half a dozen toy evergreens in cedar tubs.

It had all been in the glass case outside Dr. Steichen's office, for
anyone who could read a plan to see. Rafferty didn't know, and
she wouldn't tell him, even though they weren't their maples any
more, not *their* apartment. Once, the last spring in Oakley, she
had seen a living maple torn down. With the two little girls she
stood there, at a safe distance, while workmen on ladders cut off
the boughs, their leaf buds already swollen with life, and then
bound the giant trunk in the winch chains and went to work on it.
The torn stumps of the branches dripped sugar water onto the
men's aluminum hats and onto the racketing chain saw which
grew slippery and threatened to run amuck. At last the living
wood strained, splintered, and with a twist, ripping a window

265

from the cab of the yellow monster, it fell and lay quiet amid the sap and sawdust.

"Is that all you're going to eat?"

"I don't feel hungry."

She had had too much sun in the summer, he thought, it left her looking yellow. "Maybe you need a rest. I can't take the time, but why don't you go to the Aran Islands for a week? We can manage here."

"I don't want to go to the Aran Islands."

"Then London, Paris. A city's what you need. Shouldn't cost too much when we're this close to them."

"I don't want to go anywhere, Rafferty."

He looked at her and guessed: "You want to go home."

"I don't actually want to go home, I just wish I were there."

"Well, why don't we talk about it then? There are times when I wish we were there. Remember those two maple trees across the street? Sometimes at night, when you've gone to bed, I think about them, and it almost makes me cry." He had been surprised to find that fall hardly existed here, a dirty trick, and this would be the second they had missed.

She nodded, a little too eagerly, he thought.

"But supposing we were there, then what?" he asked. "You can't spend all your time looking out the window at trees. I'd be teaching my freshmen and you'd be getting rid of somebody at the door or on the phone. And what are you going to do about the crap in the mailbox and the crap on the radio?"

"I know."

"I don't mean that we aren't going back." It was just getting harder to visualize their return, himself putting on the dunce's cap at Oakley, or going—where? Ann Arbor, South Bend, Chicago? He still had friends from his graduate school days, some of whom could swing a little weight now. He had a clean nose, a Ph.D., a

266

book nearly written—chapters of it already in print, he wasn't just kidding himself.

"Have you written about next year yet?" she asked.

"No. There's no hurry."

It wasn't a letter he could dash off. He had to make up his mind about what he was aiming at. Dr. Steichen could have the presidency, it didn't touch what he wanted. Let the sciences have their new buildings as long as he could have the old one. The heating plant, students by the thousand, the monster cafeteria, they were nothing to him, if he could get the liberal arts, its curriculum, its faculty and students—the mistletoe on the oak.

He could see his faculty going out to the new buildings, to the antiseptic classrooms, and administering there the required *Western Civ* or *English Lit & Comp* as a doctor might give a few hours a week to a public dispensary, and returning to Old Main, to cluttered classrooms and cramped offices where his hundred and fifty or two hundred students shot from English to History to French to Latin to Philosophy, which all spun through their brains, meshing and intermeshing and lighting thousands of lights: I see, I see, I see.

But he couldn't propose that in the letter. Should he say that he had taken two years to work and now he wanted a third to go into the desert and rethink his life? There wasn't time to work it out now. Rafferty's Woollens had come closer to the precipice than he cared to admit, even to Alice, and he couldn't expect the next summer to be basically different. The tweed would impose its own rhythm as long as he was to use farmer-weavers, joining two uneconomic occupations into one living. Otherwise there could be no outworkers, just men who were weavers and nothing else, working in a factory, substituting man power for water power. That wasn't what he had come to Ireland to do.

Think big and he would go down in the collapse of his own overhead. He had seen where having two shopworkers got him.

In some things, though, it was impossible to retrench. He had spent more money than he ought to have in rebuilding the shop and might have to rent out the upper office to recoup the money. He had taken a look at his own books, and he had learned a lot.

"Do you realize," he said to Alice one night, "that the difference between expenses and income last month came to no more than the telephone rent?"

"We should be in the black this month."

"We will. I'm having the phone taken out on Monday. We're hardly into the new quarter."

"You're kidding."

"We don't need a phone. If there's something that can't wait, Brian can lock up and go out to the pay phone. There's one just outside the entrance to the mews."

"But suppose you have to phone Brian? What do you do then, send a telegram?"

"We just call the pay phone. I've the number here. Someone is sure to answer the phone, and I'll ask him to run down to number eleven for Brian."

"Great—if it works."

"It does. I was walking by the other day, and the phone was ringing its head off, so I thought I'd tell whoever it was that they weren't ringing anything but an empty pay box. Turned out to be someone who wanted to talk to Murphy, you know, the welder in number eight. When I asked him, he said he gets all his calls that way."

"I suppose it's all right then."

"How often do we phone Brian anyway? He can put through a regular call here on the days I'm not working in town."

"You're right, Rafferty," she said, conveying the opposite.

He had explained his new approach to Frank and would bide his time, let Frank see what he was doing, and then, about midwinter when the weaving was going well, he would bring up the matter of the third year.

When Frank's next letter came, it was a thick one, with two airmail stamps. Alice brought it upstairs.

"Why don't you read it to me?" he said. She enjoyed that, knowing what was written a second or two before he did.

"He's typed it himself," she said, unfolding it. "I'm afraid he's going to be funny."

"Go ahead."

"SAY WHAT'S THIS ABOUT THREE YEARS ANYWAY? AND WHAT ABOUT Al and the IRA? And what else is going on that you aren't telling me?

"What happened is that Saturday night Hel and I went to a party in that dump you call the Faculty Club. The Acorns had managed to beat State to a bloody tie, and since it's the first time we've taken on anything bigger than the B team at the Ag School, Steichen had to have a 'victory' party, just the faculty and the 50–50 Club, a new thing this year, fifty bucks for a pair on the fifty-yard line, all but ten tax deductible.

"Mrs. Steichen, Lorraine, I think they call her. (I allus think of her as Brunhilda. Now if *she'd* been on the team—) She came up to Hel and told her what a lovely house you have, with a lovely palm tree etc.

"Well, there was quite a bit of alcohol on the premises, which was contrary to Club rules, and so it had to be consumed as soon as possible. Being on O.J. and Gelusil for the old ulcer, I was unable to help, though I don't think it bothered anyone. Pretty soon Steichen got to banging Anderson on the back and talking about a bowl game in the future. It didn't take him long to get the future down to ten years and start talking about getting a real first-class coach—to Anderson.

269

"Somebody was going to play the bongo drums for us, but somebody else pinched his drums, so Pat O'Reilley, the surplus man (more about him later) sang *Galway Bay* instead, with real tears in his eyes. That reminded Brunhilda that she had to tell Hel what a lovely time she had visiting you two in Ireland, and what a lovely—that is to say, *interesting,* house your Prisma is. Anyway, Nigel, that Limey creep that Steichen has taking your place, just kept egging her on to get her to say what she really meant.

"Hel's just been reading over my shoulder, says I should cut the gossip and get down to business. Has *she* got a head. I couldn't get her out of bed in time for anything but the twelve o'clock downtown at the Cathedral. Anyhoo, Brunhilda mentioned a few details, like the patch on the patch on the sofa slipcover, and the way the dining room doorknob came off in her hand. The kitchen, she claims, is underground, sort of a cave, patrolled by a cat the size of a great Dane. And there's the gardener, he hadn't had a bath since the battle of Waterloo, and the maid with four-inch heels and a dirty apron. But the high point of the evening was her story of how she went in to the can, and there's a wrought-iron hook and hanging from it, a lot of neatly cut pieces of newspaper threaded onto a cord. Fortunately her travel guide had suggested that she carry her own supply in her purse.

"Anyway, what I'm getting at is, she stopped to take a breath, and Pat O'Reilley—I never knew you knew him—took up the story. Al, it seems, passed herself off as a loyal Irishman and got him to put her in contact with the IRA, against his better judgment. Then, after she'd accepted their help (for *what?*) she began a lot of carping criticism about the way they were doing things. She tried to get O'Reilley to withdraw his support from the IRA, and when that failed, she went to work on the contact, an old man who wasn't aware of what was happening. First she persuaded him to use your house as an ordnance depot (what Pat is doing at this point we aren't told) and then she got him to turn his coat and dump the ammo into the ocean. The old man left the IRA

270

and took his entire list of contacts with him, and O'Reilley hasn't been able to re-establish communication with them.

"So there's everybody looking at me, expecting me to explain, and all I can say is 'It doesn't sound like Al at all.' (The old boy's got the fruitcake sticking to him all over, but he's got to be building on *some*thing, and whatever it is, they're just not the kind of people you play around with, the IRA, I mean.)

"Brunhilda said you never knew about people, and Steichen said that Al was an old peach. I wouldn't care to have been in his shoes when she got him home. (Hel has been canning, and I've had a close look at a couple of old peaches in the bottom of the icebox. Sue him, I say.)

"Anyway, and now we're getting there, Steichen said that Pat was a mighty peculiar duck to represent any business enterprise. That was one I could field. I told him that Pat had the outfit running in the black, not mentioning that this had more to do with expenses being rock bottom than with production.

"And then he went on to say that you'd asked for a third year off. And there I am again, pretending to know what the devil we're talking about. Well, you know we agreed that this was to be a two-year job. I know you're doing a bang-up job, and in ordinary circumstances we could keep you on as long as you wanted to stay, but this changeover is costing a lot more than we planned. I'm taking a cut in salary myself. What I mean to say is that if you *have* to do it, we'll work it out somehow, but I wish you'd reconsider. You have nearly a year left to get it on a self-sustaining basis, and then there's your own career to think of. Three years away from it is a helluva long time. Well, so much for today's sermon.

"Love to both of you and to S & V."

ALICE COULD FEEL THE RED SPOTS BURNING HIGH ON HER CHEEK-bones. Just let Mrs. Steichen see if she would ever call her *Louise*

271

again. But Dr. Steichen might have done them a good turn by bringing Frank into the picture. Now perhaps Rafferty would see that he couldn't keep playing around with the idea of the third year.

"What you'll have to do," he was saying, "is to write a letter to Frank. Give him the whole IRA story. I don't mind being cast in the role of cardboard hero, I was only keeping it quiet for the sake of your friend, O'Reilley."

"He's not my—"

"I'm kidding."

"All right. But, listen, Rafferty, you've got to write to Dr. Steichen and tell him—"

"It's not going to cost them a cent," he said. "I'll just be getting paid for what I do. They'd have to pay someone. I'll have the wages of at least one of the beam fillers, the manager's threepence a yard, and my own weaving money. We'll be better off than we are now."

"You don't want to go on weaving like this for nearly two more years."

"I won't, not more than a special order now and then. As soon as the others are in full production I'll have enough profit without touching a loom."

She suspected that the others *were* in full production, but she couldn't take the time to go into that. "Frank certainly knows that they'd have to pay someone to replace you, so the whole point of it must be his reference to your own career. Dr. Steichen might have implied that three years was too much."

"Too much for what? Where's he going to get another Ph.D. at my salary?"

"I'd hoped he couldn't get you at your salary any more."

"Even at five hundred more? A thousand?" he said, and she felt that he wasn't applying the same voltage to that problem as he had to remaining in tweeds.

As long as he put off writing to Dr. Steichen there was a good chance that he would change his mind. Every week or two they were getting a taste of what winter would be. It was no mystery why the drawing room had not been used by the last occupiers of the house. The wind roared straight across from the mountains of Wales, came in full of raw sea air, crossed the floor, riled the light turf ashes, and mounted the chimney with a rush like water swirling out of a bath. The mysterious banging noises which had accompanied the storms were discovered to be the drawing room window weights, swinging like bell clappers in the draughts. You could tie the weights, but you couldn't stop the draughts, which came through the fabric of the house itself. And that, she said, sitting on her feet to keep them alive, could be why Prisma had stood so long in this impossible position. "The wind goes right through it, not against it."

She didn't hear Rafferty's reply. Perhaps he had only asked her what she had said, the whole exchange lost in the sounds of the wind and the loom. He no longer kept to his sprinter's pace, but he still wove for hours at a time, with his pipe clamped between his teeth as though its tiny firepot was all that kept him going. Newspapers, rolled around his legs and tucked into the tops of his high slippers, defeated the draughts, as far as they went. On top he wore the fisherman's sweater that she had made him, the high neck unrolled and pulled up to his ears.

Perhaps if he had a coal fire, instead of the turf, he would get more heat out of it, she suggested. "Can't afford it," he said. "We'll have to save wherever we can."

He had saved on the turf by getting it from one of his bogside weavers, who had thrown it off the cart into the garden and left it there.

"Why didn't you have him put it in the basement?"

"It would have been thirty-five shillings more," he said. "Johnnie and I can do it in the morning."

It rained, a downpour, during the night, and in the morning

273

Rafferty looked at the pile and said, "We'll leave it there until it dries."

Within the week, when the last of the old turf had been used, Rafferty rooted into the pile to get at the drier part. After a week or so of doing that, he and O'Connor had the turf scattered over most of the fallow part of the garden.

"It's spread right for drying now," said Rafferty, "just as soon as we get a couple of sunny days."

Eventually she and O'Connor decided that although there was less air in the basement fuel store, it was drier air, and he carried the turf in. "You know what I think," O'Connor said, after a morning of it, "I think them sods was wet when they came. Cut too late in the year. We had that class of thing during the war, you had to beg it to burn."

"I hope you're wrong," she said.

In the garden there remained a wide patch of rubble. "Leave it there," Rafferty said. "It'll make a grand manure, hold the moisture."

"I didn't think that was our problem," she said.

There were days when you could hardly talk to him without hearing some ridiculous statement. What would he be like if he stayed two more years? Already he looked different. "Fit," was what he called it, slapping the hard muscles of his stomach, but his face could have used some padding over the cheekbones and around the nose. And his skin, which had once been almost embarrassingly pink, had darkened, tanned by turf and tea and tobacco.

Wasn't there something about the effect of islands on people? Circe and the Lotus Eaters, and the very word, *insular*. He wasn't himself. Rafferty wouldn't think of taking an extra year, a thoroughly unnecessary year, from his teaching. *He* wouldn't put off writing the letter—Rafferty who had hardly ever let the sun go down on an unanswered letter, who had sent even newspaper clippings airmail, because he couldn't bear the feeling of *no contact* that surface mail gave him.

And yet she couldn't keep from asking him whether he had written, and while she listened to his answers, she knew that his convincing assurances of "tomorrow" or "just as soon as I finish this piece of tweed" meant nothing—and still she worried that he *would* do it.

If only he would delay a little longer, the weather would knock some sense into him, if the weavers or the woolman didn't do it first.

"Ah, they're doing a grand job," he would say of the weavers, when the figures didn't bear him out.

"They must be going back to bed after breakfast," O'Connor told her.

Then he got a big shipment of orange wool that he hadn't ordered, and he came home, flushed with the exertion of fighting with the switchboard operators. "My God, you try to get an express call through, and they want to know in detail why you can't wait. And there I was, standing with a handful of sixpences and some fat woman glaring through the glass."

She didn't say anything about taking the phone out of the office.

"Couldn't get through in the end. They closed the office at three-forty-five. The operator told me. Three-forty-five! It goes back tomorrow, carriage collect."

So his old fire was still there and needed only sufficient provocation to break through again. She felt better for several days after that—until he brought home a beam of orange warp and a box of orange bobbins.

"I thought you said that nobody in America would buy tweed in that color."

"I did, but I've reconsidered. These colors have grown up through the centuries. You can't separate them from the tweed. When people see the real thing, it'll win out."

275

She was looking in the wrong direction. The last straw came from the other side of the Atlantic, in the afternoon mail, and it was a bit heavier than she had been looking for, more like a mill-stone.

As she read the letter she thought that it would be just their luck if Rafferty, in Dublin, picked that day to write to Dr. Steichen. Rafferty would have to send a cable: "Disregard letter," but no letter, once read—and it would be read—could ever be really disregarded.

She dialed the number that he had left. She imagined the bell ringing there, in the curbside box, and thought of the people walking by, looking at the box, looking back over their shoulders to make sure it was empty. Would an operator interfere, cut her off? Perhaps what she was doing was against company rules.

Before she could think of more objections to herself, the phone was lifted from its hook. On the other end was a man of great courtesy, not drunk, though the fact that it was during the after-noon closing hour of the bars may have accounted for his being on the street with time to answer an untended phone. He promised to get Rafferty.

She waited, looking out the window on the landing; it was an iron grey November day that had threatened rain and produced a heavy mist instead. O'Connor—what would happen to him?—had a fire going in the rock cleft, a smudge really, for the smoke was held down by the mist, which had a prior claim on the air. The little girls and Mary were helping him, the cheeks of all three with the rouged look of Irish children, apple cheeks.

In Dublin the receiver dangled in the empty box and picked up the noises of traffic, a rumble, a short honk. What if someone came, wanting to use the phone, before Rafferty reached the box?

Outside, the smoldering fire found a few dry leaves and licked out with an orange tongue of flame. It was getting dark. If Rafferty had gone home, then Brian would surely come.

276

There was a noise in the box.

"Hello. Alice?"

"Oh, Rafferty, the man did get you."

"I told you it would work. What's up?"

"There's a letter from Frank here."

"Couldn't it have waited? We're in the middle of one of the beams."

"I was afraid you might write to Dr. Steichen before you got home."

"What gave you that idea?"

"You said you were going to write this week, and the week's nearly over."

"No, not today. What's Frank say that's so important?"

She could see now that she had made a bad mistake, better to have canceled a letter to Dr. Steichen than to deliver this news over the phone. "Maybe you'd rather wait until tonight."

"I would not."

"Well, he says that they've been having quite a bit of labor trouble over the new machines."

"We knew that."

"But it's serious. He says he's going to have to shut down the mill, permanently."

"Ah, I don't believe that."

"Well, it's what he says. And he says that the Irish division will have to be wound up entirely."

"I see," said Rafferty. There was a pause. "Does he give any reason?"

21.

THREE WEEKS HAD PASSED SINCE FRANK'S LETTER HAD HIT THEM, AND Rafferty hadn't written to Dr. Steichen. Alice could only hope that when word of the collapse had broken in Oakley, he had assumed that they would be back and that Rafferty just hadn't had time to tell him.

In Ireland where word of mouth carried news like the wind, people were not slow to work things out. "Oh, Mrs. Raftery," a voice stopped her as she hurried down the village street, "that girl of yours will be wanting a new place when you leave."

"I believe she has plans of her own, Mrs. Redmond," Alice said, and warned Mary when she got home.

There was no reason for Mary to go down with the rest of them, she told her, and Mary offered to take only enough to keep herself in bus fares while the rest of her salary piled up to be paid after their return to America.

"Oh, Mary, that might not be until next fall," Alice said. She hadn't admitted that before, even to herself.

So she ran a blind ad: *Lady, obliged to cut staff, wishes to hear of situation for industrious, young cook-general, likes children,* and Mary had gone to Blackrock and moved ten shillings up the scale.

"You'd want the money all right. Them *boys,*" Mary said when she came back to see the little girls on her first half day.

"You don't have to stick it if it's too bad. I'm still getting answers to the ad."

"Didn't I give her me word?" Mary said.

She was missing Mary more than she had thought she would, and not just for the work. O'Connor was helping with that. He had offered to take over the fires, and he had steam up in the Imperial Iron by the time she came down to make breakfast, which he now ate with the little girls before he walked them to school. Once he was up, the gate lodge wouldn't see him again until he returned at night with his hot jar bundled in a blanket, accompanied by a none-too-enthusiastic Red Eva.

In the meantime, Rafferty was winding up the company's affairs without giving a thought to his own future. It wasn't as though he were doing it for Frank, who had long since had the mill made into a limited company, his advance on his father's advice to keep the house in the wife's name. Frank had come out of it with money in the bank and a choice of jobs. The fact that he had run his ship aground in broad daylight didn't seem to affect his value as an executive—not that she wished him and Helen bad luck. He hadn't had to go for the Irish tweed, and he had never been mingy about the way he did it.

But Rafferty could have taken a few hours for himself, to write Dr. Steichen, making sure of the job in the fall, and to get in touch with his postgrad friends and ask them to keep an eye out for a second semester spot. She didn't see how he could call it ghoulish to look for a place vacated by sickness or death. Finding a good teacher at mid-year was no easy task, and he would be doing people a favor by pointing out his availability.

279

"There's plenty of time," he said.

"That's what you said last week. We have to give ninety days' notice to leave Prisma. We can't pay the rent with no income."

"I wouldn't worry."

He wouldn't worry.

"Take Brian now," he said. "He's got a real problem. He can get another messenger's job, but he's almost sixteen."

And how old was Rafferty?

"When he's eighteen his employer will have to stamp his card, and Brian will get the old heave-ho, unless he's managed to make himself indispensable."

"Yes, but now that he's back at school, he should be able to get in as an apprentice somewhere."

"Oh, I thought I told you. Brian quit school."

"He *did?*"

"It didn't work out. He'd come home from work and find his mother out, so he'd have to make his own meal. And then all the little kids would be waiting, and he'd have to feed them too. By the time he got out of the house it would be too late to go to class." Rafferty fired a bone into the flames so hard that he knocked a burning sod out onto the hearth.

"You know," she said, "he could have made his tea at the shop, fried bacon and eggs on the gas ring, and gone straight to school." Too late now, of course.

"We tried that," Rafferty said. "I brought in the groceries. It worked for a week, and then his father found out that he wasn't coming home for tea and blew his stack."

"And Brian didn't know what to say?"

"I went to his father myself. I even got the parish priest to talk to him."

"And what happened?"

"Brian's father just isn't a man of good will. He doesn't want his son to rise higher in the world than he has."

"That's going a bit far."

280

"Oh, he didn't say it in so many words. The mother's not too bad, but she's got six kids and two rooms, and she's not what you'd call well organized. If you could see that place—if Mrs. Steichen could see that place, they'd have to carry her out on a stretcher."

"It's too bad," she said, refusing to develop that picture in her mind. "But what does Brian say? Now, I mean."

"He's worried about *me*."

Poor Brian. "That makes two of us."

"Listen, Alice. Just trust me. I know what I'm doing."

THE PROBLEM WAS TO KEEP THE WEAVERS TOGETHER, WEAVING. ALL the king's horses and all the king's men had gone off and left him to put it together again.

Sometimes it was best not to try, he thought, considering the mess that had once been scraped back into its shell and moved to Byzantium, where it remained another thousand years, a bad egg. Better, perhaps, to have settled for less, as many did then, anonymous men who repaired a mile of aqueduct, fortified the barnyard, and got the corn into the ground in time.

It would be easy enough to save himself, and it was tempting to think of putting in a semester somewhere else to see if his problem was really Dr. Steichen. But after convincing the weavers that learning a craft would change their lives, he couldn't run off and leave the mess to Forbes.

"It's not your fault, Mr. Rafferty," they said. Or, "It was the same with the pigs, Mr. Raftery."

How was it the same with the pigs, he wondered. He found no echo of his carefully assumed confidence, only a quiet acceptance of the devaluation of their hard-won skills, while hope went out, covertly, like some modish outfit suddenly seen through.

Ten thousand pounds would have kept Rafferty's Woollens together. He might have done it with five. But he couldn't muster

281

much more than a thousand, even with his bank account in Oakley and all the money he hadn't drawn here—and possibly would never get.

It seemed to him that the Irish division might be profitably taken over as a working unit by one of the company's creditors. The receivers, an Oakley firm, whose last job of this kind had been a filling station stranded by a change in the course of the highway, weren't up to the idea.

Maybe he should have been grateful that they were relying on him to wind up the company's affairs. If they had sent over their own man, though, they might have been more willing to revise their inflated ideas of the company's Irish assets. It wasn't easy to give them the picture. The cost of the mews building included tax on the sale of property to non-citizens, stamp duty, conveyancer's fees, all of it unrecoverable. The cost of Willie Ryan's improvements was not the same thing as their worth. And much more.

Yes, he said in answer to their answer, in Oakley the building might be worth their valuation, but this was not Oakley. Yes, a piece of land in central Dublin ought to be worth a great deal, but they didn't actually own the land, they paid ground rent on it, and the building itself was theirs for only eighty-seven more years.

Frank, who might have been able to explain some of this, had already picked up his own pieces and gone to Denver. He wasn't even in textiles. It wasn't clear what he was in, something to do with defense, or offense, the money end of it, a vice president.

There had been Raffertys on the mill land before the railroad, before the town, before the Oakleys themselves had come on the scene. Frank's two sons would have been the fifth generation in the mill, as close to a dynasty as anyone could come in the Midwest. And now he, with a teacher's salary and only daughters, might well be the last Rafferty in Oakley.

Forbes put his fingertips together and listened.

Full payment on the looms, now, had been the latest message,

Rafferty told him. It was an awkward demand, since he had been hoping that the weavers might yet take fire and build up such a balance of unpaid weaving that they would have to be given the looms to settle the debt.

"Yes," Forbes said, and told him that they would have been all right if they had put a clause in the loom purchase contracts that, in the event of the company's failure to provide work for the weavers, the rest of the debt would be canceled. "Of course, ordinarily a company wants to protect its assets," he said.

"That's interesting, but I was hoping to find out what I can do *now*."

"Yes." Forbes broke apart the bony cage of his fingers. "There's no reason the men can't keep their looms as long as you can find someone else to employ them as weavers. We can work out the loans."

"I'll manage that somehow," Rafferty said. "And there's Brian too. Will you keep an eye out for a job for him?"

"The little boy. He worked out all right then?"

"If I'd had a couple more like Brian we'd be flying so high that it would take a lot more than this to bring us down."

"You'll give him an excellent character then?"

"The best. There's only one thing"—nothing to be lost in asking —"I've often wondered why you sent him to me."

Forbes nodded. "You see, when a client comes to arrange for the eviction of a tenant for non-payment of rent, I try to see if we can't arrange somehow for the payment of the arrears instead. And when the tenant's only asset is a fourteen-year-old boy who can't find a job . . ."

"My God, if I'd known that, I'd have had some leverage when I was trying to get his father to let the boy go to night school."

"Don't trouble yourself so, Mr. Rafferty. It wouldn't have made any difference."

"If I'd threatened to fire him?"

"The father might have let him go to school all right."

283

"And Brian might have found himself a higher place on the ladder. I call that a difference."

"For the one boy, Mr. Rafferty. We're a poor country. There are only so many places on the ladder."

He went away annoyed. Musical chairs, that was what the man was saying, and all the energies of the young went into fighting for one of the places. But he had put nine new chairs into the game, and he would see that they stayed in.

Back in the mews where Brian, irrational as a dog, still seemed happy to see him, he held out his crumb of hope. "Mr. Forbes says he'll look for a job for you."

"That's grand, Mr. Rafferty."

"Just one thing, Brian. A sense of order like yours is a rare thing around here, and so wherever you get in you've got to look for some patch of mess in the outfit and start cleaning it up. Make yourself indispensable, or else—you know what you can look forward to."

"I know me place, Mr. Rafferty."

Oh, God, what hope was there? "Listen, Brian. If you keep thinking your place is at the bottom, that's where it'll be. And I'd say, 'Go ahead. Collect your reward in the next world,' except that this world needs every little bit of order it can get."

"Yes, sir. . . . Yes, sir. . . . Yes, Mr. Rafferty."

If just one of the people he had had to disappoint had shown anger, there might have been hope. He had naturally been glad at the time that they had all made it so easy for him. But was it easy? He could have braced himself against anger and felt justified. As it was, he had to feel responsible for all of them.

He went up to the room that he had taken so much pleasure in furnishing. Only the table remained, and Frank's calendar. He had taken home his prizes, one by one, had carried them up the hill to save cartage and reimbursed the company every penny. He would take the table the first dry day and have O'Connor help him carry it up the lane.

284

The odd inches he had trimmed from the tweed were in one of Willie's cabinets. (He just hadn't had the nerve to ask Forbes about *him.*) He picked out thirty or forty of the best samples, and then realized that too many of them were his own work. He wanted to make the best representation possible, but would like to give an honest answer if the discussions got down to a weaver-by-weaver consideration of the men. There weren't more than three or four possible employers, and it wouldn't do to muff his chance with any of them.

"Ah, the hard man, Rafferty," said Fogarty, greeting him. Bogus Dublinese, Rafferty thought, put on for the Yank's benefit.

"How's yourself?" he asked.

"Grand," said Fogarty. "The news is you've had your first bankruptcy."

"It's the brother's, not mine." A little more of his annoyance than he had intended came out with the words.

"Sorry."

"What I mean is, we'll leave no unpaid bills in Ireland."

"I thought we might have our day in court."

"No." Obviously Fogarty had no idea how he felt about it.

"You'll have to come out now before you go," Fogarty said when he was leaving to catch his train. "Bring the wife out to Howth."

"Fine," Rafferty said.

The car would be gone in a week, and there wasn't a chance that they would make it.

When he got home there was O'Connor waiting for him by the kitchen fire.

"I was thinking," he said, "that if it wasn't for me wages, you'd be in a better position."

"Better position for what?" Rafferty asked. "The garden would go to hell again, and Hamilton would start up again on compensa-

tion for so-called depreciation, and we'd miss yourself, Johnnie."
He looked away from the watery eyes and down to the hearth,
and added, "—and Red Eva."

"Ah, you can set your mind at rest, Mr. Rafferty. I wasn't thinking of leaving you. I was thinking that if I was to move into the
little room be the kitchen here and I was to rent out me own little
house for three pounds ten a week, then I could pay meself, like."

It was an ingenious plan, probably legal, though dishonest.
"Well, I don't know, Johnnie."

"You should be reading your papers, Mr. Rafferty. 'Highly de-
sirable gate lodge.' That's what they call them. We could get the
money all right."

He looked at Alice, who had said nothing. It was *her* kitchen,
and she was the one who was interested in want ads and their
wording. "I don't know," he said again.

"And if I wasn't being paid, I could collect the unemployment."

"No, I draw the line at that. I'll see what Forbes has to say
about the other."

When they had gone upstairs to eat he asked Alice, "What do
you think?"

"Well, we can't get along very well in this house without him,
and I don't see how we can go on paying him."

"Yes."

"What I mean is our source of income has been disrupted, and I
don't know how much money we're going to have to spread or
how far."

It hurt him to see her trying to be decent. He would have liked
to take her into his confidence, but there were too many *ifs*. He
might only raise her hopes and then find that he could do nothing.

"Try not to worry," was all he could say.

ONE OF HIS OLD RIVALS WAS TAKING ON HIS WEAVERS, RAFFERTY TOLD
her. He had pulled it off, he said, and with Frank's list of Ameri-

can outlets for the tweed, they would have no trouble disposing of the additional output. He was tying on a new warp. He wasn't just taking off his finished tweed, as she had thought at first, he was tying on a new warp.

"I didn't know," she said cautiously, feeling her way through the eggs underfoot, "that you were still weaving."

"We can't go on living without an income. You said so yourself."

"You're working for them, too?" He nodded. Just to finish off the year—she wouldn't say it, risk putting ideas into his head. He certainly wouldn't consider taking the third year now. Where would he find time for research and writing?

"You know, you can do a lot of thinking at the loom," he said, as though he had been waiting right there for her to surface.

Yes, but thinking just run through and sent up with the turf smoke wasn't what she had in mind. In any case, she knew enough not to mention the letter to Dr. Steichen. Let the delay go on for another month or two and, if she guessed Dr. Steichen right, the fall catalogue would be printed up with Rafferty's courses there in black and white. He wasn't one to pull out then.

Rafferty hadn't said a word about the gate lodge, but he hadn't objected when O'Connor moved into the maid's room, from which it was easier for him to start the fire in the morning—and to keep the affections of Red Eva.

Rafferty must have seen, too, that they were painting in the lodge. If they had to go on with only his weaving income, its rent might easily be the margin of solvency. She had thought that she might help by knitting, until she learned the going rate and figured that by working flat out for forty hours a week, she would make two pounds.

Now that they were living on Irish wages, the balance of their diet was sliding toward sugar and starch, and it took all her imagination to keep them from falling in with the accepted way of eating: a diet based on tea, bread, and jam, with potatoes, cabbage, and fat bacon to make it a dinner, and puddings for tea, those hefty bread and scrap sausages that O'Connor kept urging her to buy.

More and more, though, she was listening to him. He had a kind of street urchin's wisdom that threw away string, but never used a match if there was a fire within reach. He could not only burn a mixture of coaldust, cinders, and water, but got more heat out of it than she could from an ordinary fire.

He found them the seaweed for half a crown cheaper than the year before, and he would go down to the village and turn an extra chipful of onions or carrots into cash. The real money lay in the apples and pears, he said. "You might get four or five pounds right there."

"I think we'll keep them, Johnnie." The fruit was almost the only luxury they still had. Apple pie, apple pancakes, baked apples, apple coffee cake.

"I like apples," Rafferty said, "but remember that stuff you used to make, crackly on top?"

"Apple crisp," she said—butter in the making and cream in the eating. "We can't afford it, unless you want to eat it with custard," she said, remembering how he felt about that.

"No, this is fine," he said, and then: "Well, we might try it once."

They were moving rapidly toward Christmas. Winding up Rafferty's Woollens was almost as tedious as putting it together had been. At this rate the second semester would have begun before Rafferty was finished (his plan, perhaps), but there was no reason he couldn't take a couple of hours to write Dr. Steichen about the fall. As far as she could see, he wasn't doing anything but weaving. "Forbes is handling things," he said. Handling what? They hadn't even advertised the mews building for sale.

That afternoon Rafferty had gone in to see him, the first time he had been in town since Brian had left. (He had found a good

288

delivery job for the Christmas season, and Rafferty had warned him to make himself indispensable.) He hadn't said that he would be late, and she was afraid he was doing the Christmas shopping, overriding her feeling that they simply couldn't afford a tricycle.

Outside it was a clear cold evening that made her think of Oakley and covering the plants there on the first frosty nights. "Ah, you won't get frost on this hill, and it wouldn't hurt if you did," O'Connor said and went down to the pub, leaving her and Red Eva alone in front of the glowing fire. The little girls were in bed, their school satchels packed and hanging on the backs of their chairs, ready for the morning, when there would suddenly be no time at all.

She heard Rafferty come into the hall above, but she wasn't prepared for the way he burst through the kitchen door to give her a one-armed hug, a bottle of wine in the other hand.

"We're all right now," he said.

"All right?" she asked, keeping a hard rein on all her hopes. "Did you write to Dr. Steichen?"

"First," he said, "I had to settle with the receivers. My idea was to get them to give me the mews building instead of our return fare and all the other money they owe us."

She nodded, as though he were making sense. He couldn't mean to start up the weaving a second time, could he? And now Dr. Steichen would have to advance them their return fare.

"You see, fixed the way it is, it'd be worth a lot to the right tenants, but in a forced sale they couldn't have got anywhere near its value. This way we both gain."

"They gain anyway," she said, in spite of herself. Did he mean to rent it? An absentee landlord?

"That's just step one, of course."

She nodded. They would be all right in a fairy story, Jack just back from trading the cow for a handful of beans, but now for the *Fee, fi, fo* and the giant's treasure.

"And then," he said, "I traded the mews building for the house."

289

"For what house?" she asked numbly.

"For Prisma, and the greenhouse, the gate lodge, and sundry outoffices and contents of the aforesaid; standing on one acre, three roods, and seventeen perches, statute measure; held on a Pembroke lease of nine hundred ninety-nine years from 1175 at four pounds per annum," he recited. "Hamilton could hardly wait to get the papers for fear I'd change my mind."

"1175?"

"I know the lease is more than three-fourths expired, but it's still a good proposition." He wasn't kidding.

"Pembroke."

He nodded, looking proud of himself.

She laid it on the line for him then: "The Earl of Pembroke who died in 1176 was Strongbow."

"You know your history all right."

She knew Rafferty's pet periods anyway. Her eyelids were hot, but she wouldn't cry. He had let go of the tiller and somebody had to do the steering. "*Rafferty*, you are what you are. You can't just get yourself a piece of paper and start thinking of yourself as a vassal of Strongbow's."

Rafferty was laughing. "Never entered my mind," he said, and pulled the steaming iron kettle, his kettle, on his crane, back from his grate. "Who'd want to be a vassal of Strongbow's anyway?"

"You went to see his tomb."

"I know, one of the *watersheds of history*. He was a terrible man."

"Well," she said. Perhaps she had gone a little far there, but even so—

"And furthermore," he said, "if it *is* one of Strongbow's leases, and I don't think it is, and if anyone has to be considered his vassal—well, the papers are in your name."

"For Prisma?"

"Yes. I know it's not exactly what you had in mind, but you've always said that you wanted a house."

290

She had reason to believe that it was one of Strongbow's leases. If she could get a copy of the Calendar of the Pembroke Estate deeds (Printed privately in 1891) she might be able to find out. She wrote and asked Mr. Hamilton what he knew. He answered that he had bought Prisma from a Mr. Doyle before the war, a man aged about fifty at the time. He said, too, that he hated to turn the house over to her with the skylight in that condition, and so he was sending out a man to "repair the catch and at the same time replace the awkward lock on the front door that the wife had always been complaining of." She wrote back that they had already caulked the skylight, and, as for the lock, it had needed only a drop of oil. (The skylight, caulked, still leaked, would always leak, but the Georgian hardware, whatever its value in the salerooms, would be removed from the house only over her dead body.)

Dublin Castle had no record of Prisma, and most of the other public records had gone in the Customs House fire during the Troubles. She couldn't even find out who had built the present house, or when, much less what earlier building the kitchen floor remained from.

All she had to do to find out that, said O'Connor, who was spending too much time with the newspapers, was to pry up a few of the floor slabs until they found the ashes. "You never saw a building site where they wasn't a fire, did you? They'd want their tea, wouldn't they?"

Once they had the ashes a simple carbon test would give them the answer, he told her. "They can pinpoint it to within two or three hundred years."

"No. I don't think we'll try that."

"We'll leave it so, then."

She was halfway out the door with the tray when she thought it well to add: "And I wouldn't want to be surprised, Johnnie. That floor's almost the only part of Prisma that I'm not worried about at the moment."

"No, you wouldn't want to touch them stones, not while we was painting the kitchen, at any rate."

"Or after."

"No, you mightn't get them back the way they was."

She stepped out into the hall then.

Well, he liked the little girls and they liked him; and they had a taste for the obvious which gave him ample opportunity for holding forth: how there came to be a hole in his boot and he halfway to town at the time; how the puddings was burnt, but the smell off them wasn't as bad as if you was to burn the milk, which itself wasn't in it with burnt cat's hair, at all.

Every two or three weeks, though, he wanted to talk to her about the meaning of life. He had always been a reader of the popular press—those very black and white newspapers, top-heavy with headlines and preoccupied with crimes of violence, sports, and acts of God—and he had managed to come up with what boiled down to "God's in his heaven, all's right with the world," except that he wouldn't boil it down.

Then, grumbling, he had first taken up one of Rafferty's discarded papers to avoid a soaking trip down to the village one evening, and now the newspapers, the *Times,* the *Irish Times,* the *Manchester Guardian,* which he collected from Rafferty (for the fire, he said), were read by the hour beneath the dangling bulb in the kitchen. "You'll ruin your eyes, Johnnie," she would say.

"Now, if you was to read that," he would say, tapping a column of solid print, "you'd have them stopped in the public house below."

It wasn't how to win an argument in the pub that had her worried. It was what she would do if she had the two of them at it, one up and one down, O'Connor with the morning papers at night, half a day behind Rafferty, like the tide cresting on a different part of the coast. Apartheid, Enosis, Kenya, Jordan, Panmunjom. O'Connor might even take Irish politics to heart.

At the drawing room door she rested the lip of the tray on the thin projection of the latch plate and reached beneath it to turn the knob. Then, bracing herself for the smell of stale tobacco and wool and turf, she pushed open the door. Rafferty was just standing there in a fleeting patch of sun and looking out over the vacant sea.

"You know," he said, turning to her, "I thought the man said *whales.*"

"Maybe he did. Bede said they were in the seas off of England, and porpoise too." She hesitated a moment. "Do you know what he says about Ireland?"

"I've forgotten."

She took the book from under the windowseat where she had hidden it in the summer and found the place: "There seldom snow longer lies than three days. And there no man in summer mows hay for winter's cold nor sheds for his cattle builds." It sounded innocuous enough now.

Rafferty nodded. "Five degrees colder and you could rewrite the history of Ireland."

And of Patrick Rafferty.

They ate by the fire, the table leg solid now, its splint hardly noticeable in that setup. She couldn't resent the loom too much, though, for without it there they wouldn't have tried to use the room in such weather. Perhaps in the spring they would carry it down. In the meantime they had moved the brass fender to give Rafferty more room for drying his turf around the fire. His spent matches, thrown from his perch at the loom, hit the barricade of turf and fell back on the outside. Within, the fire burnt weakly. She had never mentioned the wet turf, but he kept telling her, "You get a good, slow-burning fire this way."

When they had finished eating, Rafferty would return to the

293

loom, walking stiffly so as not to dislodge the newspapers from his slipper tops. He would weave until it was dark, and then he would close the shutters and keep on weaving under the ceiling light. Sometimes he would start again after dinner, weaving far into the night. And when he had finished a length of tweed, he signed and fixed to it one his employer's printed labels: ". . . your Irish tweed, handwoven by native craftsmen in their cabins by the turf fires. Go mairidh tú is go gcaithidh tú é. Do fhíodóir, Pádraig Ó Raifeartaigh."

Wahl

RAFFERTY & CO.